They turned their eyes upward at the same time. In Dawdi's barn the rafters were only three feet over their heads.

A small sprig of green with white berries dangled from a string above them.

"Is that what Mammi wants us to see?" Beth said.

Tyler kept his gaze on that sprig as if it might disappear if he looked away. "Oh," he said.

"What is it?"

He slowly shifted his gaze to her face. "It's mistletoe."

"Why would Mammi hang mistletoe in the barn? It's not even an Amish tradition." Beth's puzzlement didn't last very long. Mammi had a full bag of tricks, and she obviously wasn't above using any and all of them.

She fell silent as Tyler moved closer. Close enough that in the still of the barn, Beth could almost hear his heartbeat. "I wish your mammi hadn't done that," he whispered. "I've resisted all evening, but now that the idea is in my head, I don't think I'm strong enough to put it out." He brushed his thumb down her cheek. "Please, can I kiss you?"

Books by Jennifer Beckstrand

HUCKLEBERRY HILL

HUCKLEBERRY SUMMER

HUCKLEBERRY CHRISTMAS

Published by Kensington Publishing Corporation

Huckleberry Christmas

JENNIFER BECKSTRAND

ZEBRA BOOKS
KENSINGTON PUBLISHING CORP.
http://www.kensingtonbooks.com

ZEBRA BOOKS are published by

Kensington Publishing Corp.
119 West 40th Street
New York, NY 10018

First Printing: October 2014
ISBN-13: 978-1-4201-3360-8
ISBN-10: 1-4201-3360-8

First Electronic Edition: October 2014
eISBN-13: 978-1-4201-3361-5
eISBN-10: 1-4201-3361-6

10 9 8 7 6 5 4 3 2 1

Printed in the United States of America

Chapter One

Crouched on her hands and knees, Anna Helmuth shined her flashlight into the darkest corner of the cellar, where old storage boxes and ancient furniture gathered dust.

"Felty, dear," she called, hoping her voice carried up the stairs, through the cellar door, and into the kitchen, where her husband washed up the dishes.

He might not be able to hear her, but she could hear him singing at the top of his lungs. *"Each day I'll do a golden deed, by helping those who are in need."*

It was no use. Felty was in one of his singing moods, and Anna wouldn't be able to make him hear her. She grunted as she tried to get to her feet. Her left leg had fallen asleep, and she couldn't budge an inch. Not a single inch. She turned off the flashlight, stowed it in her apron pocket, and slowly pushed herself backward with her hands. Her knees creaked like a pair of rusty hinges as she shifted to a sitting position. Propping her hand on a sturdy cardboard box, she attempted to pull herself up. No use. Her hinter parts would not cooperate.

How had she gotten herself into this predicament? She was only eighty-two years old, for goodness sake, hardly an old lady. It must have been that extra biscuit with strawberry jam she'd eaten for breakfast.

She could still hear Felty singing. "*While going down life's weary road, I'll try to lift some trav'ler's load.*" Oh, how he loved that song!

If only he knew how badly his wife needed her load lifted at this very minute. "Felty, dear," she called again.

She might be forced to crawl up the stairs. Either that or she could take a lovely nap on the cellar floor, and Felty would notice her absence when supper didn't appear on the table.

Anna waited until he took a breath, then yelled as loudly as she could without straining her throat. "Felty, do you have Rhode Island?"

The refrain halted abruptly. Felty always attuned his ear to talk of license plates. Smiling at her cleverness, Anna heard him shuffle to the top of the stairs and open the cellar door. "Are you down there, Annie?"

"Jah, and I'm stuck. It wonders me if you could lend a hand."

Felty clomped down the steps and peered at her by the dim light from the small window.

"My knees gave out," Anna said.

Felty reached out both hands and, nearly toppling over himself, pulled Anna to her feet. Anna

"I was looking for the baby crib."

"That old crib? I chopped it up for firewood twenty years ago yet."

"Firewood?" Anna propped her hands on her hips. "Felty, that crib cradled our thirteen babies."

"And got mighty gute use. It was like to collapse with the next baby. So I burned it." Felty's eyes twinkled. "We ain't had a baby in this house for forty years, and unless you're thinking of bringing another one into the world, it was better as firewood."

"Now, Felty. We need the crib for our great-great-grandson Toby."

"Is he coming for a visit?"

"He and his mother are going to live with us. They'll be here tomorrow."

Felty massaged his forehead just above his right eyebrow. "Annie, what are you up to?"

"Amos has been gone over a year now, and it's time we found Beth a new husband."

"Beth told her mother she doesn't want a new husband."

"Well, that's silly. I'm sure her mother didn't believe that. Every girl wants a husband, and Beth has a son to consider."

Felty wrapped his arm around his wife of sixty-three years. "I lost a lot of sleep over your last match, Annie-banannie. The doctor says I need a nap every day."

"Do you remember Tyler Yoder?"

"Of course I remember him. Our grandson Aden stole his fiancée."

"Lily and Tyler were never right for each other. But Tyler and Beth are a match made in heaven."

"Made in heaven or in an Amish mammi's day-dreams?"

"Now, Felty, every match we've ever made has been a success."

Felty grunted. "In spite of us, not because of us."

"Beth needs our help. She's obviously not very gute at picking her own husband."

Felty shook his finger. "Don't speak ill of the dead."

Anna turned around and started climbing the stairs. "I didn't say a word against Amos. It was more a criticism of Beth."

"Where are you going? I still haven't agreed to this."

"Seeing as Tyler hasn't set foot here since church five months ago, I've got to pay Aden a visit. I need an excuse to get Tyler to Huckleberry Hill. Aden still feels guilty about marrying Tyler's fiancée, and when I tell him I've found Tyler's match, he'll be eager to help."

"Annie, I don't think I can stand any more love-birds disturbing my peace."

Anna stopped halfway up the stairs. "So, you

admit they'll fall in love." She grinned. "We should buy a crib so the baby doesn't have to sleep in a box."

Felty chuckled softly and followed Anna up the stairs. "I slept in a bureau drawer until I turned three."

"What a lovely thought, Felty. I can imagine that you were an adorable baby, like Beth's son, Toby. Cute, lively, and in need of a father."

"Every child should have a father. Especially our only great-great-grandchild."

"I knew you'd come to see it my way."

Felty shook his head in resignation as he paused at the top of the stairs to catch his breath. "Did I hear you say something about Rhode Island?"

Chapter Two

Tyler Yoder jumped out of his skin as his open-air buggy came around the bend and he saw a small child standing in the lane directly in the path of his horse. "*Ach, du lieva!*" he yelled, as he pulled hard left on the reins to keep Dobbin from trampling the little boy. The horse swerved sharply and came to a stop a mere three feet from the child.

The toddler didn't seem to understand how close he'd come to death. As the dust settled, he stared at Dobbin with one finger stuck up his nose and a big grin that revealed a mouth full of tiny teeth. His feet were bare and his orange-auburn hair perched wildly on top of his head. Tyler had never seen such an adorable child, but why he had the presence of mind to notice, he would never know.

His legs felt like pillars of gelatin as he set the brake and slid out of the buggy. Breathless and shaking, he ran, or rather stumbled, toward the little boy, who couldn't have been more than two years old. Tyler glanced in the direction of the Helmuths' house. What was this child doing out here all by himself?

The boy's eyes grew as wide as buggy wheels when he saw Tyler coming toward him, and he turned and ran in the opposite direction, pumping his chubby little arms and giggling with glee. He must have thought Tyler wanted to play tag.

Tyler sped up but didn't catch him before the toddler lost his balance and tumbled to the ground. The boy immediately voiced his indignation with an ear-piercing wail. When he caught his breath, he held it so long, Tyler feared he might hyperventilate. The second wail proved louder and more pathetic than the first. Tyler wrapped his hands around the boy's waist and helped him to his feet. The child's whole face turned damp as wetness spouted from his eyes and nose.

Unsure of what to do, Tyler pulled a handkerchief out of his pocket and began mopping up the little one's face. "There, there. No need to cry," he said, in the most comforting voice he could muster. He caressed his little hand and patted him on the head while whispering, "Hush, hush."

The boy stopped crying as suddenly as he had begun. He popped his finger into his mouth, whimpered halfheartedly, and stared at Tyler with wide blue eyes. Tyler lifted the little boy's trouser legs. His knees were red, but the skin wasn't broken, and judging from the fading bruise on his forehead and the small scab on his elbow, he'd been in a few tussles with the ground before. Children this age weren't called "toddlers" for nothing.

"Let's see what we can do about your trousers," Tyler said, brushing the dust and gravel from the boy's padded bottom and straightening his pant legs.

The boy held out his hands, and Tyler lifted him into his arms. He rested his head on Tyler's shoulder and seemed to settle in for an extended stay. "Has it been a hard day already, little guy?"

Tyler snapped his head around as he heard a door slam behind him.

A young woman, gliding like a fast-moving tornado, stormed across the front yard. "How dare you?"

She snatched the toddler out of Tyler's arms and held the boy's head protectively against her chest. Tyler remembered her. She was the Helmuths' great-granddaughter Beth, and she used to live in Bonduel. She'd married a man from Nappanee, Indiana, who had passed away recently. Tyler hadn't laid eyes on Beth for three or four years.

At the moment, Beth looked more like a badger than the Helmuths' great-granddaughter. She practically spit out her words. "Toby is just a baby. You never spank a baby."

"Spank?" Tyler was stunned into silence.

"I turned my back for one minute, and then I looked out the window and saw you spanking Toby. Never touch him again or I'll come at you with a hot poker." She bounced Toby on her hip as if to comfort him, but he wasn't crying. He didn't even seem upset. Grinning at Tyler, he grabbed onto his own ear and squeezed it with his chubby little fingers.

Beth whirled on her heels, stomped across the front yard in half a second, and marched up the porch steps. She nearly ripped the door off its hinges before slamming it behind her.

Tyler kneaded the back of his neck. It was going to be a long day.

Beth closed the door with such force that it rattled Mammi's front window. She'd done it. She'd stood up to that man and told him what was what. Her heart beat with exhilaration and indignation. The gall he had spanking someone else's child! And a helpless toddler, to boot.

Mammi stood at the kitchen sink, elbow deep in dishwater. "Is everything all right, dear? You gave me quite a start."

Beth held tight to Toby, while he struggled to free himself. "I'm sorry, Mammi. Toby must have escaped out the front door. When I looked out the window, a man was spanking him. I ran right out to fetch him." Her legs quivered like overcooked spaghetti. She sat down to catch her breath.

Mammi's eyes widened in disbelief. "Who spanked my little punkin pie?"

Someone tapped on the front door. Beth's heart pounded double time as she stood and peeked out the window. "Him. He's the one."

Mammi bustled to Beth's side and stood on her

tippy toes to get a good view of the horrible man standing at the door, waiting to be let in as if he hadn't just offended the entire family.

Beth was horrified by Mammi's reaction. Mammi burst into a grin the size of the sky, clapped her hands, and almost tripped over her feet trying to reach the door. She flung it open and flung out her arms to greet the visitor. "Tyler Yoder, you are a sight for sore eyes yet."

Beth's arms tightened around Toby as Tyler walked into the room, his steps tentative, his brow dark and furrowed. Tyler Yoder. He *had* looked slightly familiar. Beth remembered seeing him at gatherings and *singeons* before she married Amos and left Bonduel, but she didn't remember him very well. After she had met Amos Hostetler, she hadn't noticed any other boys, even the good-looking ones. Despite her hostility, she eyed Tyler appreciatively. He'd turned out quite nice to look at.

But he was still a dirty rat.

Tyler took off his hat and glanced at Beth as if she would pounce on him. "I'm meeting Aden here."

"*Cum.* Sit down," Mammi said. "Beth made some cookies. Would you like a cookie?"

Beth wouldn't stand for being in the same room with such a person, even if Mammi acted as if an angel had crossed their threshold. "I'm going to my room," she said, still gripping wiggly Toby in her arms.

Tyler jumped to attention. "Wait. I'm not sure why you're so mad at me, but I want to apologize."

"Apologize? Since when does a man like you apologize?"

"A man like me?" He seemed more puzzled than angry at her insult. "What do you mean?"

"A man who hits little children."

He bowed his head and looked as if he had been stricken with some very bad news. His humility surprised her. "I would never hit a child."

"I saw you from the window."

He fixed Beth with an earnest gaze. "I don't want you to think I'm looking for an argument, but that's not what happened. I almost ran over him and—"

Beth felt the heat rise in her cheeks as if she'd swallowed a boiling pot of tea. "You almost ran over him?"

"I didn't expect to see a baby playing outside unsupervised."

Beth pressed her lips into a hard line and bounced Toby up and down with renewed intensity. "So now you think I'm a bad mother?" She tightened one arm around Toby and poked Tyler forcefully in the chest with her finger—just to back him up a bit. "Let me tell you something. It's not easy to raise a son by myself. Don't judge me until you walk in my shoes. And don't preach to me either."

Tyler took a step back. "I'm sorry if you think I'm preaching. I'm just grateful I stopped the horse in time."

"Were you mad because he spooked your horse? Is that why you spanked a twenty-month-old?"

With her hand still on the doorknob, Mammi stood frozen in place, grinning as if she thought their confrontation was wildly entertaining.

Tyler's frowned deepened. "I didn't spank anybody, and may the good Lord forgive me if I ever do." He lifted his hands in surrender. "What do you think you saw? I brushed the dust off his trousers. He fell down, and I helped him up. No spanking involved. He gave me shock, but I wasn't angry."

Beth examined his expression and found only sincerity there. His eyes and face didn't hold one spark of anger. She hadn't expected that. Even the smallest things used to set Amos off.

Toby pushed away from her and reached out to Tyler. Beth's jaw dropped to the floor, and she took a step back.

Toby only struggled harder against her grip. "Dow, dow," he said.

Beth reluctantly set her son on his feet, and Toby immediately stretched out his hands for Tyler. Tyler backed away and Toby followed him, whining to be held. He backed Tyler to the wall, and Tyler acted as if a guard dog had cornered him.

Her mouth curled in amusement. Perhaps she'd been a bit hasty. Maybe what she thought she'd seen wasn't what she'd actually seen. It was possible that Tyler had only been trying to help.

Tyler cocked an eyebrow and twitched his lips

upward. "I'll pick him up if you promise not to attack me with a hot poker."

Beth knew she must be blushing clear to the tips of her toes. She'd made a complete fool of herself. Tyler's intense scrutiny only succeeded in heightening her embarrassment. "Go ahead. He's taken with you already."

Tyler scooped Toby into his arms, and Toby wasted no time in snuggling against Tyler's shoulder.

"I'm sorry I got mad." Beth studied Tyler's solemn expression. She shouldn't have accused him so harshly. "I'm really, really sorry."

"I'm not mad."

"I hurt your feelings."

"Nae."

"But you look so serious," Beth insisted.

"So I've been told."

Mammi finally shut the door and gave Tyler's arm a pat. "Tyler is not inclined to smile, but a finer man you'll never meet."

Not inclined to smile? Mammi must be trying to make her feel better. If Tyler hadn't been attacked by a crazed mother, he'd be inclined to smile. Beth felt the need to wipe that serious look off his face. Surely he would smile if he knew she bore him no ill will. "I panicked when I couldn't find Toby. When I glanced out the window and saw you with him, I guess I wasn't thinking straight."

"It's okay. I would have been frantic if I had lost my son." He played with Toby's silky soft fingers.

"He must have an angel watching over him. Dobbin stopped just in time, praise the Lord."

"Praise the Lord, indeed," Mammi said. "I have to get used to having a little one again. I forgot to shut the door on my way in from the garden." Mammi's eyes twinkled as her gaze darted between Beth and Tyler. "I think I'll go see what Felty is up to." She practically skipped down the hall without another word.

Toby reached for the floor. Tyler set him down. A grin played at his lips as he watched Toby toddle to the rug and pat Mammi's dog, Sparky. Beth tilted her head and gazed at Tyler. He might be of a solemn disposition, but he seemed inclined to smile at Toby.

Tyler's piercing look caught her attention. "He has your eyes," he said.

Beth wanted to smack herself as she felt a blush warm her face. She should have passed the shy schoolgirl stage years ago. "Denki. Most people tell me he looks like his father."

"There's a lot of you in him too."

His gaze intensified and made Beth squirm a little. "He has my temper," she said.

The hint of a smile traveled across his face before he cleared his throat and snapped out of whatever thought had distracted him. "Are you in town for a visit?"

Beth recited her carefully rehearsed explanation. "We're staying with Mammi and Dawdi until we can find a place of our own in Bonduel."

"I'll keep my eye out. There was a nice little

cottage north on one-seventeen, but it sold three weeks ago."

"Out by the Millers' farm?"

Tyler nodded. "You remember that old barn?"

"Jah. Mamm said it burned down six months ago."

"A blessing in disguise. If the fire hadn't taken it, it might have toppled in a wind storm and hurt somebody."

Beth laughed at the memory of that old barn, so rickety that it creaked in a breeze and so charming that *die youngie* gathered there almost every week. "Toby could have given it a good shove and knocked it down. We had some fun gatherings there." Her mind wandered back to the days of volleyball and *rumschpringe* and independence— blissfully happy years before her marriage. "Amos complained that I loved that rope swing more than I loved . . ." She lowered her eyes before she finished her sentence. She didn't want to think of Amos today.

Deep lines of concern dug themselves into Tyler's face. "I was sorry to hear about your husband's car accident."

"We are comforted that he is with God." Another carefully rehearsed response.

"With a new baby, you must have been devastated. How long has it been?"

"Over a year, last June. Toby was not six months old."

The deep compassion in his eyes surprised her. "It must be hard to be left all alone like that with a baby to care for. I'm sure it was a great comfort to have Amos's family share the burden of your grief."

"Jah" was all Beth could muster. She had stayed in that oppressive house for months, aching to return to Bonduel, knowing she would be callous indeed to up and leave the family so soon after Amos's death. Amos's mamm, Treva, had been battling cancer when Amos passed away. No matter how Beth had yearned to be away from the Hostetlers, she couldn't have abandoned Treva, as sick as she had been.

Tyler misinterpreted the pain that surely must have shown on Beth's face. He radiated genuine sympathy. "You must miss him very much."

I don't deserve your kindness, Tyler. I was overjoyed to have escaped Nappanee, Indiana, and the Hostetlers.

Noncommittal answers were almost second nature to her now. "He is with God now. I rejoice in that."

In more ways than one.

My heart is blacker than the bottom of the deepest well.

An awkward silence followed. Beth refused to say more about Amos than necessary, and it appeared that Tyler had run out of words of consolation. Either that or he didn't want to stir up Beth's painful memories unnecessarily. Well, she had plenty of bad memories but probably not the kind Tyler imagined.

He studied her face for several seconds before clearing his throat. "Anna said you made cookies."

"Oh . . . yes." She retrieved the plate from the

counter and held it out to him. "I'm not that good of a cook, but they do have chocolate chips in them. Chocolate makes everything taste better."

Toby saw the plate of goodies and skipped to Beth's side. Beth sat down and handed him a cookie. Tyler sat next to Beth at the table and lifted Toby onto his lap.

"Be careful," Beth said. "Toby likes to take a bite, spit it into his hand, examine it, and then put it back in his mouth. He ends up quite messy."

Tyler scooted Toby to a more secure position onto his lap. "I'd consider it an honor to be smeared with cookie goo. Babies don't grant their affection to just anybody."

Beth couldn't seem to pull her gaze from the sight of Toby cradled safely in Tyler's arms, arms that clearly did heavy work. A man didn't get muscles like those by sitting around and yelling at his wife all day.

The memory felt as if someone had poked her, compelling her to rise from her chair and giving her a reason to pull herself from Tyler's gaze. "Would you like some milk?" She quickly collected herself and shot him a teasing grin. "You might have to soak them for a few minutes. My cookies always turn out dry. Not on purpose of course."

Tyler snatched one from the plate and took a hearty bite. "These are delicious. Just the way I like them."

Beth tried not to take too much satisfaction in what he said. He was only trying to be polite. She poured milk into two cups and set both on the table. "One for Toby and one for you. Just in case."

Tyler helped Toby drink his milk, which dribbled down his chin and the front of his shirt and dripped onto Tyler's trousers. Tyler didn't even flinch.

As they ate, Beth tried her best to wipe Toby's face after every bite of cookie so Tyler's shirt wouldn't be a complete mess. He actually grinned when Toby waved his hands back and forth and bits of soggy cookie ended up in Tyler's shiny black-brown hair.

"Oh, Toby," Beth said. "Look what you've done."

A rag proved insufficient to clean up Toby's gloppy hands, so Beth carted him to the sink. Once Beth washed Toby's hands under the running water, she set him down to play with Sparky. "Now," she said, glancing at Tyler and dampening a dish-towel, "let's see what we can do about your hair."

Tyler propped his elbow on the table and rested his chin in his hand. "I kind of like it. Birds can land on my head and eat."

Beth giggled. Standing behind him, she used the towel to pluck Toby's mess from Tyler's hair. This close, she could catch his manly scent. He smelled of freshly mowed hay at autumn time. The distracting aroma took her to a grassy meadow, where she pictured herself picking wildflowers while she strolled hand-in-hand with Tyler Yoder. She jerked her fingers from his hair and unwittingly pulled out four strands by the roots.

With his chin still resting on his hand, he glanced

at her out of the corner of his eye. "It must be in there like glue."

"Sorry. I got carried away. It won't happen again."

"I don't mind."

She finished his hair, took the dishtowel to the sink, and busied herself rinsing it out so she could gather her unruly wits. She'd promised herself that she would never, ever consider another boy again for any reason. That promise was always fresh in her mind. To be sure, Tyler smelled wonderful, but no amount of tempting fragrance should weaken her resolve.

I must be coming down with something.

Tyler looked slightly flushed as he stood, donned his hat, and grabbed another cookie. "I don't think Aden is going to show up, and Dat is waiting for help at the dairy. Will I see you at *gmay* on Sunday?"

"Lord willing."

He strode across the room to where Toby played with three balls. Tyler squatted to be eye level with him and laid a light kiss on his cheek. "Good-bye, Toby. Stay out of the road."

Toby waved and called forth a smile from Tyler. "Bye-bye."

Beth pursed her lips to keep from smiling as Tyler glided out the door.

He had eaten three cookies and hadn't taken one swig of milk.

She took a deep breath and reminded herself of her promise. She didn't want a man in her life ever again. She felt perfectly happy being alone, answering to no one but God.

Beth didn't pay any particular attention to what went on out the window as Tyler jumped into his open-air buggy and drove away. He had a beautiful horse. And very nice posture. And an able hand at the reins.

She barely noticed his departure or her heart drumming a cadence she hadn't heard for a very long time.

Chapter Three

Beth glanced out the window and groaned softly. She shouldn't have gone to church on Sunday. The vultures were already circling.

She wiped the ketchup from Toby's face and hands before lifting him out of the high chair to let him run free around the great room. Running free was Toby's favorite activity.

Beth's too.

Getting down on her hands and knees, Beth picked up the remnants of Toby's breakfast. Toby liked to feed himself, but when he had his fill, he hurled his leftovers off the tray. The floor never stayed clean.

Mammi came from outside with her egg basket. Her eyes twinkled, but her lips parted in an expression of befuddlement. "Oh, dear, Beth. You have a visitor."

Beth stood and threw away the last of Toby's toast. "I saw."

"What are you going to do?"

Beth huffed in exasperation and stifled a sorry grin. "I don't want to hurt his feelings, Mammi, but he's old enough to be my dat."

Mammi slumped her shoulders. "He brought flowers."

A pathetic giggle burst from Beth's lips. "I wish men wouldn't feel the need to kill a perfectly good plant for me."

Mammi propped her hands on her hips. "These eager suitors need to make way for your true match. You'll never get a chance to fall in love when all these other men make pests of themselves."

"I can take care of myself. I don't want a husband." The very thought dampened her spirits. In Nappanee, unwanted suitors had swooped in after the one-year anniversary of Amos's death. She had refused three men before July had come and gone.

"Well, I know you don't want Alvin Hoover. I'll march right out there and tell him to go home."

"Nae, Mammi. I'll talk to him."

"Do you think a knitted potholder would make him feel better?"

"Jah, everybody loves your potholders."

Mammi peeked out the window. "A sweater might be better. As pretty as you are, you're bound to break his heart."

Beth dried her hands and kissed Mammi on the cheek. "I'm as plain as the nose on your face. The men in Bonduel have poor eyesight."

Mammi giggled. "They can see well enough."

"Alvin Hoover wants a housekeeper more than he wants a wife."

Mammi pulled a bright yellow potholder from her closet. "I think the poor man doesn't want just any wife. He's hoping for a pretty one."

Beth tied her bonnet under her chin. "I'm as plain as an unvarnished fence post."

Mammi would not be persuaded. She winked and handed Beth the potholder. "Alvin Hoover must be partial to fence posts."

Beth arched an eyebrow in amusement and stepped outside.

Broad and firmly built, Alvin Hoover didn't stand quite as tall as Beth, but he must have considered himself tall enough to have a chance with her. Strands of gray hair peppered his chestnut-brown beard, and a decidedly deep furrow set directly between his eyebrows.

He held his bouquet of flowers at his side with the blooms pointed toward the ground as if he were planning on sweeping the dirt with them. He chatted cheerfully with Dawdi about the weather, like old men always did.

Beth's dat would be indignant if he could hear her thoughts. *Forty-five isn't old. Alvin Hoover is in his best years*, he would say. Dat was forty-eight. He considered anyone under sixty to be in the prime of his life.

Alvin squared his shoulders when he caught sight of Beth. He lifted the bouquet directly in front of him as if he were posing for a picture. "Well, hello, Beth."

Dawdi placed a hand on Alvin's shoulder. "Gute to talk to you, Alvin. Let me know when you slaughter that hog, and I'll ready the smokehouse."

Dawdi turned his back on Alvin and walked toward Beth. When Dawdi came close, he stopped and took her hand. "Just so's you know," he whispered, "this isn't the one your mammi wants."

Beth smiled. Dawdi always seemed to know precisely what he was talking about, even if no one else did.

Alvin stepped forward and handed Beth the flowers, a mixture of black-eyed Susans and daisies that he'd probably gathered from his pasture this morning.

"Denki, Alvin. These are very pretty."

"I saw them and thought of you," he said. "Because you're cheery like a garden of yellow pansies."

Beth sorely needed a drink of water. Her mouth tasted as dry as a pile of dead leaves. She had met Alvin on Sunday. Would he have the nerve to propose to her today? And how would she ever deflate his hopes without sounding callous or ungrateful?

Or completely and utterly uninterested.

"Benji and Alvin Junior picked them for you," Alvin added.

Beth cringed. Alvin Junior was nineteen years old, four years younger than Beth. And then there were Alvin's other six children to consider, children in need of a cook and housekeeper.

Beth found the thought unbearable—not the thought of children, but the thought of being sought after, not because Alvin loved her or cared for her, but because he needed a woman, preferably young and strong, who wouldn't mind working herself to death. Since she'd been married before, Alvin must have believed she was either less picky or more desperate than most girls her age.

She felt more than a little awkward as Alvin fell silent and stared at her. She cleared her throat and handed him the potholder. "My mammi wanted you to have this."

He looked at the potholder as if he had no idea what to do with it. "Denki," he said, stuffing it into his pocket and strolling toward the house. He inclined his head and shrugged his arm as a hint that she should follow him. She did, reluctantly. "My wife's been gone three years, you know."

Yes, she knew. In five days, this was Alvin's third visit, and he had mentioned his late wife no less than ten times. "Yes. I'm very sorry for your loss. Mammi tells me she was a wonderful-gute cook."

"Her butterscotch pies were always the first to sell at auction."

"I am a very bad cook. Amos always used to tell me so."

"Thanksgiving was my favorite holiday because of her chestnut apple stuffing. Delicious."

If she didn't poke fun at herself, she'd probably burst into tears of frustration. "I made stuffing from a box once, but it didn't come with chestnuts."

Alvin halted and rested his hand awkwardly on the porch railing. "Beth, your lot in life cannot be easy. You have a son to care for and no way to support yourself."

Beth held her breath. She hated having to refuse a marriage proposal so early in the morning. It would put a damper on her whole day, but she could see no way around it.

How had Tyler Yoder known how badly she needed an interruption at this very moment? He rode up the lane on his dapple-gray horse like a hero from a storybook come to rescue the fair maiden.

"Tyler," she called, waving and jogging toward his horse as if he were her best friend in the world.

Tyler, ever so serious, nodded before dismounting. "How are you? Is Toby well?"

"Jah. He is running around inside with Mammi."

"Gute," Tyler said, leading his horse to the barn.

Beth stood at the edge of the grass, pretending to be very interested in Tyler's trek to the barn. If she could avoid Alvin for a few more minutes, Tyler's presence would prevent him from proposing. She bit her bottom lip. Maybe she should go to Alvin right now and get it over with. Why prolong the suspense?

Because she was a coward, that's why. Right now, she didn't have the guts to deal with Alvin's reaction. She wanted to give herself some time to prepare an appropriate refusal so she didn't hurt

Alvin's feelings any more than she had to. He had already lost his dear wife.

Tyler emerged from the barn, and Beth walked with him to the porch. She still clutched the flowers in her hand as if she were holding a flashlight, not quite sure what to do with them.

"I came to help Aden," Tyler said, "if he shows up. He says I got the day wrong last time, but I think he's the one who's mixed up." Tyler stopped as if he'd run into a wall. "Hello, Alvin. *Wie gehts*?"

Alvin practically tripped over his feet in an effort to shake Tyler's hand. "I'm fine, fine." His eyes darted between Beth and Tyler, and his smile melted like butter in a frying pan. "You paying a call?"

In puzzlement, Tyler stared at Alvin until understanding flickered in his eyes, and he stuttered his reply. "Nae . . . nac. I'm here to see Aden."

Beth wanted to laugh out loud. Tyler was trying to be tactful and encouraging at the same time. He didn't realize that Alvin's suit was a lost cause. It would have been better if Tyler had pulled her into his arms and kissed her wildly—to send the clear message that Beth was unavailable. That would do it. Alvin would run for the hills.

Beth shivered involuntarily. The thought of kissing Tyler was not all that unpleasant. He had such a handsome face and a steady way about him. What girl wouldn't be tempted?

Had she lost her mind?

"I came to help Aden build a chest of drawers for his wife for Christmas," Tyler said. "We're putting it together here because Aden wants it to be a surprise."

Alvin unclenched his jaw. "Christmas will be here before we know it. Only four months."

Mammi opened the front door and clapped her hands together as if dismissing a class of scholars. "Well, Alvin, Beth and I must go."

Dear Mammi. Always so accommodating.

Alvin shaped and reshaped his lips as if searching for the perfect word to release from his mouth. "Oh."

Not a bad choice of words, considering how Mammi's dismissal must have thrown him for a loop. He had come to make a marriage proposal, for goodness sake.

Alvin soon recovered his composure and smiled pleasantly. "I can see this is an inconvenient day for a social call. I will return next Tuesday. When does Toby take a nap?"

Tuesday. She had until Tuesday to come up with a kind yet firm refusal. Guilt niggled at her like a mosquito buzzing next to her ear. "Toby usually goes down at noon."

Alvin nodded cheerfully. "I will see you at noon on Tuesday."

She couldn't match his enthusiasm. "Okay."

He tromped away, and Tyler gazed at Beth with an apology on his face. "I'm sorry if I interrupted something—"

"You didn't," Beth said with a finality in her voice that indicated she would rather not discuss Alvin

Hoover ever again in her lifetime. She watched as Alvin climbed into his courting buggy and rode away. The more the distance grew between him and Beth, the better she felt. She grinned at sober-faced Tyler. "I noticed you rode your horse today. Was that in case you ran across a little boy playing in the middle of the lane? A horse is easier to stop than a buggy."

Tyler furrowed his brow and turned his face away, as if studying the whitewash on the barn. "Of course not. Some days I like to ride."

Beth liked seeing him squirm. He was too polite to mention that unfortunate incident ever again, but she suspected it was precisely the reason he had ridden his horse to Huckleberry Hill.

"You think I'm a bad mother, don't you?"

He snapped his head around to look at her and growled when he saw the amusement in her eyes. "I like riding my horse. And toddlers are gute at escaping even the most careful mothers."

"It's so fun to tease someone who doesn't know how to be teased."

His lips turned upward into a half smile. Quite an accomplishment. "Why does something have to be wrong with me? Maybe you don't know how to tease."

She laughed. "You could be right. But I must tell you, I have years of practice."

Tyler inclined his head toward her. "Then I have a lot to learn from you."

He said it with a voice as smooth as honey, as if

he looked forward to her lessons. A warm sensation spread to the tips of Beth's fingers.

Toby poked his head out the front door and saw Tyler. "Mommy!" he squealed.

Beth felt her face glow. "He only calls people 'mommy' if he likes them. Congratulations."

"I'm surprised he remembers me." Tyler bounded up the steps and scooped Toby into his arms.

From inside, Dawdi shuffled to the door, humming one of his many tunes. "Tyler, you are just the man I want to see. Can you help me set up this new-fangled contraption?"

"Of course." Tyler put Toby on his feet even as he whined to stay in Tyler's arms. "I'll be back in no time at all, Toby."

Beth tried not to let Tyler's gentle ways make an impression on her, but any kindness to Toby, even from a man, softened her heart to jelly.

Tyler followed Dawdi into the house. "It's called a Pack 'n Play," Dawdi said. "It ain't nothing but a crib, but a stranger crib I never saw."

Mammi's eyes sparkled like the sky on a starry night. "He's a nice young man, ain't not? And quite taken with Toby."

Beth decided to skirt the issue. "Who wouldn't love Toby?"

Of course Tyler was a nice young man. Beth had once thought Amos was a nice young man too.

"Who indeed?" Mammi said, as she slipped Toby's arms into the small green sweater she'd knitted for him. "Did Alvin get a chance to propose?"

Beth curved her lips and shook her head. "He

tried." She studied the limp bouquet of flowers in her hand. "Am I wicked for not wanting to marry him?"

"Wicked? Of course not. Alvin needs a wife. You're available. That's as far as he's thinking." She fastened the sweater buttons up to Toby's chin and gave the wiggly little boy a kiss. "Alvin needs Suvilla Mast. She's four years older than him and has four children, all grown. She sits a bit broad, but so does he. They would get along very well together." She sighed and looked as if the very thought of Suvilla Mast and Alvin Hoover wore her out. "There's always so much matchmaking to be done."

"That won't stop him from coming back on Tuesday."

"Nae. You'll have to let him down easy. He's worn out from all them *kinner* he's caring for. He needs a wife right quick."

Mammi went back into the house where she retrieved her bonnet and black sweater and a light yellow sweater for Beth. "Should we pick some of the huckleberries this morning? We can gather enough to make Christmas jam tomorrow, and the family can pick the rest of the berries on Saturday."

"I would love to pick today." Beth gazed at the clear blue sky of late August. They wouldn't need sweaters, but she didn't mention that fact to her mammi. Mammi loved seeing her grandchildren wear her knitted gifts. Beth slipped the sweater around her shoulders. Black was the traditional sweater and coat color that all Amish wore, but when it came to knitting, Mammi either forgot or ignored the rule. Beth shrugged. Mammi had gone to a great deal of work to knit her a yellow sweater. She would wear the yellow sweater.

Tyler and Dawdi reappeared on the threshold, and Tyler immediately lifted Toby and gave him a squeeze. "Toby's new bed is ready."

"All Tyler did was push the center down. I should have thought of that," Dawdi said.

Tyler stared intently at Beth and didn't look away when she caught his eye. "That's a wonderful-pretty sweater," he said.

Hoping her ears hadn't turned bright red, Beth reached for Toby, and Tyler flew him down the steps like an airplane. He even supplied the airplane noises. Toby's giggles bubbled from his lips as Tyler placed him in Beth's arms.

"Mammi and I are going to pick huckleberries," Beth said. "Denki for your help." Especially the part where he'd come just in time to fend off a marriage proposal. "I hope Aden comes soon so you're not left waiting again."

"Come on, Sparky," Mammi called. The dog waddled out of the house as if she had just awakened from a nap.

Worry etched tiny lines around Tyler's eyes. "It's quite a walk to the huckleberry patch. Can you manage Toby by yourself?"

"He loves to explore the woods."

"Does he ever wander off? It wouldn't be easy to find him if he wandered off. Do you have a bell or something you could tie to his arm?"

A smile tickled Beth's lips. "Like a cow?"

"Jah. We sometimes use bells on our cows when they graze."

The laughter tripped out. "I will keep a careful eye out."

Mammi handed Beth a bucket, and the two of them strolled toward the path into the woods.

Undeterred by her teasing, Tyler followed. "Aden saw a bear there last year. You should take a frying pan." That deep furrow right between his brows was adorable.

Beth strolled blithely down the path. "We'll make lots of noise, and Sparky will scare off the bears."

She and Tyler glanced at Sparky, who shuffled lazily after them as if merely lifting her feet were a monumental chore. Beth and Tyler locked gazes. Beth giggled. Tyler frowned.

He held up his hand to motion for Beth to stop. "Wait. Wait a minute. We've got to think about this. I'm worried you're putting yourself in unnecessary danger."

"When I was a little girl, I used to go to the huckleberry patch by myself all the time." She leaned closer to punctuate her next words. "I ran all the way. With scissors. While being chased by three bears and a cat. And I didn't wear sunscreen."

Tyler didn't even flinch. Didn't even crack a smile. She would definitely have to help him with his sense of humor. With a frown still firmly riveted to his face, he took Toby from Beth's arms, grabbed her bucket, and walked briskly into the woods. "I'm coming with you."

"What about Aden?" she said, grinning and struggling to keep up with him.

He glanced back at her while sustaining his breakneck pace. "I wouldn't consider myself any kind of a man if I let two women and a baby traipse into the woods by themselves." He halted abruptly and pinned her with a concerned look. "And you shouldn't run with scissors." Without another word, he turned and marched adamantly down the path.

Beth was laughing too hard to argue.

Chapter Four

Huckleberries had taken over Mammi's kitchen. With Tyler's help yesterday, they had picked five bucketsful, enough to make seven or eight dozen half-pints of huckleberry jam to sell at the Christmas bazaar. Making that much jam was quite a production. With mashing, stirring, boiling, and processing, it would take them all day.

Although it was hard work, Beth always looked forward to jam making day, especially when she did it with Mammi and her mamm, Sarah. It had been four years since she'd been part of a jam frolic. They would spend the day stirring, visiting, and laughing, and she loved seeing the bright purple jam glistening in the jars when they finished. And the jam tasted wonderful gute. Neither Beth nor Mamm were known for their cooking skills and Mammi was the worst cook of all, but jam only had five ingredients. It was hard to mess up.

Besides, Amos wasn't here to remind Beth of her

poor cooking skills. Food tasted better without the constant criticism.

Dawdi and Sparky's job was to entertain Toby while Mamm, Mammi, and Beth worked.

After checking for stems, Mamm rinsed the berries in the colander. Once the huckleberries were cleaned, Mammi deposited them into every available bowl in the kitchen. The table and counters were soon a sea of shiny purple berries ready for processing.

Beth rinsed out the galvanized metal bucket. Every last huckleberry had been washed. She glanced at Dawdi, who sat in his recliner with a box of crackers and a can of Easy Cheese. He sprayed the pasty cheese onto a cracker and handed it to Toby, who eagerly ate crackers while playing with his blocks. Sparky cheerfully cleaned up Toby's crumbs, which often turned out to be whole crackers with generous globs of smeared cheese.

"You doing okay, Dawdi?" Beth asked.

"Right as rain," Dawdi said, popping a cracker into his mouth. "This cheese is the weirdest stuff I ever seen."

Beth smiled. Everybody looked perfectly content on that side of the room.

Mamm filled a measuring cup with water while Mammi pulled a large saucepan from under the sink. "Moses stacked the sugar in the cellar last time he came," Mammi said. "Can you manage, Beth?"

"Jah, of course."

Beth skipped down the cellar stairs and had no

trouble locating the three large bags of sugar that Moses had stacked against the wall. She propped her hands on her hips. How would she ever lug a fifty-pound sack of sugar up the stairs? What had cousin Moses been thinking?

She stooped and wrapped her arms around the top sack as best she could. Using all her strength, she managed to lift it a few inches before her arms gave out. Unless she wanted to break her back, she'd have to find another way. Huffing in exasperation, she grabbed the sack by two corners and grunted as she strained to slide it off the pile. It fell with a thud onto the cement floor, sprinkling grains of sugar as it landed. Hunched over like an old man, she dragged the sugar to the bottom of the stairs, leaving a grainy trail behind her.

Breathing heavily, she attempted to yank the sack up one stair at a time and almost toppled head over heels. Was it possible to rip her arms out of their sockets? Maybe she would have to leave the sack down here and bring the sugar upstairs one cup at a time.

"Can I help?"

She turned to see Tyler Yoder at the top of the stairs, with Toby in his arms and that deeply concerned frown on his face, as if a great tragedy had befallen her and he wanted to help any way he possibly could.

His expression made her smile. She took a deep breath. "Never wrestle with a bag of sugar. It shows no mercy."

He came down the stairs carrying Toby. "Are you hurt?"

"Nope. Just humiliated." She flashed a smile, hoping to coax him out of his distress. She thought maybe his eyebrows moved apart a fraction of an inch. Maybe not. The cellar was sort of dim.

"That's a lot of sugar," he said.

"It takes more sugar than berries to make jam."

He nudged her elbow and slipped Toby into her arms. "He wanted me to pick him up the minute I walked in the door. I hope that's okay."

"Of course. You were his berry-picking buddy yesterday."

In one swift movement, Tyler reached down and hefted the heavy bag over his shoulder. Beth's tongue stuck to the roof of her mouth, and she didn't even try to pull her gaze away as she instinctively hugged Toby tighter. Muscles had always been a weakness of hers. She pressed her lips together so a girlish sigh wouldn't escape her lips. She'd rather not make a fool of herself so early in the morning.

Tyler tromped up the stairs with Beth and Toby following close behind. He propped the sack on the counter. "Is this a gute spot?"

"Wonderful-gute," Mammi said, her eyes twinkling. "I'm glad you came by when you did. Beth needs a strong young man around the house."

Tyler merely nodded and sprouted that worried look on his face again, as if all of the Helmuths' problems had just become his problems.

Beth felt as if her cheeks had burst into flames. She bent over and put Toby on his feet. It gave her an excuse to hide her face momentarily. Mammi had been on her side about Alvin Hoover. Surely she wasn't trying to shove Tyler Yoder on her. Both Mammi and Mamm knew perfectly well that Beth had chosen to remain single permanently.

Beth's lips twisted in annoyance. Her refusal to marry wouldn't stop Mammi from trying to find her a husband. Dawdi had told Beth that Alvin "wasn't the one Anna wanted," which clearly meant that Mammi had somebody else in mind. But it didn't matter how big Tyler's muscles were or how much he helped with Toby, she was immune to every good quality. She refused to marry ever again.

It was as simple as that.

Beth's mamm took some scissors and cut the top off the sugar bag. "We could use some strong arms, if you can stay, Tyler," she said.

"Mamm," Beth protested, suddenly irritated beyond endurance. "We don't need Tyler's help making jam." She looked at Tyler. "I'm sure you've got more important things on your schedule today," she added, in case he thought she wanted to get rid of him.

One side of his mouth turned down. Beth wasn't the only one irritated. "I'm waiting for Aden. Again. He assured me he'd be here at ten o'clock. That's why I came at ten-thirty." He rolled up his sleeves. "How can I help?"

Mamm turned on the water and started filling the sink. "Wash bottles."

Beth was tempted to point out that it didn't take big muscles to wash bottles, but they'd already reeled Tyler in. Mammi had told Beth that Tyler liked helping people. He couldn't very well back out now. He plunged his hands into the water and started washing.

"How old are you, Tyler?" Mamm asked.

"Twenty-three."

Mamm nodded in satisfaction. "Same age as Beth."

"How very nice," Mammi said, gushing like a geyser.

Beth clenched her teeth.

Mamm was just getting started. "Tell me about your dairy. Is it making gute money? Can you support a wife and children?"

"Jah," Tyler said, unsuspecting of where Mamm's questions led. "I planned it all out last year before I got engaged."

Beth tried not to let her eyes pop out of her head. "You're engaged?" Unexplainable disappointment sneaked up on her, which she immediately quashed. How could she possibly feel disappointed? Tyler may be solidly built, but she didn't in a million years want to marry him.

Tyler's expression deflated. "Not anymore."

Studying his face, Beth clapped her mouth shut and determined not to ask more questions. Some sad story had to be behind a broken engagement, and she wouldn't force Tyler to relive the memories.

Mamm had no such reservations. "His fiancée ended up with your cousin Aden."

Beth couldn't keep her eyes from popping out of her head. "That was you?"

Tyler washed the jars with increased vigor. "Yep."

"I heard the story, of course, but Mamm never told me the name of the jilted fiancé."

Tyler turned one shade darker and glanced at Mamm. "I suppose you wanted to spare my feelings by not repeating it?"

Mamm nodded. "I suppose I did." She waved her hand as if brushing aside the topic. "That's all water under the bridge. The important thing is that when you do find a girl to love, you're ready to provide for a family."

"That's right," said Mammi, winking at Beth. "Somewhere out there is a beautiful girl who needs a pair of strong arms to take care of her."

It was Beth's turn to blush. The scheming had begun.

Tyler regarded Beth as if he were trying to comprehend her past and future by looking hard enough. She cocked her eyebrows and pursed her lips to scold him for staring.

He quickly looked away. "These are done, Sarah."

Mamm picked up one of Tyler's bottles and examined it. "Good enough." Mamm never sugarcoated her praise. "Beth, take Tyler to the cellar, and each of you bring up an armful of bottles. With all these berries, we'll use them, sure as you're born."

Tyler dried his hands and followed Beth down the stairs.

"We wouldn't need extra bottles if you hadn't helped us gather so many berries yesterday," Beth said as they reached the bottom of the stairs.

"Thanks to you, Mammi and Dawdi will sell a lot of jam this year."

Tyler shook his head. "I mostly watched out for Toby and for bears."

Beth smiled. Halfway into their walk into the woods yesterday, Tyler had picked up a stick and started banging it against the trees to scare away any critters lurking in the shadows. "I've never seen anyone quite so vigilant about bears and snakes."

"Snakes have been known to eat small children."

The laughter bubbled from her lips. "Not typically in Wisconsin."

"You can't be too careful."

"I'm glad Aden never showed up so you could come with us."

"Unless he's in the hospital with two broken legs, I plan on giving him a stern lecture about the importance of keeping his appointments."

Beth led Tyler to the shelf where the extra half pints sat. "If he weren't my cousin, I might not believe that Aden actually exists. He hasn't shown himself once since I've been to Huckleberry Hill."

Tyler grinned. "Don't take it personally. Right now, he thinks he and Lily are the only two people in the whole world."

Beth checked her laughter. Such thoughts must be at least a little painful to Tyler, even if he smiled about them.

"If we put these jars in a bucket, we won't have to make so many trips," she said.

They looked around and found three dust-covered buckets stacked together underneath one of the shelves. Beth picked up the stack and blew some of the dust off the top bucket. "I haven't had a chance to redd up down here. The dust is thick."

"You take gute care of your grandparents."

"They take gute care of me and Toby."

"I'm glad they do." That worried frown came back, accompanied by a deep furrow right between his brows as if someone had taken a plow to his forehead. "Do you like living here?"

"There isn't a better place on Earth. Mammi and Dawdi moved here when I was seven years old. I have fond memories of berry picking and maple syrup time. When I was growing up, we spent many summer days playing volleyball or helping Mammi and Dawdi in the vegetable patch."

"How long do you think you will stay?"

She would stay forever if she and Toby weren't such a burden on Mammi and Dawdi. "I need to earn some money first, but I'd like to find a small house in Bonduel."

He pressed his lips together. "It's hard for a single mother to make it on her own. Most think it best to remarry."

Beth couldn't look at him. She concentrated on prying the buckets apart. They were stuck tight.

His frown looked as if it had been stapled to his face. He held out his hand. She gave him the stack of buckets, and he pulled the top one away from the others as easy as you please. "I'm sorry. I should stay out of your troubles."

"Don't apologize. I want to be strong enough to support myself and Toby."

"I could help you, if you need money. The dairy makes enough for me to put a little away each month."

Beth laughed as if she'd been holding it in a long time. His offer didn't offend her. In a strange way, it brought her comfort. "Mammi said you have a kind heart. She wasn't exaggerating."

He relaxed his dire expression. "I didn't say that to beg for praise."

"I know."

Tyler shook his head adamantly. "I don't want you to think better of me than I deserve. I just want to help." He placed two more jars in the bucket and glanced at her out of the corner of his eye. "What about your late husband's family? Can they help?"

Beth turned her face and fixed her gaze out the small cellar window. "Their help comes with strings attached."

"What do you mean?"

What would Tyler say if he knew what she really thought of her in-laws? "I'll not be a burden to anyone."

They loaded jars into two of the buckets, and silence prevailed until Beth talked herself back into good humor. She squared her shoulders and flashed a smile at Tyler. "Denki. I'll never forget your generous offer."

"I want to help."

"You needn't worry about me. I have a plan." She put one last jar on the top of her stack. "Forgive me for saying so, but I'm a gute seamstress. I can whip out a dress on my old treadle machine in less than two hours. Kapps take even less time. I have done the figuring. If I make three dresses a day and sell them for forty dollars each, I can make a gute living. Enough to buy a house and keep chickens if I want."

Tyler took her bucket. It wasn't that heavy, but he insisted. "You want to make dresses for Amish women?"

"And Mennonites and German Baptists. And even the *Englisch* want the Amish dresses. The Englisch will pay the most." She studied his somber face, and her hopes sank. "You think it's a bad idea. Amos thought it was a bad idea."

"Nae, I think it is a wonderful-gute idea. Everyone would buy. My mamm hates to sew. She would love it if someone else made a dress for her."

"Do you think the bishop will approve?"

"My dat is the bishop. He'll approve." He placed his buckets on the floor and shoved his hand into his pocket. "It wonders me if you would sew a dress for my mamm for her birthday. Purple is her favorite color." He pulled out two twenty-dollar bills and stuffed them into Beth's fist.

A thrill passed through her as she stared at the money in her hand. "You want me to make your mamm a dress?"

He cracked a smile. "It's worth the forty dollars to see how wide your eyes are."

"I can't take your money. I haven't even officially started the business yet."

"You have now."

She tried to give the money back, but he refused

to take it. Her insistence and his refusal became a sort of tug of war as she tried to shove the bills into his hands, and he raised them in the air so Beth could not reach them. They both laughed as she backed him against one of the cellar walls. He was cornered, but he wouldn't lower his hands.

Beth, giggling uncontrollably, finally threw the money at him. It fell at his feet. He snatched it off the floor and stuffed it into one of the empty jars sitting in one of the buckets.

"I haven't even made the dress yet," Beth insisted between giggles. "Pay me when I finish."

Tyler was breathless with laughter. "You need money for fabric, and I don't think Toby has the cash to loan you."

Beth slipped the bills out of the jar and smoothed them in her hands. "My first customer." Her lips curled in satisfaction. "I think I'll put your name on a plaque over my sewing machine."

Tyler chuckled. "Be sure to spell it right."

"I'll make a very nice dress for your mamm," Beth said. "But I might have to charge you extra for the wrinkled money you paid your bill with."

He picked up the buckets and stomped up the stairs. "Charge me anything you want. Your dresses are probably worth twice what you're asking."

It turned out that Tyler's muscles came in handy making jam after all. He lifted boiling-hot pans of jam off the stove and poured their contents into bottles. He packed boxes with finished jam and lugged them downstairs for storage until Christmas. Between batches, he took Toby outside and chased him around the yard when Dawdi ran out of energy to look after him.

Tyler had to leave at three to milk cows at his dairy. Aden hadn't shown up again, and Beth began to suspect that Aden was in on Mammi's scheming. Why else would he invite Tyler to Huckleberry Hill and then not show up himself? She'd have to give her cousin a good talking-to.

Beth couldn't help but be touched. Aden may have tricked Tyler onto Huckleberry Hill, but Tyler's gute heart had compelled him to stay and help with whatever project she happened to be working on that day.

Amos certainly wouldn't have been so kindhearted.

Thoughts of Amos jolted Beth back to reality. No amount of scheming by any of her relatives would convince her to waste her life on another husband. Not even someone with big muscles and an adorable frown.

She'd be much better off on her own.

Chapter Five

Tyler strolled into Aden's barn with his hands in his pockets. His friend sat at his workbench studying a book by the light of a kerosene lantern. Even though a bright autumn sun glowed outside, the barn was mighty dim for reading without a lamp. "You should drag a recliner out here if you want to be more comfortable."

Aden burst into a smile when he saw Tyler. He hadn't stopped smiling since he'd married Lily. It was a wonder that someone so deliriously happy could keep from floating off the ground. "I'm trying to figure out how to use my new composter."

"What's to figure out? You dump leaves and peelings in and get compost out six weeks later."

"Not this composter. It's complicated. It makes tea and does all sorts of fancy things." Still grinning like a cat, Aden stood, strode to Tyler, and shook his hand firmly.

Tyler sighed in mock relief. "I'm so glad to see

you haven't broken your legs. Or your ankles. Or even your toes."

Aden raised an eyebrow in puzzlement. "Nae. I'm walking around just fine."

"Lift up your sleeves," Tyler said. "I want to see your hives."

"I don't have hives."

"Shingles? Chicken pox?"

Aden, realizing Tyler's game, chuckled and shook his head.

"The croup? Or measles? What about fibromyalgia?"

"I'm fit as a fiddle, thank you very much."

"So," said Tyler, folding his arms and looking his friend up and down, "it wonders me why you have missed three appointments with me on Huckleberry Hill. I assume you still want help with Lily's Christmas present."

Aden would not stop grinning. Tyler found his amusement slightly annoying. "A few unexpected things came up. I hope you made good use of the time you spent waiting for me."

"I picked huckleberries one day and made jam the next."

"Gute. Picking huckleberries is hard on Mammi's back." Aden leaned against a wooden pillar. "Did you meet my cousin Beth?"

"Oh, jah, I met her."

Aden didn't take his eyes off Tyler's face. "She's pretty, ain't not?"

"Sure. And feisty. Keeps me on my toes."

Aden smirked. "I knew you'd like her."

Tyler eyed Aden suspiciously. "Did you?"

Aden cleared his throat and suddenly became very interested in his boots. "Everybody likes Beth."

Tyler groaned as realization caught up to him. "Please don't tell me you and your mammi are in cahoots to match me and Beth."

"Okay, I won't tell you."

He put a hand on Aden's shoulder. "Look, I know you still feel guilty about stealing my fiancée."

Aden sighed. "I suppose I do."

"Well, don't. Lily is much happier being your wife. And I don't feel bad anymore. Lily is a wonderful-gute girl, but we never would have suited. I'm glad she came to her senses before it was too late. I was embarrassed, to be sure, but I have a thick skin. I got over it."

Aden kicked the pieces of hay at his feet. "I want you to be happy as I am. You deserve a girl like Beth."

Tyler shrugged off such a thought. "I gave up the notion of romance a long time ago, Aden."

"And it's my fault you did."

"When Lily broke our engagement, I realized that I'd been chasing after an illusion."

"You're wrong."

"No, I'm not. I got swept away by infatuation when I should have been more levelheaded."

Aden pressed his lips into a hard line and shook his head. "Why don't you admit that the rejection stung and that it's painful to think about trying again?"

"Romance doesn't work for everybody, Aden. You don't need to feel bad about that."

"So you're giving up on Beth?"

"Beth is Anna's and your idea, not mine."

Aden sat down at his workbench. "She's a wonderful-gute cousin."

Tyler couldn't argue with that. He liked Beth a lot. It was nice to have a friend he enjoyed being with, someone who actually tempted him to smile occasionally. "I worry about her, trying to pull through life without a husband. She shouldn't have to struggle like that while she's still grieving the loss of her husband."

Aden snorted. "Amos? That grumpy toad? Amos didn't deserve her."

With an ear-splitting bark, Aden's giant of a dog came barreling into the barn. Before Tyler could fend him off, the dog jumped up and propped his paws on Tyler's shoulders.

"Pilot, get down," Aden said.

Tyler nudged Pilot off him and ruffled the curly fur on the dog's head. "It's good you're so lovable, Pilot, or I might find you annoying."

Pilot trotted to Aden for some love. Aden held Pilot's face in his hands. "Jah, no one can resist your cuteness."

Tyler rolled his eyes. That dog would never learn to behave with Aden as his master. Aden didn't have a stern bone in his body.

Breathless and flushed, Aden's wife and Tyler's former fiancée, Lily, appeared at the door of the barn. "Pilot, you little sneak. How did you slip out of that knot?" When she stepped farther into the barn, she caught sight of Tyler and hesitated for a fraction of a second. After almost a year, it still felt a bit awkward between them even though there was no ill will on either side.

With satisfaction, Tyler noted that the sight of Lily didn't upset him at all. He was finally over her and his juvenile dreams of giddy romance.

"Hi, Tyler. Sorry about Pilot. He's supposed to be having a bath."

Tyler smiled, hoping to put her at ease. "It's Aden's fault. He lets Pilot walk all over him. Or rather, jump all over him and every other poor soul who happens to set foot on your property."

Aden grinned and brought his face within inches of Pilot's nose. "You wouldn't hurt a fly, would you, boy? Tyler's just being crabby."

"Oh, sure. This is *my* problem."

Laughing, Aden patted Pilot's neck. "At least you're man enough to admit it."

Lily marched up to Pilot and grabbed his collar. She and Aden briefly brushed hands, and the look they gave each other didn't escape Tyler's notice. Romance came naturally to some people. It just wasn't Tyler's thing.

"I don't know how, but Pilot can sense when I'm about to give him a bath," Lily said as she pulled him toward the open barn door. "He's a master of escape."

"It's chilly outside," Aden said, obviously trying to keep the concern out of his voice.

Lily looked up at him and winked. "Don't worry. I'll make the water nice and warm. He'll love it."

Aden didn't take his eyes off Lily until she disappeared from sight. "Isn't she beautiful? I am blessed beyond measure." He glanced at Tyler, lowered his eyes, and cleared his throat. "Sorry. That was insensitive."

"I don't want you to spend one more minute worrying about it." Tyler pulled up a milking stool and sat down next to Aden. "I'm sincerely happy for you. God sent you a wonderful-gute wife, and I hope I am as fortunate someday."

"But you just said you've given up on marriage."

Tyler shook his head. "I still want to get married. I just don't believe in romance anymore." He propped his elbows on his knees. "Mamm says that unmarried men over the age of twenty-five are a nuisance. I only have two years left before I become insufferable and annoying. I'd rather find a wife."

"But you don't want a romantic relationship?"

"What I really need to find is a good woman to share my life. A companion and helpmeet. No romance required."

Aden nudged him in the shoulder. Hard. "Then why not Beth? You'll never find a harder worker or a girl who's more fun to be with."

"She still misses her husband."

"I already told you, Amos was a toad."

Tyler knew better. He had seen the look of pain that flitted across Beth's face every time she mentioned Amos's name.

Aden nudged him again. *What?* Did he think Tyler hadn't been paying attention? "It's plain as day that my cousin needs someone to care for her, and Toby needs a *fater*."

Aden was right. Ever since that first day on Huckleberry Hill, Tyler hadn't been able to stop worrying about how Beth would support herself and care for her small son. She'd wear herself to a frazzle in a matter of months. She needed help.

It concerned Tyler that Toby would never have a dat to teach him how to fish or show him how to plant and harvest crops. A boy should grow up with a *fater*.

"Amos has been gone for almost a year and a half," Aden said. "You wouldn't be offending anybody's notions of what's proper and what's not."

"I might be too late. Alvin Hoover's already set his sights on her." Tyler's mouth went dry at the thought of Alvin courting Beth.

Aden grimaced. "Alvin's old. What young widow wants to marry someone who will make her a widow again in twenty years? She'd definitely pick you over Alvin."

Before he could raise another objection, Tyler pictured Beth in his mind and clamped his mouth shut. Beth was a gute woman who had the qualities he wanted in a wife. It seemed too good of an idea not to at least consider.

Beth needed someone to take care of her. Even if the sewing business did well, she would only be able to make enough dresses to barely eke out a living. He could help her rear Toby, and Beth could lend a hand at the dairy. A mutually beneficial arrangement.

Because she still loved her first husband, she wouldn't crave the romance Tyler felt so disillusioned about. She'd already married for love once and wouldn't need the devotion and fervor of a first relationship.

"It doesn't hurt that she's pretty," Aden added.

"In other words, you're still scheming to match me with your cousin."

"It's not scheming if you're in on it. It's more like a secret plan."

Tyler chuckled. What would Beth think of their secret plan?

The more he thought about it, the more he liked the idea. Beth was certainly pretty. She didn't need to be pretty, but Tyler considered it a nice bonus. And she could make him laugh. He'd laughed more in the last two weeks than he had in the last twelve months. She would keep him laughing, and he would keep her safe.

Chapter Six

Beth's heart sank as she saw Alvin from the window. Another bouquet of flowers, another awkward conversation. Some men were annoyingly persistent.

She'd considered baking cookies yesterday with salt instead of sugar or offering him a bowl of Yankee bean soup with mushy beans and slimy ham. Since his first wife had been such a good cook, one fallen angel cake would surely chase Alvin Hoover away.

Instead, she decided the best course of action would be to tackle the problem head-on, without hesitation and without apology. Not waiting for Alvin to knock, she stepped onto the porch before he would have a chance to invite himself in and make himself comfortable.

"*Gute maiya*, Beth."

"*Gute maiya*, Alvin."

He marched up the porch steps and presented her with the flowers. "I gathered these myself.

Shall we sit?" He hesitated as he glanced around the covered porch. The lack of a place to sit seemed to confuse him momentarily. "Oh. Never mind. I expected rocking chairs or a porch swing."

Beth always felt more comfortable when the mood was light, although she hadn't noticed if Alvin had a sense of humor. She smiled. "Mammi says porch rockers are for old people, and she doesn't consider herself old yet."

Alvin smiled weakly as his gaze swept the porch for a second and third time. Did he think a loveseat would appear if he wished hard enough? He finally gave up and stared at Beth as if the absence of a place to sit derailed all his plans.

"We can sit on the steps," Beth suggested and sat before he had time to think of a better plan, like going inside. Keeping Alvin safely out of doors made for an easier getaway after she rejected him.

He smiled uncomfortably and grunted as he lowered himself to the step. Beth had forgotten that not everybody was as young as she, but he was only forty-five, for goodness sake. Was he too stiff to have a sit on the porch step?

He scooted to the middle of the step, cramming Beth tightly between him and the railing. "Beth, I have something very important to ask you."

She thought of cutting him off right there so she wouldn't have to sit in embarrassment while he professed his imaginary love. But she thought better of it. Let him say his piece so he couldn't claim that she hadn't given him a chance. That was what

Wallace Schwartz had accused her of after she had refused him.

Wallace had been the first in Nappanee to propose to her once her mourning period had passed, but he hadn't given her flowers like Alvin. She had gone to the market to do her weekly shopping, and in between ringing up a box of toddler cookies and weighing a head of purple cabbage, he'd mentioned that he needed a wife and she needed a husband and how about it?

Beth laced her fingers together and wrapped her arms around her legs, pressing her bouquet between her hands and knees. It would soon be over, and Alvin Hoover would never bother her again.

"Something to ask me? I hope you don't want my recipe for bread pudding. My late husband took a match to it the last time I pulled it out of my recipe box."

Alvin didn't even acknowledge her joke. Okay. No sense of humor.

"Barbara has been gone three years. Alvin Junior and Maysie Lynn are a big help, but those kinner will get me laid down yet."

Beth's thoughts wandered, and Tyler's face came unbidden to her mind. Tyler, unselfish to a fault, would never ask a girl to marry him simply because he needed someone to watch out for his children.

"I have a big farm and strong hands. My children will never go hungry."

Beth did her best to be sensitive to the compliment of a good man asking for her hand in marriage, even out of convenience. She tried to have sympathy for his feelings, though she didn't return them.

"The moment I laid eyes on you at gmay, I knew you were the one I wanted to share the rest of my life with. I know Barbara would approve." He took off his hat and tried to grab her hand, but since she wasn't about to unclasp her fingers, he ended up holding her wrist. "Will you marry me?"

Beth would suffocate if she didn't put some distance between them. She stood and faced Alvin, holding her flowers like a shield. "Alvin, any woman would be pleased to have you for a husband. You are a fine man with much to offer. I am very grateful that you consider me a fit mother to your children." She took a whiff of the flowers to give Alvin a moment to let her words sink in. "I am confident you will find a suitable wife, but I can't cook and I have a very bad temper. I would not make you happy."

Now he sprouted a grin. "What a tease you are. Your lightheartedness is one of the things I love about you."

Blast! It was her own fault he didn't take her seriously.

"Nae. You misunderstand. You will be happier with someone else, and I don't ever want to marry again."

This time, Alvin took her seriously, praise the Lord. He wrinkled his forehead in concern. "But you have a son to consider. You don't want him growing up without a father."

"The good Lord saw fit to take my husband.

Perhaps it is His will that Toby grows up without a father." She didn't know why she brought God into it. God had done nothing to stop her from marrying Amos. She couldn't trust what He *saw fit* to do with anybody.

"Not when He sends you a man to take your deceased husband's place."

Beth huffed in exasperation. How foolish to give him a reason he could argue with. She had wanted to make it quick and painless. "Alvin, truth be told, I don't want to marry you."

His countenance fell, and he stood more slowly than he had sat down. "I'm not so old, you know."

"No, not so old." She didn't know how else to defend herself. Of course she thought he was too old, but that didn't matter. She did not want to marry, period.

"If you're holding out hope for a younger man, I fear you'll never marry. No single man with a lick of sense will want to take on another man's child, no matter how pretty his mother is."

Beth tried very hard not to be offended. In his irritating way, Alvin only wanted to persuade her. "I know you'll find a wonderful-gute woman to mother your children," she said through gritted teeth.

Falling silent, Alvin folded his arms and shifted his weight from one foot to the other while glaring at Beth. Probably counting all the reasons she'd make a horrible wife. Would it be rude to urge him to go away?

Once again, Mammi saved the day. She threw

open the door and gave Beth and Alvin that twinkly smile that diffused even the tensest situations. "Alvin, I have a favor to ask. I've been so busy with jam and huckleberries and grandchildren that I almost forgot a promise I made to Suvilla Mast." She came down the steps and handed Alvin a white envelope. "She is learning how to knit and asked me for instructions for the honeycomb stitch. She's been waiting on them for weeks, and if she doesn't get them soon, her daughter will go without a Christmas present. Could you drop these off to her on your way home? She lives in the two-story clapboard house down the road from the Lampings' gift shop."

"It's not really on my way," Alvin stuttered. Mammi's change of subject had caught him off guard.

"Oh, thank you. It would mean so much to both of us. Knitting gives Suvilla such comfort. She's so lonely with her husband gone and all her kinner grown and moved away. She's not out of her forties yet and is still fit as a fiddle."

Alvin glanced at Beth as if trying to decide if their conversation had truly come to an end. Narrowing his eyes, he tapped his hat onto his head and pulled his bouquet from Beth's grasp. Without a word of good-bye, he stomped to his buggy and drove away with all the haste of a spurned boyfriend.

Beth bit her lip to keep from laughing. It was a virtue to be frugal. Lord willing, Alvin would find a gute home for those flowers.

Chapter Seven

Tyler scooped the last of the crispy bacon onto the tray and spooned half the bacon grease out of the pan. Then he poured pancake batter into the grease to form four perfectly round pancakes. Nothing better than pancakes flavored with bacon grease. He set the orange juice and bacon on the table and stepped back to admire his handiwork. Two crisp white plates sat on yellow placemats with a knife, fork, and spoon resting in their proper places. At home this morning, Mamm had helped him fold four yellow cloth napkins into the shape of flowers. He set two of them on the plates and the other two sat at the empty places at the table, in case Toby was extra messy. Toby's high chair sat between the two chairs at the table, and his plastic cup and plate waited on the tray.

Girls liked to be a little fancy now and then. He hoped his table decorations would send Beth into fits of delight.

He quickly turned back to his pancakes and

flipped them over one by one, each perfectly golden-brown and saturated with bacon grease. It had taken quite a bit of finagling to get Anna and Felty out of the house without Beth knowing about it. He'd hired a driver to pick them up early this morning and take them to the Denny's in Green Bay. When he had told Anna that he needed to be alone with Beth, Anna had actually squealed with glee and wished him happiness.

Felty, on the other hand, had looked more concerned than Tyler had ever seen him—even on the night Lily had broken off their engagement. "Don't get discouraged" was all Felty had said.

Tyler looked at the clock. Six-fifteen. Anna said Toby arose, without fail, at six. Hopefully, Beth would smell the bacon and emerge from her room at exactly the right time.

Toby toddled into the kitchen first. When he saw Tyler, he ran into his arms. "Mommy."

Tyler threw Toby into the air three times while Toby squealed and giggled. Tyler plopped him into the high chair and poured some orange juice into his sippy cup.

He heard the sound of bare feet on the wood floor and looked up as Beth shuffled into the kitchen. She wore a lavender dress without shoes or a head covering. Her long chestnut hair fell gracefully over her shoulders and almost to her waist. He couldn't help himself. Tyler stared like a hungry child in a candy shop. Beth's hair shone like liquid chocolate, and he wondered what it would feel like to run his fingers through it.

Beth yawned and then realized that it wasn't her mammi standing in the kitchen. She opened her eyes wide and took two steps back. "Oh."

Giggling, she retraced her steps and disappeared down the hall. In less time than it would have taken Tyler to don his boots, she returned, wearing shoes and stockings and with her hair tucked into a prayer covering. Tyler yearned for another glimpse of that hair.

"You know," she said, "you should really tell me when you're going to show up in my kitchen. It is entirely your own fault that you saw me without a kapp."

"Sorry. I wanted it to be a surprise."

"You surprised me, all right, but there is a very thin line between a surprise and a heart attack. Are you trying to send me to the hospital?"

How come no one else could make him smile so easily?

Beth kissed Toby on the cheek and gestured to the table. "What is all this?"

"I wanted to make you breakfast."

A shadow flitted across Beth's face before she replaced it with a grin. "Are you trying to tell me that I shouldn't cook for myself? Amos said I didn't even know how to boil water. Once I knew he didn't like the way I made it, I quit serving boiled water for supper."

"It's a special day. I wanted to make a special breakfast."

Beth raised her eyebrows and showed that charming dimple. "Ooh. Special breakfast."

He suddenly felt as if he'd been stricken with pneumonia and were struggling for every breath. He didn't need to be nervous. Beth wasn't intimidating in the least. Then again, it wasn't every day a boy asked a girl to marry him.

"I have something I want to ask you." He took the sunflower from the vase and handed it to her. Girls liked getting flowers.

Beth's smile disappeared faster than a Popsicle on the pavement in mid-July. She looked at the flower as if he had given her a snake.

A feeling of dread washed over him. Maybe she didn't like flowers so much.

Maybe he should reconsider.

He'd already told Beth today was a special day. He could pretend it was his birthday.

No, he had a plan. He felt good about the plan. This was not the time to abandon the plan.

He sat down and began his carefully rehearsed speech. "Last year at this time, I was published with Lily Eicher."

She cocked an eyebrow. "You made me breakfast to commemorate your engagement?"

"No," he stammered, "I want to explain . . ."

Her face fell. "I'm sorry. I didn't mean to make light of it. You must have been heartbroken."

"I suppose I was. I thought I loved her, but looking back, I can see we weren't right for each other, and she and Aden are so happy. The thought of it doesn't hurt anymore. The thing that stung the most was my complete humiliation."

Toby reached for a pancake. Beth cut one up

and poured syrup on it. "I'm sure Aden would never embarrass you on purpose."

"Of course not. He and Lily were both so nice about it. They even offered to postpone their wedding so people wouldn't feel sorry for me. But they needed to be together. I wouldn't ever want to stand in the way of real love."

Beth twirled the flower with her fingers. "You're quite noble, Tyler."

"I got a valuable lesson from the whole thing. I was like a moony teenager with Lily. Her rejection made me realize that romance is fake—a trick to get people to marry each other."

"You're right. All a man has to do is behave well enough to convince some girl to marry him, and then she's stuck for life."

Tyler studied her face. Was she teasing him again? "But I still want to share my life with someone. What do you say?"

"About what?"

"Will you marry me?"

Beth looked as if he'd chewed up his napkin and swallowed it whole. "Wha . . . why? What are you talking about?"

"I need a companion and helpmeet who will work beside me and be my friend. I know you'd be a good wife."

Beth slapped the sunflower against the edge of the table. Petals flew everywhere. "You think I'd make a good wife?" she said, her voice rising in pitch with each word.

Tyler flinched. Was she angry or just surprised?

"Jah. The way you care for Toby and look after your great-grandparents—"

Petals kept flying. "What makes you think for one minute that I'd want to marry you?" she practically snarled at him as she reduced the sunflower to a barren stem.

He hadn't expected quite this reaction. He'd bought yellow napkins and made bacon, for crying out loud. "You're fun to be with. I think we'd get along very well together."

She folded her arms and grunted her disapproval.

"If you think I'm expecting you to adore me, you don't have to worry about that. It's obvious you're still very much in love with Amos."

Pain darkened her expression.

"I can't pretend to be able to replace the bond you shared with Amos, but we could at least offer each other companionship and comfort in our later years. Besides, I worry about you and Toby. A widow's lot in life is hard, no matter how young or old she is. I want to help you out."

After tossing what was left of the sunflower on the table, Beth picked up a piece of bacon, ripped it into shreds, and deposited it on Toby's tray. "So, you think I can't take care of myself. That you've got to swoop in and rescue me."

Tyler had never been thrown quite so far off-balance before. Thoughts and ideas flew around his head like a flock of birds, not the least of which was that Beth looked stunningly beautiful when she was angry. Not a gute time to mention that. "Now I've made you angry."

Beth stood and began to pace. "You certainly don't want to marry a girl with a bad temper."

Toby, sticky with syrup and not in the least upset, pumped his little hands in the air and yelled, "No, no, no," as if he were chastising Tyler and making his own arguments against him.

"I don't mind a temper. It means you care about things."

She threw up her hands. "Do you never have an unkind thought about anybody?"

"I try to be—"

"Because I am thinking some very unkind thoughts about you right now."

"You have every good reason to."

Tyler caught sight of a fleeting grin before Beth plopped into her chair and buried her face in her hands.

He bent over to peek at her. "Beth? Are you okay?"

He heard a muffled growl behind the hands. "You are the most frustrating person to be mad at. If you fought back, I'd feel a lot better about myself."

Tyler didn't know what to do. He didn't have much practice at fighting back. "Okay. What do you want me to say?"

A giggle escaped Beth's lips. "Just . . . just stop talking."

"Can I just tell you—?"

"Nope," she said, with her face still buried in her hands.

Tyler shut his mouth and tried not to move a muscle except when Toby pointed to the bowl of scrambled eggs. "Mommy."

Tyler picked up the bowl and mouthed, *Do you want these?*

"Mommy."

He spooned eggs onto Toby's tray and watched as Toby gathered them up in his chubby little fingers and popped them into his mouth. He spit each bite out, played with it, and put it back in his mouth for further tasting.

Beth finally lifted her head and wiped an errant tear from her cheek. Tyler's throat sank to his toes. He hadn't meant to make her cry. "Beth, I'm really sorry."

She held up her hand as if to stop traffic. "I'm fine. I cry when I'm angry. Don't apologize."

"I cry when I'm angry too."

Beth twisted her lips into a wry grin. "You do not." She shook out his exquisitely folded napkin and blew her nose on it. "In a few days, we're going to laugh about this. Well, I'm going to laugh about it. You're going to sort of smile about it."

Tyler confirmed her prediction by smiling. He couldn't help it. She was so cute.

"Look at that," Beth exclaimed. "You're smiling already."

"I'm thinking of bacon."

"Even if we're mad at each other, we shouldn't let this food go to waste."

Tyler wasn't mad. He felt like smacking his own forehead. Stupid, stupid, stupid.

They said silent grace, and Beth helped herself to a pancake. Her lips curled in pleasure when she bit into it. "Hmm. Delicious. They taste like bacon and maple syrup."

Tyler didn't know if he should eat. Would she be cross if he saved her all the biggest pieces of bacon? "My mamm's recipe."

Beth smothered her eggs with pepper but no salt. "Do you know yours is the second proposal I've had in the last twenty-four hours?"

"You're kidding."

"Alvin Hoover." She picked up the sunflower that she had beat the petals off of. "He brought sunflowers."

Tyler had never felt so foolish in his entire life.

"I'm sorry I overreacted. You caught me off guard, that's all. I thought I had you figured out. I didn't want you to turn out to be like all the others."

"The others?"

"Wallace Schwartz proposed at the market where I bought groceries. He had three children and five cats that needed a loving mother's care. Yost Byler was a sixty-year-old bachelor. He wanted someone to look after his ailing father. He tried a little harder than Wallace. He brought me zucchini from his garden and Mary Ellis romances from the library. But when he started knocking on my bedroom window late at night, that's where I had to draw the line."

Tyler managed a smile, even though he felt like a creep. "Were there 'other' others?"

"Amos's twin brother Isaac ran them off."

"I'm glad somebody watched out for you."

"Not Isaac. He told everyone that I was engaged to him."

Tyler's mouth fell open. "What did you do?"

Beth's dimple disappeared, and her hand trembled slightly as she put down her fork. "I begged him to leave me alone, but he was nasty about it, insisting I had a duty to marry him because he is Amos's brother. Then his mamm said if I truly loved their family, I would agree to a marriage. The pressure made me miserable. When Mammi's letter came, I packed my bags and got out of there right quick."

Beth had asked if Tyler ever got mad. Jah, he did. He couldn't stand the thought of anyone bullying Beth. He balled his hands into fists and took several calming breaths. "I'm not like the others."

She laid her hand on his arm. His skin tingled at the touch. Any widower, bachelor, or young unmarried man, for that matter, would be a fool not to wish for Beth as a wife. Of course her suitors were many. "Oh, I know you're not like the others. Alvin told me he wanted to take care of Toby and me, but he didn't mean it. The other men saw how marrying me would benefit them. They didn't take the trouble to find out how I felt or what I wanted or what would be in my best interest. You, on the other hand, are willing to sacrifice your entire future to help a struggling widow."

"I don't see it as a sacrifice." He looked into those deep blue eyes. Not a sacrifice at all. "But I didn't really consider your tender feelings either."

Beth withdrew her hand and snorted dismissively. "Jah, tender. That's twice in the last couple of weeks I've almost bit your head off."

"I shouldn't have asked. I don't usually rush into things. I'm sorry."

She jabbed the dead sunflower in his direction. "Enough apologizing."

"And I don't think you're helpless. You are smart and feisty, and you can do anything you put your mind to."

A soggy piece of pancake flew through the air and hit Tyler in the cheek. Beth giggled. The side of his mouth curled in amusement as he took his cheery yellow napkin and wiped the side of his face.

"I guess Toby's done," Beth said, laughing as if nothing had upset her. She carried flailing Toby to the sink and washed his face and hands before letting him loose on the floor. Toby immediately toddled to Tyler and wanted to be picked up. "Mommy," he said.

Tyler bounced Toby on his knee and played peekaboo while Beth finished her breakfast. She ate five pancakes. At least some of his plans hadn't turned out disastrously.

"Tyler," Beth said, nibbling on the last strip of bacon, "I hope you're not too unhappy."

"No," he replied insincerely. In all his planning, he hadn't anticipated feeling so disappointed.

"If you're eager to find a wife, I'd be happy to help. I grew up here and know many of the girls in the other districts who you might not be familiar with. I could arrange meetings if you think it would help you choose a suitable wife."

Tyler pretended to be deep in thought. Did he want a wife? That was why he had proposed to Beth. She wouldn't have him, so why shouldn't he look elsewhere?

Even though it went against all his carefully laid plans, he was beginning to suspect that not just any wife would do.

"Okay," he said. "If you think you are a gute judge of character, I'll let you find me a wife."

Beth's eyes sparkled. She pulled a paper and pen from Mammi's pencil drawer. "Gute," she said, sitting back at the table and writing something at the top of the paper. "What qualities do you want in a wife?"

Tyler rubbed the stubble on his jaw. "Most importantly, she must have a temper. I will not even consider levelheaded girl. I want a wife with fire in her bones."

Beth jotted down some notes. "Oh, you are in for trouble." She looked up at the ceiling as if expecting trouble to fall from the sky.

"I like trouble."

"You do not. You're saying that to make me feel better."

Concern for Beth's feelings made him frown. "Is it working?"

She didn't look up from her paper. "Jah. It is."

The front door opened an inch at a time, and Anna and Felty stuck their heads through the crack as if they were spying on someone. Felty stood above Anna so that their heads appeared to be stacked on top of one another.

Anna raised her eyebrows, her eyes wide with curiosity. "Are we interrupting?" she whispered loudly.

With Toby tightly in his arms, Tyler leaped to his feet as if he'd been caught doing something he shouldn't, relieved that Anna and Felty had come to diffuse the tension floating in the air. This whole proposal thing had turned out to be a disaster. "We are just finishing up. Do you want some pancakes?"

"Tyler fixed me a very nice breakfast," Beth said. "We've had a wonderful-gute visit."

Jah. Wonderful-gute. He'd made Beth cry, Toby had hurled pancake everywhere, and Beth had butchered a perfectly good sunflower.

Anna glanced up at Felty with a smug gleam in her eye. "I told you."

Felty, looking unconvinced, sauntered into the great room. "You're a wonder, Banannie."

"I didn't expect you back so soon," Tyler said.

Anna sat at the table and helped herself to a pancake. "Roy got a flat tire halfway there."

Felty patted the pocket of his trousers, where he always kept his small notebook. "Even though it was half a trip, I saw some gute license plates."

Anna reached out and patted Tyler's arm. "Felty has played the license plate game with himself every year for the last forty years. He hopes to see all fifty state plates every year."

"I have eight yet to find before the end of December."

"Anyway," said Anna, "we're back because Roy didn't want to drive all the way to Green Bay on his spare. I worried about ruining your special day, but there was nothing for us to do but turn back and hope you'd had enough time to ask what you needed to ask." Her lively eyes danced as if she already knew all the answers to the questions in her head.

A frown flitted across Beth's face. She knew full well what Anna hinted at. But as Tyler had already observed, she couldn't stay upset or serious for long. She leaned toward her mammi and grinned mischievously. "We've decided that I am going to find Tyler a wife."

The smile lines around Anna's mouth etched themselves deeper into her face. "I've already found Tyler a wife."

Beth lifted her chin but kept that playful glint in her eye. "Well, Mammi, it's not me."

"Of course it is, dear. Who else?"

Tyler wished for nothing more than to crawl into a very deep hole. The deepest hole in the world. Could his embarrassment be more complete?

Beth glanced at Tyler and actually giggled. What was there to laugh about? "You are about seventeen shades of red, Tyler. We better stop talking about this or you're bound to turn purple."

"Okay," said Anna, wiping her mouth on one of

Tyler's garish yellow napkins. "But I don't see why you won't accept an entirely suitable husband."

Beth's face lost its luster. She lowered her eyes and drew meandering, squiggly lines on her paper. "You know why."

Tyler felt a wrench in his gut. Beth would always adore the memory of her late husband. He certainly couldn't and wouldn't compete with that.

Felty sat at the table and smacked his palm against it. "The very gute news is that I found Delaware. This is the best day I had all week, and it's not even seven o'clock."

Tyler frowned. It was the worst day he'd had all year, and it wasn't even seven o'clock. He hoped it wouldn't go downhill from here.

Chapter Eight

Awkwardly holding a hunk of cheese in one hand, Tyler tapped on the door. He wasn't sure if he should have brought cheese, but what other sort of gift should a dairy farmer bring on a first date? Should he have brought a gift at all? Eva Raber was from Ohio. Maybe she'd be offended.

Tyler scratched at the hair tucked under his hat. Why had he agreed to this ridiculous scheme? He wanted a wife, but he certainly didn't need help finding one. Beth had been so eager to help him, and he would have agreed to anything to keep her from bursting into tears at breakfast last week. If Beth wanted to couple him up with every single girl in Bonduel, then he'd endure every girl in Bonduel. Beth had seen enough of heartache in her life. He'd do just about anything to bring her a little happiness.

Sarah Beachy, Beth's mother, opened the door and propped her hands on her hips. "Tyler Yoder. Come in."

Sarah stood just shy of six feet tall, only a few inches shorter than Tyler. He followed her into the kitchen, and she motioned for him to sit at the table and then sat across from him. She studied him as if he were a Holstein she might consider buying. "I hardly see any folk from your district anymore, unless they're having a baby. Last week when we made jam, I remember thinking, 'Tyler's put on some muscle since I last saw him.' I always thought you were too skinny."

"*Denki*," Tyler said, unsure of the proper response. Had he just thanked her for thinking he was too skinny?

Sarah's husband, Aaron, came into the kitchen, thumbing his suspenders and examining Tyler as closely as Sarah had. Aaron, a lean and slight man, stood almost three inches shorter than his wife.

Sarah nudged a chair out from under the table for him. "*Cum*, Aaron. You remember Tyler."

Aaron sat and stroked his beard. "Jah, he looks fine. He'll do fine."

Sarah rested her elbows on the table and clasped her hands together in front of her. "Beth tells us you asked her to marry you."

Tyler almost choked in astonishment. "Uh . . . jah . . . I did."

"You shouldn't have done that," Sarah said. "Not without consulting us first."

Aaron nodded.

"I apologize. I realize how foolish—"

"She may have already been married once, but

we're still her parents and would appreciate being asked our opinion."

"Of course. I made Beth very upset and—"

Sarah gave Tyler's arm a motherly pat. "Aaron and I have talked it over and have decided it's a gute idea. So, the next time you propose to her, you don't need to consult with us. You already have our approval."

Tyler wondered if his eyes would pop out of his head. "You . . . you . . . ." He gathered his wits. "Denki, but it doesn't matter now. Beth told me she doesn't want to marry ever again."

Sarah waved away his explanation as if she were swatting a fly. "Stuff and nonsense. She had a very hard time of it first go-around. She's not sure she should give the good Lord a second chance. I keep telling her that the good Lord is her only chance."

Tyler thought about Beth's tearstained face at the breakfast table and a lump lodged in his throat. He hadn't meant to stir up painful memories for her. "I can't imagine losing someone so close."

Aaron grunted while Sarah snorted her displeasure. "Better days are ahead for both of you."

"Jah," Tyler said. "I think Beth's new business will do well."

Sarah rapped her knuckles in the table. "I mean for the both of you together. You're a fine young man, Tyler, but you got too eager. Beth won't jump into the pool until she's checked to make sure it's filled with water. Then she'll have to be certain the water's warm. And then she'll want to know there's a gute swimmer to catch her. You'll have to be patient."

What exactly did they want him to be patient about? He certainly wasn't going to ask a girl to marry him if she didn't want to be asked. Tyler looked from Sarah to Aaron. "Are you . . . are you going to introduce me to your new neighbor?"

Sarah slapped her thigh and jumped from her seat. "Oy, anyhow. I forgot about Eva. She's waiting for you in the back."

Tyler grabbed his cheese and let Sarah lead him to the back door. He peered out the screen at a girl dressed in brown who sat at the picnic table nibbling her fingernails. The table had been laid with a red-and-white checkered cloth, paper plates and cups, and an unruly vase of sunflowers. Tyler groaned inwardly at the sight of his flower nemesis. He wondered if Eva ever got angry enough to snap off the heads of innocent flowers and use their stems as bullwhips.

It didn't matter if she did. He didn't plan on giving Eva any reason to hurl, flail, or otherwise destroy the flowers. He'd come for an enjoyable, friendly picnic with a girl he thought he might want to get to know better. And under no circumstances would he ask her to marry him. Surely the flowers were safe.

Tyler could hear Felty singing inside.

"*To be a child of God each day, my light must shine*

along the way. I'll sing His praise while ages roll, and strive to help some troubled soul."

Tyler knocked, and he heard Anna call from inside, *"Cum reu."*

He opened the door and for a moment thought a stiff wind had come through the room and up-ended everything in its path. Beth, with a pair of scissors in one hand, stood at the kitchen table examining a piece of fabric and a pattern spread across the top of it. Piles of scraps sat on each kitchen chair, and fabric fibers and bits of cotton floated through the air like dandelion parachutes.

While Sparky napped at her feet, Anna sat in her rocker stitching ties onto a crisp white kapp. Tiny scraps of white fabric collected at her feet or came to rest on Sparky as she let them fall. Sparky didn't seem to notice the disturbance.

Five bolts of sky-blue fabric sat on the sofa with a deep purple propped against the end table.

Leaning forward in his recliner, Felty played ball with Toby. Their game consisted of Toby throwing the tennis ball wherever he wanted to and watching it bounce around the furniture. Felty would clap at the appropriate moments, and Toby would fetch the ball to throw again.

"Tyler," Beth said, blooming into a radiant smile that he didn't deserve, considering how he'd made her cry two weeks ago.

But he sure liked that smile and the dimple that came with it.

He shut the door and hung up his hat. "Aden promised me he'd be here this time."

Beth snipped at an errant thread. "He brought a load of good oak yesterday. He had better get to work soon, or Lily won't get that chest of drawers for Christmas."

As soon as Toby saw Tyler, he opened his mouth in a breathless smile, pumped his little arms, and ran to him. Tyler threw Toby into the air and twirled him around the room.

Beth laughed at Toby's delight and seemed to glow from the inside when she looked at her son.

Propping Toby securely in one arm, Tyler reached into his pocket. "I have something for you."

"For me?"

He held out his small stack of papers. "Three more women in my district want dresses. They wrote down their measurements, and I promised I wouldn't look."

The blush seemed to travel up her face as she bit her bottom lip and grinned. Tyler had never seen a more appealing sight. "You didn't have to do that," she said.

Anna tied a knot and cut her thread. "You should hire him as a salesman."

The warmth in Beth's blush seemed to intensify. "Tyler, you're so kind. You've brought me half my customers."

"Your dresses sell themselves. My mamm wore hers to gmay on Sunday, and everyone wanted to know who made it. I told them where they could get one just like it."

Anna shuffled to the table and ran her hand over

Beth's fabric. "I don't wonder but you'll need that rotary cutter."

"Rotary cutter?" said Tyler, bouncing Toby on his hip.

"It looks like a pizza cutter," Beth said, "but it cuts fabric and manages straight lines extra quick."

"Like as not, you could use a new machine too," Anna added.

The thought of buying a new machine seemed to amuse Beth. "I'll have to make a mountain of dresses before I can do that."

Anna tossed the finished kapp into a paper bag on one of the chairs. "We better get these orders caught after. A mountain of dresses sounds like quite a bit."

Beth seemed likely to float off the ground. "But look at how much we've done already." She gave her mammi a mushy hug and a kiss on the cheek "Thanks to you and Dawdi. And Tyler."

Tyler was sort of disappointed that Beth's gratitude didn't overflow into a kiss for him too. "I didn't do anything."

"You talked Mattie Yutzy into ordering five dresses and three matching shirts. That'll keep me busy for a week." Her gaze could have sweetened a whole bucket of cream.

Before too much time had passed, he realized he was grinning like an idiot. Clearing his throat, he trained his eyes on the lane out the window. "Where could Aden have got to?"

"Bah, bah," said Toby, which was his word for ball, milk, and Sparky. Tyler let Toby down, and he immediately found his tennis ball underneath Anna's rocker.

Anna searched through two other paper bags and pulled out a tie-less kapp and a pair of ties. "I've finished five of these already this morning."

"Oh, thank you, Mammi. You are so gute to me."

Anna settled herself into her rocker. "It's years of knitting experience. I ain't never seen a stitch I couldn't master."

Felty sat back in his recliner. "Annie-banannie, sometimes your fingers get to going so fast, they're a blur."

Anna cut herself some thread. "Maybe you just need new glasses, Felty."

Tyler pulled a broom from the closet and began sweeping the floor. Beth's reaction was immediate. He might have just given her a whole stack of bacon-flavored pancakes for as delighted as she looked. He wasn't sure why she acted so happy. He was sweeping the floor, not donating a kidney.

"You don't have to do that, Tyler."

"If you're going to make a mountain of dresses, everybody's got to do his part. And I can't sew to save my life. Besides, I might as well make myself useful while I wait for Aden."

She stifled a grin. "I want to hear about your first date. Or is it none of my business?"

Tyler swept with vigor. "You volunteered to find me a wife. You should know how it went so you can start narrowing down your list of girls."

Beth cocked an eyebrow. "Narrowing down? Didn't you like Eva?"

Tyler refused to say anything bad about anyone. "She makes excellent fried chicken. And coleslaw. She's a very pleasant young woman."

"Mamm says Eva wasn't quite what we expected."

He looked up from his sweeping. If Sarah had already filled Beth in on the details, he wouldn't have to say a word. "Your mamm already told you."

"I was curious to know how you got on." Beth seemed to turn a bright shade of red instantly. She averted her eyes and concentrated very hard on the pattern on the table. "Mamm says Eva is a quiet little thing."

"Some people are naturally shy. There's nothing wrong with that."

"Shy?"

Tyler concentrated very hard on his pile of scraps and thread. "She wouldn't speak."

"At all?"

"She pulled out the food and poured me a mug of hot chocolate and looked as if she would throw up when I asked her a question. So I stopped asking. I didn't want her to be sick all over her own picnic. That probably would have scarred her for life."

The corner of Beth's mouth turned upward. "You're always so thoughtful."

Tyler thought of Eva's ghost-pale face and horrible posture. "Do you know if she was a sickly child?"

"I don't know much about her."

"Neither do I." He stopped sweeping and laid a hand on Beth's arm. She stared at his hand and froze as if she were made out of stone. "I have to apologize for something. You need to know the worst about me. I might have hurt Eva's feelings."

"What did you do?"

Tyler spoke past the lump in his throat. "I fell asleep."

Her eyebrows nearly flew off her face. "What?"

Tyler groaned. "It was a warm day."

Beth threw back her head and laughed—a deep, throaty laugh that made all of Tyler's discomfort worth the trouble.

"After I ate a piece of pie, the silence made me drowsy. I get up at four every morning, you know. When I woke, probably twenty minutes later, she was gone. She'd even managed to pull the table-cloth out from under me without waking me. Very skilled. She probably sat there and listened to me snore for twenty minutes."

"She should have kicked you under the table. That's what I would have done."

Tyler stifled a grin. "You would have smacked me over the head with a sunflower."

Beth gasped and pretended to be offended. "You would have deserved it."

Tyler laughed at the indignant expression on her face. "Yes, I would have. Before I left, I wrote Eva a note of apology and asked your mamm to deliver it for me."

Beth's eyes sparkled, making it impossible for Tyler to look away. "So, I suppose you won't be wanting a second date with Eva Raber."

He chuckled. "She won't be wanting a second date with me."

Beth suddenly became intensely interested in the cut of the fabric on the table. "Okay. I'll see who else I can come up with."

Tyler found himself more eager to tell Beth about his next date than to actually go on his next date. More than anything, he wanted to make her laugh again. He wanted to share the laughter with her. Beth should always be laughing.

It didn't bother him in the least that Aden didn't show up. Again. He spent a very pleasant morning in the Helmuths' company while waiting for his tardy friend. While Beth cut fabric and told him funny stories about Toby; Tyler swept the entire great room, played ball with Toby, and helped Anna thread needles. He even changed Toby's diaper with a little help from Anna. He'd never changed a diaper before and determined it was a skill he should master. It wasn't too bad or too hard. And Anna corrected him before he put the clean diaper on backwards.

Toby rubbed his eyes with his little fists as Tyler placed him in Beth's arms.

"He's had a busy morning," Beth said. "He's earned his nap."

Tyler planted a kiss on Toby's forehead. There was nothing softer than a baby. "Are you coming to the Millers' bonfire on Friday?"

"Jah. Mammi and Dawdi wouldn't miss it."

"Can I save you a spot?"

Beth blushed and caressed Toby's cheek. "Okay." Their gazes locked until Toby made a fist and started knocking on Tyler's shoulder. "Mommy," he said.

Beth lost her smile and took a step away from Tyler. "Why don't I find you a date to the bonfire? Lots of girls go."

A lump of coal settled in the pit of Tyler's stomach. Oh, yes. Beth wanted to find him a suitable wife. Beth, who had been crazy in love with her late husband, wanted nothing to do with Tyler Yoder's marriage proposal.

He thought of Lily and Aden. He'd made a fool of himself once. He'd never make that same mistake again. All he wanted was a good woman to give him some companionship and a family. He didn't need the teasing and the laughter and the butter-flies in his stomach whenever he laid eyes on her.

And he certainly wasn't going to let Beth Hostetler break his heart.

Chapter Nine

In the dusky light of sunset, Tyler looked as if he were waiting to greet a funeral procession, but then he was naturally of a solemn disposition. Never mind the fact that the last few times she had seen him, he had been playful and merry. Tyler Yoder's normal state was serious and steady.

Still, Beth wished he would conjure up a smile so she knew he was happy to see her. But maybe she had no right to hope for a smile. He wasn't her date tonight. Maybe he wanted to save all his charm for Lorene Zook.

When Dawdi set the brake, Tyler opened the door. He helped Mammi out of the buggy before reaching into the backseat for Toby. Beth handed Toby out and descended from the buggy without any help from anybody.

Toby patted Tyler's cheek. "Mommy."

There was the smile she wanted. Toby could summon a grin from the grumpiest of old men.

Beth zipped her coat and retrieved the extra

blankets from the buggy. It would be chilly tonight. She handed a blanket to Tyler, who wrapped Toby up as tightly as Toby would allow.

Tyler pointed toward the massive pile of leaves and branches already burning brightly. "I spread out a blanket for you over there. And I brought some camp chairs for Anna and Felty."

Why did her face feel so warm when the temperature was so cold? "You didn't need to do that."

He frowned. "I told you I'd save you a spot."

As Tyler led them through the crowds of people to the blanket, Beth breathed in the heavenly scent of burning leaves and steaming hot chocolate. The air felt crisp and tart, like a cold Granny Smith apple fresh from the tree. The fire, which must have recently been lit, blazed with intense heat that would soon give way to crackling coals perfect for hot dog roasting.

The blanket sat close enough to the fire to enjoy some of its warmth, but not so close that they would feel like they were roasting. Seven young men stood guard around the perimeter of the fire making sure that no little ones got too close until it had burned itself down.

Toby refused to be contained inside the blanket. He struggled with Tyler until Tyler set him on his feet and fastened the coat around his tummy. Holding onto Toby's hand, Tyler opened a shoebox and let a pile of colorful blocks tumble to the blanket. Toby clapped his hands and immediately began throwing the blocks in every direction.

Tyler glanced at Beth. "I hoped this would keep

Toby occupied for a few minutes, at least. He'll be wanting to charge the fire before too long."

Beth glowed with gratitude. She'd never met anyone as thoughtful as Tyler Yoder. And she wasn't even his date for the evening.

Dawdi and Mammi took Mammi's potluck pasta salad to the food table. Mammi called it "Pimento Surprise." Beth hoped somebody would eat it, mushy pasta and all, so Mammi's feelings wouldn't be hurt. Dawdi helped Mammi to her chair and sank into his. "Denki, Tyler. This chair will save my backside weeks of soreness."

"Gute," said Tyler, catching Toby's blocks as they came at him. "I figured you'd have a much better time if you didn't have to sit on the hard ground."

Mammi reached into her bag and pulled out five vibrant scarves. She handed a yellow one to Dawdi and a blue one to Tyler. "We're going to stay nice and warm. Come here, Toby."

To Beth's surprise, Toby obediently toddled to Mammi and let her wrap a fuzzy red scarf around his neck. He handed her a block as payment.

Beth's scarf was a lovely lavender color that felt so soft, she closed her eyes and nuzzled it against her cheek. When she opened her eyes, Toby sat in Tyler's lap while Tyler glued his eyes to Beth's face. He quickly looked away and busied himself constructing a block tower for Toby to knock down.

The blocks held Toby's attention for nearly ten minutes. Then he decided he wanted to run in no particular direction. Toby always wanted to run.

Tyler jumped to his feet. "I'll follow him. We'll

be back in a few minutes to roast hot dogs." He dogged Toby's every step as Toby toddled over other people's blankets and into other people's conversations. Beth watched as little old ladies and young mothers alike reached down to pat Toby on the head or pinch his cheek as he walked past. Everyone smiled at Tyler. Mammi said he was the community's favorite bachelor—although at twenty-three, he could hardly be called a bachelor yet.

Beth stiffened as Toby tripped into a gaggle of girls standing near the food table. They cooed and sighed at Toby and took quite an interest in Tyler. Beth couldn't hear what they said to him, but they were definitely flirting. Luckily, Tyler had Toby to look after, and Toby was in no disposition to wait while Tyler flirted with anybody.

A broad and balding man approached Beth's blanket and after glancing quite pointedly at her, reached out a hand for Dawdi. "I hear you had gute huckleberries this year."

Beth didn't know the man, but he looked to be older than she by at least ten years. He had no beard. *This* was a true bachelor.

"Vernon," Dawdi said. "I haven't seen you since syrup time."

Vernon didn't wait for an invitation. He plopped himself down on the blanket next to Beth and stared at her while he talked to Dawdi. "I caught sight of you leaving the market last week with your granddaughter." He pumped both eyebrows up and down vigorously as he regarded Beth. "They tell me you're a widow."

Beth had to hold her breath to keep a groan from escaping her throat. She could see that to an unmarried, older man, a young widow was like honey to a grizzly bear.

"I am available to come to dinner on Wednesday," Vernon said. "I love pork chops and chowchow."

She had to admire his audacity. His pushiness made her want to giggle. It also partly explained why Vernon hadn't married yet.

Tyler seemed to come out of nowhere with Toby in his arms. He wasted no time in plopping himself between Beth and Vernon. It was a tight fit as Vernon was forced to scoot to the right to make way for him. "The fire is ready for hot dog roasting," Tyler said, acting as if nothing were out of the ordinary, even though he had practically sat on Vernon's lap.

Vernon opened and closed his mouth like a trout out of water before standing, giving Tyler a confused nod, and disappearing into the crowd.

Tyler, with Toby in his lap, didn't move one inch from Beth, even though Vernon's absence had opened up oodles of room to his right. He frowned in concern. "Are you okay? A pretty girl is never completely safe from wife-hunters. I'll try to do a better job of keeping them away."

Beth grinned in spite of herself. "I'm fine. He only said about three words to me."

Tyler nodded solemnly. "Vernon Schmucker has asked out every girl between the ages of eighteen and thirty-five who lives within thirty miles of town. An unsuspecting widow like yourself would have gotten a marriage proposal before the fire burned itself out tonight. And I know how marriage proposals upset you."

His closeness should have made her feel uncomfortable. Instead, she savored his warmth. "You're very kind to watch out for me."

"I was watching out for Vernon. To save him from getting pummeled by a sunflower. Or a roasting stick."

Beth cuffed him playfully on the shoulder. "I didn't bring any sunflowers."

Tyler grimaced. "Then I'm glad I stepped in. I would hate to see what damage you could do with a roasting stick."

The laughter burst from her lips. "Just hope you never find out."

Tyler reached for one of the sticks he had brought and handed it to Toby. "*Cum*, Toby. Let's roast a hot dog." He stood and took Toby's hand and helped him skewer a hot dog from the food table.

They went to the fire, now a toasty pile of glowing coals, and Toby attempted to get too close. Tyler squatted and wrapped both arms around Toby's chest. Toby squeaked in protest and struggled against Tyler's arms until Tyler leaned down and whispered something in his ear. Toby stopped fussing and stretched his stick toward the fire while Tyler softly spoke to him. Beth couldn't imagine that they were close enough to the fire to even warm Toby's hot dog, but she could see that Tyler was not about to let him get any closer and risk burning himself. He was careful like that.

The reflection of glowing coals danced in Toby's wide eyes. Beth felt a little hitch in her throat. Toby wasn't a baby anymore, and he looked more and more like Amos every day.

The dying fire lit Tyler's features as he watched over her son. What kind of a father would Tyler be? Amos had never changed a diaper or gotten up in the middle of the night with Toby, and he had refused to lift a finger around the house. His contribution had been criticizing Beth for everything she did and telling her how she could have done it better. Being married to Amos had nearly crushed her spirit. She shuddered. That chapter of her life was over. She'd never have to answer to a husband again. And no matter how many times people told her that God wanted her to remarry, she would hold firm. He hadn't protected her the first time. She wouldn't put her happiness in His hands ever again.

Tyler helped Toby put his hot dog in a bun and squeeze ketchup on it. They walked back to the blanket together, with Tyler carrying both the stick and the hot dog. Better not to take any chances with Toby's dinner.

Tyler sat and put Toby between him and Beth. "Can he eat the hot dog like this or do we need to cut it into small pieces?"

Beth smiled. "I'll make sure he takes small bites."

"I blew on it."

"Denki," Beth said. Tyler was a more attentive mother hen than she was.

He got up on his knees. "Felty and Anna, would you like me to roast a hot dog for each of you?"

"What a nice young man," Mammi said.

Tyler opened a small cooler that sat next to the camp chairs. "Felty, I brought something for you. And for Anna and Beth, too, if you'd like." He pulled a package from the cooler and opened it. "Do any of you like bratwurst?"

Dawdi leaned forward to get a better look. "Fresh?"

Tyler nodded. "From the sausage shop."

Dawdi sighed. "I think I've died and gone to Heaven. Bratwurst is one smell my nose recognizes." Because of an accident as a child, Dawdi had almost completely lost his senses of smell and taste.

Tyler pulled a bottle of stone-ground mustard from the cooler. "And we can't eat it without this." He went to the food table and found a four-pronged hot-dog roaster. "What about you, Anna? Do you want a bratwurst?"

Mammi tapped a finger to her chest. "Not gute for my digestion."

"Beth?"

Why did Tyler have to make himself so completely irresistible, when she was trying so hard to find him a wife? "Jah, I would love one, thank you."

Tyler threaded three bratwursts and one hot dog onto his roasting stick and tromped to the fire. If she hadn't been occupied with Toby, she would have gone to stand by him. A person so thoughtful should never have to cook bratwurst all by himself.

In between feeding Toby bites of hot dog, she

studied Tyler's profile by the light of the fire. She was quite taken with his dark lashes and square jaw. He stared into the glowing embers and held the stick completely still, looking like a man at peace with himself. Would he ever berate his wife for burning the stew or missing a stain on his favorite shirt?

Beth looked away. She would never know if he was a good husband or not.

Toby ate his entire hot dog and drank a full cup of milk. He pointed at the fire and Tyler several times and said, "Hot, hot," over and over again. His eyes drooped and his head swayed, and Beth made a pillow out of her scarf and lowered his head to it. She pulled his pacifier from her coat pocket and gave it to him. He rubbed his eyes, rolled onto his tummy, and fell fast asleep.

Tyler returned with the bratwursts. He pulled another package out of his cooler. "Brat buns," he said. "It's a crime to eat a brat without one."

Beth went to the food table and filled two plates with an assortment of salads and desserts. Dawdi and Mammi shared one plate, and Beth and Tyler shared the other.

Tyler handed Beth her perfectly cooked bratwurst in a bun. "Denki, Tyler."

He shrugged and sat next to her. "Toby finally conked out."

"Thanks to you, he got to run all his energy out."

"He ran all my energy out. I don't know how you keep up with him. I'll bet you're exhausted by the end of the day."

Beth felt like she had spent the evening thanking Tyler for one thing or another. "This is delicious, Tyler. Amos's mother used to make bratwurst every Friday night."

Tyler pressed his lips together. "Did she?"

Beth lowered her eyes. She hadn't meant to say anything about Treva. There were too many bad memories associated with her.

"Tell me about her."

"What?"

"Tell me about your mother-in-law. What is she like? I can imagine she was devastated when her son passed away."

"Jah. Her boys mean everything to her." Beth didn't know what else to say.

"She had cancer," Mammi volunteered.

Tyler gazed at Beth with deep concern flickering in his eyes. "Oh, I'm sorry."

Beth fiddled with a curly lock of Toby's hair. "Colon cancer. She was diagnosed just weeks before Amos died."

Mammi was more eager to talk about Treva than Beth was. "Beth cared for her from sunup to sundown for over a year."

Tyler regarded Beth with awe. "How did you manage with Toby?"

How had she managed? The cancer had given Treva immense power over Beth's life. Beth had felt so sorry for Treva that she had felt obligated to obey her demands. Treva's other children hadn't lifted a finger to help her because she was so unpleasant. Beth had been the only one willing to endure her, because she'd already felt so guilty that Treva had lost a son. Once Amos passed, Treva had treated Beth like a servant. Beth had longed to return to Bonduel, to the comfort of family who loved her. After several months, Treva had started feeling better, and Beth had gotten up the courage to tell Treva she wanted to move back to Wisconsin.

Treva had accused Beth of not loving her, of being cold and heartless for even thinking of leaving her mother-in-law to die a lonely and forsaken death.

So Beth had stayed, far longer than she had truly been needed, compelled by guilt she hadn't deserved, even though Treva had been in remission. Even though her own children could have, should have cared for their mother.

Living with Treva had proved as painful as living with Amos. In Treva's eyes, Beth couldn't do anything right. The sheets she washed always came out gray, the dinners she cooked tasted like pig slop, and the way she looked after her own baby was a disgrace.

Beth had been silent too long. Tyler eyed her with a piercing blue-gray stare as if he were trying to read her thoughts.

"It . . . it was difficult," she finally managed to say. "Treva needed so much looking after."

"Is she doing better?"

"Jah, fit as a fiddle." Beth brushed some crumbs from her lap as if brushing aside the topic. She didn't want to waste any more emotion on Treva

Hostetler. "I wouldn't have left her if she still needed me."

"Of course you wouldn't have." Tyler rarely altered his expression, and yet his whole face conveyed undeniable compassion. "But she wanted you to marry Amos's brother. You had to go."

"Jah." Beth whispered to keep her voice from cracking into a million pieces. Tyler understood better than he thought he did.

He put down his plate and leaned close to her. "I'm sorry she made it so difficult for you." He reached across sleeping Toby and caressed her cheek with his fingers. His touch felt heavenly, like a tingly kiss of rose petals against her skin. "You're upset." He furrowed his brow. "Was she unkind to you, Beth?"

Beth held perfectly still, not wanting to break the tenuous connection between them, even as she fought the need to tell him everything. She didn't want him to discover her wickedness. The words caught in her throat. "I was very unhappy."

His fingers travelled to the nape of her neck. She closed her eyes and let the sensation of his touch course through her. His closeness felt so good. He bent closer and whispered in her ear, "You're safe now."

At that moment, Beth did feel completely safe. Worries about Toby and her new business melted with the touch of Tyler's hand. Something deep inside reassured her that she would always find safety with Tyler.

She opened her eyes. The firelight flickered on

Tyler's face as he stared at her lips. Did she dare tell him how she had never felt sure of Amos and so could never be sure of any man, not even Tyler?

Especially not Tyler. Tyler, so thoughtful and accommodating, wanted to be helpful—to everyone. Did he see her as someone to be loved or someone to be rescued?

Well, she didn't need his rescue. She could take care of herself.

Beth jerked away from him and leaped to her feet. "Stop it, Tyler. Just stop."

He widened his eyes in shock. She could have laid him flat with her pinky finger. "What . . . what did I do? I'm sorry."

She stomped off in no direction in particular, leaving Toby sleeping on the blanket. He would be fine with Mammi and Dawdi nearby. She had to clear her head of Tyler Yoder. Of men in general. She didn't want a man; she didn't need a man. She wouldn't hang her happiness on a man ever again.

She found herself walking amongst the deserted buggies and horses parked in Miller's field. She petted the nose of a beautiful chestnut mare that whinnied softly to her and then moved down the line of horses, giving each of them a little affection as she passed.

"My sewing business is doing very well," she said to a dappled grey that nodded his head thoughtfully when she spoke. "I can support Toby and myself on my income. I can save on rent if I find a small house. We don't need a lot of room." A milky white got her attention next. "I have it all planned out, you know. I've added everything up carefully. I'll take gute care of Toby."

"You can talk to the horses, but you can't talk to me?" Tyler strolled toward her in the gathering darkness with his hands behind his back and his hat pushed back as if he'd been smacking himself in the forehead. He raised an eyebrow, but she could see the unguarded worry in his eyes. Of course he had already blamed himself for her outburst.

How could she ever stay mad at someone so annoyingly forgiving?

A grin pulled at Beth's mouth. "The horses don't fight back."

"I don't fight back."

"No, you don't. I find it irritating."

Tyler raised one hand in surrender. "I asked you once to tell me how to be less irritating. You haven't given me anything to go on yet."

Beth patted the milky white's neck. "I'll get back to you on that."

Tyler took his hand from behind his back. He held a wilted sunflower in his fingers. "I scoured Miller's pasture to find this, in case you want to smack me with it."

Beth laughed and took the pathetic wildflower. For someone so serious, Tyler certainly knew how to tickle her funny bone. "I've brought this on myself. You'll never trust me around flowers again."

Tyler took off his hat and slapped it weakly against his leg. "Beth, I'm sorry for whatever I did. The last thing I would ever purposefully do is hurt you."

"You didn't hurt me. You annoyed me."

"Did something I said make you think of Amos? I know how much you miss him."

She wished he wouldn't bring up Amos. She didn't miss Amos at all, and it made her feel guilty that Tyler believed her to be a better person than she really was. She popped the head off her sunflower and ground it into the dirt with her heel. "For goodness sake, Tyler. It doesn't have anything to do with Amos."

"It doesn't?"

"I'm not a homeless puppy."

Puzzlement flooded his expression. "I never said you were."

"You want to help everybody because you are a naturally nice person, but I refuse to be one of your projects. I don't need rescuing. Like a puppy."

"I'm not fond of dogs."

"I'm not helpless. You don't have to bring bratwurst to make me feel better."

"I thought Felty might like it."

"We all liked it. You're so thoughtful."

He scratched his head. "You're not upset about Amos?"

"Nae."

His lips twitched. "You are annoyed because I'm nice to you?"

Beth rolled her eyes. "Well, when you put it that way, I sound like a crazy woman."

Tyler chuckled softly. "Jah, you do."

She growled and smacked him on the shoulder with what was left of her sunflower.

He laughed louder. "I'm glad you found a use for

that." He put his hat back on his head and grew more serious. "I'm not going to stop being nice to you, Beth."

"And I'm not going to stop being irritated."

"Gute. I love that spark you get in your eyes when you're mad at me. I love trying to figure out what I've done wrong and then apologizing profusely."

"You do not."

"Yes, I do."

They walked back toward the bonfire together.

A lump lodged in Beth's throat as she thought about a topic she'd been avoiding all evening. "You don't seem all that curious about your date tonight," she said.

Tyler stopped walking. "I was having such a nice time, I hoped you'd forgotten."

"Of course not. If you want to find a wife, we've got to get busy."

Tyler huffed out a breath and folded his hands across his chest. "Okay. Who is she?"

Beth swallowed hard. "Her name is Lorene Zook, and she gets off work at eight. I told her to meet us here."

"Okay."

"She's not shy like Eva Raber."

"Okay."

Three girls charged toward Beth like a small herd of cattle. The middle girl, Lorene, had big teeth and a mole right in the center of her chin. Beth bit her bottom lip. A boy like Tyler wasn't so shallow as to care about appearance.

Lorene stuck out her hand while the girls on

either side of her giggled uncontrollably. "Hi, Tyler. I'm Lorene. I know you don't know who I am, but I know you. Your dat is the bishop in the west district. You came with him when he preached to our congregation in April."

Beth nibbled on her lip and waited for the eruption.

Tyler shook Lorene's hand and formed his lips into a passable grin—an amazing feat for someone who didn't smile all that often.

"I'm twenty-one," Lorene said. "But just barely. My birthday was last week."

Tyler nodded cheerfully. "Happy birthday."

"My brother said I'm an old maid now, but I say there's plenty of fish in the sea."

And then it came. Lorene exploded with laughter. In Bonduel, Lorene was known for one thing. She didn't just laugh. She cackled like a high-pitched duck with volumes that could rival the loudest car horn.

Tyler flinched at Lorene's ear-splitting guffaw but stood his ground. A boy like Tyler wasn't so shallow as to care how loudly Lorene could laugh. He'd work hard to get to know her instead of dismissing her first thing.

"Do you like to roast marshmallows?" Tyler stuttered.

Lorene clapped her hands in delight. "I love roasted marshmallows. Do they have stuff for s'mores? Let's make s'mores."

Tyler motioned to the food table. "Okay then, Lorene. Let's go find the marshmallows."

He let Lorene and her friends lead the way with only one backward glance at Beth. Would Lorene's friends be tagging along all night?

Beth nibbled on her thumbnail as she watched them go. All right. She admitted it. Lorene was not the likeliest of prospects for Tyler Yoder, and she had known it the minute she'd arranged the date. But Tyler should meet a whole range of girls, shouldn't he? The unsuitable candidates only helped him narrow down his choices. Beth provided him a great service.

Beth returned to the blanket, where Mammi and Dawdi sat staring into the dying fire. She reclined next to Toby and stroked his little carrot top. She didn't need anyone else but Toby in her life. She'd never be lonely, and she'd never risk being so miserable again. Surely God wanted her to be happy after all she'd been through.

Over and over, Beth heard Lorene's incessant laughter echo into the wide night sky. Tyler must have been keeping her entertained.

Tyler deserved to have a good time. She hoped he was having a good time.

But not really.

Chapter Ten

Tyler and Aden carried the boards into Felty's barn and laid them on the floor next to the circular saw that sat in the corner along with Felty's other woodworking tools.

Tyler took off one of his work gloves and wiped the sweat from his brow. It couldn't have been more than fifty degrees in the barn, but the wood Aden had chosen for the chest was heavy, and they both panted with exertion. "I'm glad Lily will get her dresser this year," Tyler said. "I thought you might never show your face on Huckleberry Hill again."

Aden grinned like an idiot. Always the grinning. Why couldn't he stop with the grinning? "I had to give you and Beth enough time to fall in love. I figured I'd still have time to finish the dresser after you got engaged."

The sharp stab of regret surprised him. He'd never be engaged to Beth Hostetler. But Aden was teasing. He expected a joking response. "Very funny," Tyler managed to say.

"How is that going? Does Beth meet your requirements for a gute life companion? Which is a stupid plan, by the way."

Tyler cocked an eyebrow and frowned at Aden's insult. "Beth and I are finished already."

"What do you mean? Take some time to get to know her."

Tyler grimaced. "I already proposed, and she already refused and that's the end of it."

Aden scraped his jaw off the floor. "You already . . . ?"

"I didn't see any point in wasting time once I made up my mind."

Aden's eyes danced with amusement. "And she said no?"

"She offered to help me find a more willing partner."

Aden laughed. "That's Beth. Always so unselfish."

"Or eager to get rid of me." Tyler couldn't share in Aden's mirth.

Aden quit laughing and studied Tyler's face. "You're disappointed. I should have known. Beth's no ordinary girl."

Tyler shrugged his shoulders as if he didn't really care. "It's a pain to have to spend the time finding someone else."

"Oh, jah, I'm sure that's the worst thing ever, having Beth derail your carefully made plans."

"She wasn't ever really a part of my plan until you talked me into it."

Aden's smile was too wide. "Go ahead. Blame it

on me. It's plain you have absolutely no interest in my pretty cousin."

"I don't."

The door swung open, bringing cool October air with it. Beth blew into the barn like a black nimbus cloud, waving a pizza cutter in the air like a torch. "Tyler Yoder, look what came in the mail today."

Aden glanced from Beth to Tyler. "I'll go see if Dawdi wants to help us with this wood," he said and hastened out the door as if there were a fire. Or a looming thunderstorm.

Tyler realized what Beth held in her hand. He smiled innocently and feigned ignorance. "Somebody sent you a pizza cutter?"

Beth shoved the offensive tool at Tyler. "You know very well what this is. It's a fabric rotary cutter. The newest model. It came with a cutting mat the perfect size for cutting out dresses."

"Who sent it?"

Beth folded her arms. "The return address is conveniently smudged."

"A tool like that could come in handy in your line of work. Why are you mad? It's a real nice gift."

Beth sighed in exasperation. "I already told you, Tyler. I don't need to be rescued, and I don't need your help."

Tyler took two steps back in case she decided she wanted to smack him with her sharp new toy. "Maybe since you won't accept gifts from people, someone wanted to send it to you anonymously so you wouldn't be offended. And then somebody hoped he wouldn't be here when you received it."

Maybe he wanted you to have a chance to cool down so you wouldn't bite his head off."

Beth narrowed her eyes, sniffed indignantly, and sat on a nearby milking stool. The storm came to rest. She let a grin escape her lips. "You are impossible. And I don't bite people's heads off."

"Maybe the lady at the fabric store told this particular person that you could cut out dresses twice as fast with a rotary cutter. Maybe he wanted to do something nice for you—no hidden motive or devious plot involving homeless puppies."

Beth laughed as if she couldn't keep her amusement cooped up any longer. When she wasn't laughing, she seemed to be on the verge of bursting into laughter every moment.

Tyler pulled the other milking stool next to her and sat down. This way he could look into those intelligent, expressive eyes of hers. "And maybe you didn't check the package carefully. It might be addressed to Toby. The mat and cutter could have been meant for him."

"How silly of me not to think of that."

"I can't wait to see how fast you'll go now."

Beth's eyes sparkled with a hint of a tease. "So, you don't think I'm all that fast with a pair of scissors."

"What are you talking about? You wield a pair of scissors like my dat handles a milking machine."

Beth stretched her legs and turned her toes inward. "If Amos thought I was bad at something, he'd give me a gift to help improve my skills. Our first Christmas, I asked for a new sewing machine. He gave me a frying pan because he said I needed lots of practice in the kitchen. After Toby's birth, he gave me a diet book because no wife of his was going to be fat."

Tyler was stunned. How could Amos treat his own wife that way? His stomach tied itself in a knot. Beth didn't deserve that.

Beth forced a laugh. "I have a nice set of pans, anyway."

She didn't fool him. Her flippant remark hid a mountain of pain. But she had loved Amos, hadn't she? Maybe she had been able to see past his harshness. If she had, she was a better person than Tyler could ever be. The thought of Amos presenting Beth with a saucepan on Christmas morning stoked a fire inside him. No wonder Beth hated gifts.

He placed his hand over hers. He couldn't resist the feel of her skin. "I bought you that fabric cutter because an expert needs the right tools."

She blushed and lowered her eyes before curving her lips into a mischievous grin. "So, you admit your guilt."

He coughed dramatically. "I mean, if I wanted to give you a rotary cutter, it would have been because I wanted to be nice." He squeezed her hand. "Please don't judge me by what Amos did or said. I'm not Amos."

She slumped her shoulders. "I tend to overreact."

"Just a little."

"You're right. I'm sorry."

Tyler leaned back and widened his eyes. "I'm right?"

Beth smiled and groaned. "Yes, I admit it. You're right. I'm wrong. Don't rub it in."

Tyler shook his head. "I don't want to be right at the expense of your happiness. If you feel better about it, I don't mind being wrong."

She burst into that throaty laugh he loved so much. "Oh dear. I've dug a very deep hole, haven't I? You're afraid to stick one toe in my pool."

"I'm not afraid, just wise." Tyler withdrew his hand from hers. He should behave properly at least some of the time. "Since I've already irritated you today, I have an important matter to discuss."

"Will I be further irritated?"

"I hope not. I want to talk to you about the date I had on Friday night."

Beth pursed her lips to keep from smiling. "Oh. Your date. How did you like Fern?"

"I'm trying to be good-natured about the whole thing—"

"You have been."

He raised his eyebrows. "But a thirty-five-year-old? Is that the best you can do?"

"Fern Newswenger milks three cows a day. I thought you might have something in common."

"She's more than ten years older than I am. Don't you think that's stretching things a bit?"

Beth always giggled as if she couldn't contain herself. "Oh, all right. I admit even I knew Fern wasn't going to work out."

"She cut my steak for me at dinner and insisted

on driving the buggy." Tyler chuckled. "It was like taking my aunt on a date."

"You have to admit she was better than Eva."

Tyler threw his hands in the air. "I give up. No more dates."

Beth drew her brows together. "No, no, you can't quit now. You've only had three dates. I'm in the narrowing-down process."

Tyler pinned her with a playfully sober gaze. "Let me narrow it down for you. How about a girl between the ages of nineteen and twenty-four whose laugh can't be heard in three counties."

"You didn't like Lorene?"

"She was lovely, absolutely lovely, but I prefer a quieter existence than the one I am bound to get with Lorene Zook."

Tyler loved making Beth laugh. He only kept up with this dating idea because it gave him an excuse to see Beth.

"Okay. I will find someone else, but have you ever considered that maybe you are too picky?"

"Eva Raber put me to sleep. I think we can do better than that."

"If you keep falling asleep on dates, no one is going to want to go out with you."

"And if you keep sending me mature and seasoned women, I might choose to become a bachelor, like Vernon Schmucker."

"I'll work very hard to see that, Lord willing, you don't turn into Vernon Schmucker."

He never smiled more than when he was with Beth. "Denki. I'm relieved. Now, can we go in the house and try out this new tool of yours? I don't know who gave it to you, but he must be a very nice young man. I hope you appreciate his present."

She gifted him with a dazzling smile. "I do appreciate it, but I might be tempted to rip the petals off a hundred sunflowers if he ever does it again."

"It's fortunate for him that it's almost wintertime. No more sunflowers until next summer."

Chapter Eleven

Lydia Kiem brought a suitcase on their date. That should have been Tyler's first clue that something was going to go horribly wrong.

They sat across from each other at a table at Luigi's and stared at their menus. Lydia kept pulling her cell phone out of her pocket and checking it for messages. Tyler tried to make pleasant conversation, but it was obvious she was more interested in her phone than anything Tyler might have to say.

Her appearance had surprised him when he'd picked her up earlier this evening. She wore blue jeans and a Green Bay Packers T-shirt and let her brown hair tumble around her shoulders in soft, wavy curls.

Lydia met the requirements Tyler had given to Beth. She was twenty years old, didn't laugh excessively, and seemed to have her wits about her. Tyler made a mental note. He had neglected to put "baptized" on that list. Lydia was definitely not a church member.

Tyler didn't mind if Lydia was still in *rumschpringe*, but did she have to flout her Englisch clothes and Englisch cell phone when out on a date with a devoted Amish boy? Maybe he expected too much. After all, Lydia acted polite and could carry on a relatively normal conversation.

"What do you want to eat?" Tyler said. "The pasta is very gute."

Lydia chewed on her fingernail and glanced at her phone for the tenth time in five minutes. "Do you think I could have a big plate of cheese fries?"

"Of course," Tyler said. "Anything you want."

It hadn't even crossed his mind to put *healthy eater* on the list.

The waitress ambled to their table to take their order. "What's in the suitcase?" she asked, pulling a pen out of her apron pocket.

Tyler was eager to hear Lydia's answer. Had she felt the need to bring a collection of books with her in case the date got boring?

"Nothing," she said.

Okay, whatever was in that suitcase was none of Tyler's business.

The waitress shrugged, flashed a curious grin at Tyler, and held her notepad at the ready. "What would you like to eat?"

"I'll have the lasagna," Tyler said.

"Can I have cheese fries and a Diet Dr. Pepper?"

"Sure," said the waitress. "We're a little backed up in the kitchen, just to let you know, but I'll bring it out as soon I can."

A little backed up? Lydia acted as if she wanted to eat immediately and take her suitcase and get out of here. Was he really that dull of a date? She checked her phone again, shoved it into her pocket, and curled the wrapper from her straw around her finger.

Tyler took a drink of his water. "So, I hear you like to ride horses. Do you have your own horse?"

Lydia chewed on another fingernail. "No, but we have two horses the family always rides."

Lydia had seemed so eager to come on this date. She had greeted Tyler with breathless excitement at the door, introduced him to her parents, and smiled sweetly as if she thought a date with Tyler Yoder might be kind of fun. Tyler had assured Lydia's dat that he would have her home by ten, and Lydia had practically bounded down the porch steps. She'd asked him to wait before she'd sprinted to the toolshed, retrieved her strange suitcase, and joined him in the buggy. Maybe the ride to Shawano had been enough time with Tyler to decide she wasn't really interested, because she made absolutely no effort now.

Not that Tyler was really broken up about it. If Lydia wasn't interested, she wasn't interested. And Beth would love to hear all about the mysterious suitcase.

Tyler heard the telltale beeps that could only mean Lydia had a text message. She whipped the phone out of her pocket and flipped it open. She must have read something she liked, because she did a sharp intake of breath and beamed from ear to ear.

"What are your horses' names?" He was grasping at straws now.

Lydia clapped her phone closed and looked at Tyler with something akin to pity in her expression. "Look, Tyler. You are a super nice guy, and it was wrong of me to use you like this, but I couldn't see any other way. My boyfriend is here to pick me up."

"Your boyfriend?"

"He got jobs for both of us in Milwaukee."

"You're going to Milwaukee?"

"Two weeks ago we made a plan to go away together and get married. This whole date thing with you was a perfect way to get out of the house without creating a big scene with my parents. I'm really grateful."

Tyler couldn't believe what he was hearing. Had he fallen asleep again? Was this bizarre conversation part of a dream? "You're jumping the fence?"

"Jah."

"Right now?"

"Jah. With Brandon. He's got a new Jeep."

Tyler frowned. "But I told your dat I've have you home by ten."

"He'll get over it. I left a note under my pillow. They'll find it when I don't come home tonight."

Tyler had no idea what to do. He'd never been party to an elopement. Or a fence-jumping. "You're still my responsibility."

Lydia rolled her eyes. "Don't worry, Tyler. My

parents aren't going to be mad at you. I've always been a difficult child." She leaned closer. "I want to be happy. You understand that, don't you?"

"Of course. I'm sorry you don't feel like you can be happy in our community."

She pressed her lips together. "Me too."

"Are you sure? Maybe I could take you back to your house, and we could talk to your parents about this. I know they love you. Don't you think you'll break their hearts?"

"I've thought about this for years, Tyler. I'm not going back." She reached across the table and patted his hand. "But you're very nice to be concerned."

A boy who looked like he lifted weights for a living walked through the door and scanned the restaurant. He caught sight of Lydia and jogged to their booth. With a look of hurried anticipation, he gave Tyler a cursory nod. "Hey."

Tyler couldn't do anything but stay cool and nod back. "Hey."

"Ready, Lydia?"

Lydia handed him her suitcase and slid out of her chair. "Thanks for your help, Tyler." She laced her fingers with her boyfriend's, and they swept out of the restaurant together.

"Don't you want your fries?" Tyler called.

Seconds after Lydia stepped out the door, the waitress set Tyler's order on the table. "Good news," she said. "This came up a lot faster than I had hoped."

Tyler stared at his lasagna and Lydia's heaping plate of cheese fries. He couldn't help it. The chuckle started deep in his throat and rumbled out of his mouth like a locomotive.

When he imagined Beth's reaction, he laughed until he cried.

Chapter Twelve

Nine o'clock. Beth sat at her treadle machine and put the finishing touches on Mary's wedding dress. Dawdi had been kind enough to give her machine a place of honor in the great room right next to the sofa so she could sew while Toby played.

Mammi and Dawdi had gone to bed, but Toby was still up. He'd taken an unusually long nap this afternoon and wasn't ready to throw in the towel yet. He threw his ball around the room and kept up a steady stream of words that Beth couldn't understand. He occasionally yelled, "Ball," and sometimes "Mommy." Another few months and that child would be talking her ear off.

She leaned back in her chair, snipped the last errant threads, and held the dress up in front of her to get a good look. Mary had asked for a royal-blue dress for her wedding. It had turned out very nice. In two weeks, there would be wedding bells for Mary and Beth's brother, Aaron Junior. Beth had made the dress as a wedding present.

She looked at Toby. He smiled at her and yawned. Time for bed. For both of them. Beth did not do well the next day when she stayed up too late.

Someone knocked on the door. Her heart jumped to her throat at the thought that it might be Tyler coming to report on his date. He had come once before later in the evening, and they'd shared a pleasant visit and a warm cup of hot cocoa.

Beth hung the finished dress over the back of the chair and went to the door. She put her hand to the nape of her neck to make sure there were no stray wisps of hair peeking out from under her prayer covering.

When she opened the door, her throat constricted, and she found it impossible to breathe. Isaac Hostetler, her late husband's twin brother, leaned against the doorjamb with a cocky grin on his lips. "Hello, Beth."

She wanted to slam the door in his face, but couldn't find the courage or the strength to do it. She couldn't find her voice, either.

He didn't seem as tall as she remembered him. Tyler stood a good three inches taller, to be sure. But he still had the same confident air about him that Beth found maddening. And intimidating. Isaac and Amos had always been so sure of themselves that Beth had surrendered all her self-confidence to them.

Isaac handed Beth a gift wrapped in blue paper and tied with a white bow. "I brought you something."

Beth took the present reluctantly. All of Isaac's kindnesses came with conditions.

"Open it," he said.

The involuntary trembling had started the minute she'd laid eyes on Isaac. Frustrated with her shaky fingers, she hastily opened his gift.

"It's a calendar of daily Bible verses," Isaac said with a self-satisfied smile. "I went through a lot of trouble to find the perfect one."

Beth winced when she found she couldn't speak without her voice cracking. "Denki. Denki, Isaac. I like calendars."

"I know." His gaze pierced her skull. "You've perked up a bit, Beth. When you left Indiana, you were pale and thin. You've got some of your color back. Not all, but you don't look like a ghost anymore. Maybe someday you'll be pretty again."

She flinched as he reached out and patted her cheek. "I missed you, Beth."

Beth folded her arms around her waist. Why did she let him make her feel so small? It had been the same with Amos. He had always made her feel powerless to fight back.

"What are you doing here?" she squeaked, wincing at how insignificant her voice sounded.

"I came to see how you're getting along without me. Not very well by the looks of it."

Grinning with self-assurance, Isaac stepped past Beth and into the house. He tossed his hat on the kitchen table and hung his coat over one of the chairs. He thought he had the right to make himself at home.

He gazed around the room and caught sight of Toby standing by the sofa. "Toby," he said, spreading his arms wide as if expecting Toby to run into his embrace. "You got so big."

Beth tensed. She didn't want Isaac near her baby.

Toby screwed his face into a scowl and pointed a scolding finger at Isaac. "No, no," he said.

Beth held her breath as Isaac marched to the sofa and scooped Toby into his arms. "Toby, Toby," he said, hugging him while Toby struggled to break free. To Beth's relief, Toby didn't cry. Instead, he pushed against Isaac's chest while grunting and repeating, "No, no."

"Aren't you happy to see your favorite uncle?"

"No, no."

Isaac finally gave up the hope of getting any affection. With a sheepish and irritated twist of his lips, he placed Toby on the sofa and patted his head. "That kid looks more like Amos all the time." He winked at Beth. "Or more like me."

Beth hurried to the sofa and stood between Isaac and Toby. "He's growing up right quick."

Isaac tapped her nose with his index finger. "Growing up without a father, Beth. You know that's not right."

"We get along fine."

"Amos would have wanted Toby to have a father, and he would have wanted me to take his place. Why did you leave us, Beth? We treated you good after Amos died." Isaac slid his hands around Beth's waist. "I've missed you."

Beth turned her face from him and stiffened. She'd fended off many of his unwelcome advances in Indiana. She had learned that if she remained still and didn't try to resist his touch, he would soon grow frustrated and release her. Even Isaac wouldn't cross a certain line of propriety.

"Marry me, Beth." When she didn't respond, he pulled her closer until his face came within inches of hers. "I love you. I want to spend the rest of my life with you."

She pressed her lips into a firm line. He stared at her for a few moments before scowling and nudging her away from him. Stepping back, he shoved his fingers through his hair.

Beth took a deep breath and willed her pulse to slow down.

Isaac looked around the room. "It's a mess in here," he said resentfully. He pointed to her sewing machine and the fabric that sat on the sofa next to Toby. "What's all this?"

"My sewing business."

Isaac laughed bitterly. "You were always talking about starting a sewing business. But you're not smart enough to make this work, Beth. You can't sew a straight stitch to save your life." He threw his arms out wide and made a sweeping gesture around the room. "I told you. You don't have to do all this. I will take care of you. Come back where you belong and marry me."

The hurt and abuse of three years with Amos almost choked her. She wanted to lash out, to tell Isaac how much she despised him, how much she resented his family for crushing her spirit and trampling her dreams. But fear stole her voice. Isaac and Amos had always frightened her. When she wanted to be strong, she always found herself cowering in a corner.

Beth shook her head. "My grandparents need me."

"Mamm needs you too. Don't you care about her?"

"Of course. I nursed her for over a year after Amos died."

Isaac turned red in the face. With his fair complexion, he looked as if he were on fire. "That's so typical of you, Beth, to make it sound like a prison sentence. My mamm took you in and let you stay in the dawdi house even after Amos died. She deserves your gratitude, not your selfishness."

"I . . . I can't leave. I've got several orders for dresses yet."

Scowling, Isaac stomped to the table and swiped his hand over the top, sending her patterns, fabrics, and scissors crashing to the floor.

Beth recoiled as her heart beat a wild cadence. Toby started to bawl hysterically. She reached behind her and smoothed her hand over Toby's hair. If Isaac meant to harm her, she didn't dare pick Toby up.

She hoped Mammi and Dawdi would sleep through the racket. Isaac's behavior would distress them. They did not need to partake in her troubles.

Isaac returned to her side and shoved his face within inches of hers. "You are a stubborn, prideful woman. If you don't forsake your wickedness, you will burn in Hell."

Beth held her breath. Isaac seemed to be within seconds of striking her across the face.

Please, Heavenly Father, don't let him hurt my child.

The most beautiful sound in the world reached her ears.

"If I were you, I'd get away from her."

Beth caught her breath. Did God really answer prayers so immediately?

With all the noise Isaac had made, she hadn't even heard him come in. Tyler stood in the open doorway with his arms folded across his chest. He looked an awesome sight. The tense muscles of his arms bulged against the confines of his navy-blue shirt. His eyes flashed with the violence of a thousand winter storms and the intensity of barely contained rage.

Isaac snapped his head around and glared at the intruder as Toby, still bawling, slid from the sofa, pumped his little legs as fast as they would go, and made a beeline for Tyler. "Mommy!" he cried. Tyler gathered Toby into his arms and kissed his cheek. Beth wanted to sob with relief.

"What do you want?" Isaac growled.

Tyler pinned Isaac with a steely gaze. "Maybe you should step away from Beth. It's clear she doesn't welcome your touching."

Isaac didn't lose his snarl, but he took a small step backward. "It's none of your business."

Although she wanted Toby as far from Isaac as possible, Beth felt palpable relief when Tyler moved to her side with Toby firmly in his embrace. He placed the whimpering Toby carefully in Beth's arms and positioned himself between Beth and Isaac. "Take Toby to your room, Beth, while I show this man where the door is."

Beth moved away from Tyler, but in the opposite direction of her room. To get there, she'd have to pass Isaac. What if he lashed out and hurt Toby?

Isaac balled his hands into fists as his face glowed red as a beet. "Don't try to keep me from what's rightfully mine."

Tyler contained his rage, but Beth could see it deepen in the lines of his face and the set of his jaw. "So far as I know, you have no claim on Beth. And I will not stand for your cruelty. Get out now."

Tyler placed a firm hand on Isaac's arm. Isaac reacted by throwing a punch squarely at Tyler's mouth.

Beth screamed as Tyler's head snapped back. He didn't go down, and he didn't fight back. Holding up his hand to stop Beth from coming to him, he fingered his bloody lip and raised his hands in surrender. "I won't fight you," he said. "I'm a man of peace. If you want to hurt me, let's go outside so the baby doesn't see."

Isaac massaged his knuckles and shot Tyler a glare that could have curdled milk. He turned on his heels, snatched his hat and coat, and stormed out the door.

Breathing heavily, Tyler nodded to Beth. "I'll make sure he leaves. Get Toby in the other room." He cupped his hand over her elbow. "And get yourself in the other room where I know you're safe." When she didn't move, he frowned. "Please?"

Numb with shock, but not about to abandon Tyler, Beth followed him to the threshold. He screwed up his mouth in vexation, gave her an exasperated huff, and shut the door behind him.

Peeking out the window, Beth saw Isaac tromp across the frost-covered grass. Tyler followed him halfway and stopped. Beth let out a breath as if she'd been holding it for ages. Isaac had finally given up.

Suddenly, Isaac turned and yelled something to Tyler. Beth couldn't hear him, but even in the semi-darkness, the nastiness in his expression was unmistakable. Without warning, he charged at Tyler and plowed him to the ground.

Beth gasped as Isaac hit Tyler again and again. Tyler did his best to shield his face from the blows but did nothing to fight back. The panic tore through Beth's chest. Maybe it wasn't right, maybe her vow of nonviolence demanded that she do nothing, but she refused to stand by and let her brother-in-law hurt Tyler.

Sobbing uncontrollably, she ran to her room and set Toby in his crib. He reached for her and cried as if his heart would break, but he'd be safe until she got back.

She ran to Mammi's closet and pulled out the broom. She could beat Isaac back with it or give him a good smack over the head if she had to. Unable to quell her tears, she burst from the house ready to do battle in the middle of the night.

Isaac had disappeared. Tyler sat on the ground with his elbow propped on his knee, holding the left side of his face in his hand. She sprang off the porch and ran to him. His lip and nose were bleeding and a goose egg was already forming at his eyebrow.

In breathless alarm, she knelt beside him.

He peeked at her out of his good eye. "Did he hurt you?" She didn't answer, just kept sobbing as she brushed her fingers across his lip. "Beth, are you okay?" he insisted.

"Jah, jah, I am fine."

"Was that Amos's brother?"

"Jah. Isaac. His twin in every way."

Tyler glanced at the broom clasped in her fingers. "Do you want me to sweep something?"

Chapter Thirteen

She offered her shoulder to lean on, but he stood on his own accord and hobbled slowly into the house. Toby's cries of distress immediately greeted them.

"Sit down," Beth said. "I'll tend to your face."

He ignored her request. She followed him as he limped down the hall into her room and scooped Toby out of the crib. Toby, his entire face soggy with moisture, immediately rested his head on Tyler's broad shoulder and hiccupped pathetically.

They went back into the great room. He sat at the kitchen table and patted Toby's back while whispering comforting words into Toby's ear.

Toby might be soothed, but Beth could not be comforted. Crying softly, she dampened a dishtowel and pulled a small first aid kit from the drawer. Scooting a chair close to Tyler, she began sponging off his lip and nose. "Your nose isn't bleeding anymore."

"Did he hurt you?"

"No," Beth said. "He asked me to marry him."

He kept one arm tightly under Toby and reached out for her hand. "I'm so glad he didn't hurt you."

"He wouldn't stop hitting you," she whimpered.

"I'm okay, Beth. Really. He spent his rage right quick, especially when I didn't fight back. He only hit me four or five times. And not that hard. I can tell he doesn't milk cows." He flexed his bicep and made Beth smile involuntarily. "My arms are about twice as thick as his. Because he beat on me, he wasn't even thinking of harming you or Toby. That's what I wanted."

Beth shuddered. "I'm glad Toby is safe, but I can't be happy that you got hurt."

"I was sorely tempted to hit him back, but I held my anger. Jesus said to turn the other cheek. But it crossed my mind to wonder what to do when I ran out of cheeks."

Beth giggled through her tears. "You gave him your nose."

Tyler gently ran a finger up and down Toby's arm. "What were you planning on doing with that broom?"

"I was going to conk him on the head."

Tyler frowned. "I'm glad you didn't get the chance. He could have turned on you in an instant, and then I would have been tempted to break my vow of nonresistance."

Beth finished wiping the blood from his face as she felt she might overflow with gratitude. "Isaac seldom had a kind word to say to me. I don't know why he'd ever want to marry me."

"I do."

"Both brothers always had hot tempers. . . ." She lowered her eyes and let her voice trail off. There were many things that Tyler need never know.

A deep line appeared between Tyler's brows. "Beth." He took her hand and caressed her fingers one by one with his thumb. His soft touch tingled all the way up her arm. He cleared his throat. "Did Amos ever hit you?"

Her heart felt as heavy as a blacksmith's anvil. "Nae. He never did."

Frowning, Tyler bent his head over to meet her eye. "Is that the truth?"

She nodded. Amos, with all his faults, had never struck her.

He turned her hand over and stroked her palm. "But he was unkind to you?"

Beth snatched her hand away and practically leaped to her feet. She turned her back on him and opened the freezer. "You need some ice for that eyebrow."

"Beth." His voice was as soothing as chamomile tea. "Will you tell me about Amos?"

She swiped a tear from her cheek and reached into the freezer for a small chunk of ice. "Do you have a headache?"

Tyler braced Toby against his chest and stood up. The poor little guy had zonked out in the comfort of Tyler's arms. "I'll go lay him down," Tyler said before tromping down the hall and disappearing into Beth's room.

Beth rinsed out the dishtowel and splashed cold

water on her face. She still needed to tend to that lip. She pulled the ointment from the first aid kit.

Tyler came back, rubbing the uninjured side of his face and peering at Beth with a doubtful glint in his eye.

She motioned for him to sit on the sofa and brought the ointment and the ice wrapped in a towel. Sitting next to him, she handed him the ice. He hissed as he dutifully placed it against his eyebrow. "I'll bet he hurt his hand on this one. I have a thick skull."

Beth squeezed some ointment onto her finger and dabbed Tyler's lip. He riveted his gaze to her face while she worked in silence. She couldn't endure that probing look for long. "I want you to know, I wasn't glad that Amos died."

"I didn't think you were."

She swallowed hard. Might as well share the worst of it. "But I was relieved. Extremely relieved."

"Oh, Beth."

She took a shaky breath. "And now you know. A woman who is relieved when her husband dies has a heart as black as coal."

She half expected him to turn away from her or find an excuse to go home. Instead, he slid his arm around her shoulders. She should have resisted his pity or his attempt to rescue her or whatever it was, but weariness overtook her. She leaned her head on his shoulder and melted into his warmth.

"If Amos was anything like Isaac," he said, "I would have been relieved too."

"In many ways, I deserve the blame."

"No. Don't ever say that."

"I am not very good at cooking or keeping house. Amos got so frustrated with me. But why couldn't he have been more patient?" Water flowed anew down her cheeks.

Tyler set his ice down and wiped the tears from her face.

"He criticized everything I did. The chicken was too tough, the clothes weren't ironed properly, the toilets were cleaned wrong. I was too stupid to read a recipe or understand the Bible."

He brushed his thumb across her bottom lip and whispered gently. "Hush. I can't listen to any more of this. It makes me furious."

"My mamm urged me to stand up for myself, but I was too weak."

A smile played at his lips. "I've seen you stand up for yourself plenty of times."

"I'm not afraid of you."

"I'm very glad to hear it."

"But wives must submit to their husbands. I tried to be meek and submissive, but in my heart I resented him. He could sense it. My ill will made him all the more angry." She lifted her head off his shoulder and folded her arms. "That is why I refuse to remarry. I won't submit myself to anyone ever again."

Tyler's face briefly clouded over. "You're forgetting the other half of the marriage vow." He pulled his arm from around her and reached for Dawdi's

Bible on the table next to the sofa. He leafed through the pages of Ephesians and raised his un-injured eyebrow. "Will I put you to sleep if I read a few verses?"

He managed to coax a half smile out of her. "You're the one who falls asleep on dates."

"*Husbands, love your wives, even as Christ also loved the church, and gave himself for it.* Did Amos ever love you the way Christ loved his church?"

"I don't know."

"*So ought men to love their wives as their own bodies. He that loveth his wife loveth himself. For no man ever yet hated his own flesh; but nourisheth and cherisheth it, even as the Lord the church.*" He laid the Bible back on the table. "No husband should ever treat his wife the way Amos treated you, because such be-havior is the grossest sin." He brushed his finger against her jawline and sent sparks shooting through her whole body. "The grossest sin, Beth. A husband must have the deepest humility when he takes a woman to wife. He is charged with treating his wife as Jesus would treat her."

"So you can see how risky it is for any woman to entrust her happiness to an imperfect man."

"And yet women do it all the time."

Beth looked down at her hands. "Because they don't know any better."

"Because they trust God."

Beth wanted to agree with him, but she had seen too much of real life. "That didn't work for me."

"Maybe it did, and you don't recognize it."

Beth refused to be convinced. "You're not making any sense."

Tyler shrugged in resignation and put the ice back on his eyebrow. "I got hit in the head one too many times tonight."

Her eyes blurred with tears yet again. "I don't know what would have happened if you hadn't been here. Thank you."

"I've never been so glad for a bad date in my entire life."

She clapped her hand over her mouth. "Oh no. What happened?

"Lydia's boyfriend showed up at the restaurant, and they eloped. He had a new Jeep."

"They eloped? What do you mean they eloped?"

Tyler grimaced. "She told me that she had been planning on jumping the fence for weeks and that a date with me had been the perfect time to put her plan into action."

"She was thrilled when I asked her to go on a date with you."

He smiled wryly. "And that didn't make you suspicious?"

"Not at all. You're quite a catch, Tyler Yoder."

He knit his brows together. "At least to some girls."

"I had no idea any of this was brewing. Poor Lydia! I feel so bad for her family."

"I went to her parents as soon as she walked out on me."

"What did they say?"

Tyler shook his head. "Her dat lectured me for

twenty minutes. I apologized, but I don't know what I could have done short of tying myself to the top of the Jeep. Her mamm was understandably upset, but neither of them seemed all that surprised."

"They were probably hoping you would convince her to settle down. If anyone could have done it, it would have been you."

"Nae. I can't compete with a new Jeep."

Beth swallowed the lump in her throat. "I promise I'll do better, Tyler. The next girl will be everything you could ever want. You deserve a wonderful-gute companion in life."

He took the ice from his eyebrow and stared at her. A hint of some intense emotion flitted across his face before he released a huff of air and stood up. "I don't think you can find me what I'm looking for."

"Give me another chance," she heard herself say. Did she mean give *her* another chance or give her another chance to find someone? She couldn't really decipher her own feelings. She ran her hand across her forehead. Tyler was proving to be a greater temptation than she had anticipated.

He frowned and turned away from her. "You do what you think is best."

"I just . . . I just want you to be happy."

"Do you?"

"Of course. I'll do everything in my power."

He turned back and gazed at her, that deep emotion returning to his expression. "And I'll do everything in my power."

His intensity made her heart race. And then he

relaxed and melted into a smile. Reaching out a hand, he pulled her from the sofa. "The gute part of the date was that Lydia didn't eat her cheese fries. I thought you might like them."

Beth gave him a half smile. Did he ever go one minute without thinking of something thoughtful to do? "She must have been in quite a hurry. How could anyone abandon cheese fries?"

Bleary eyed, Mammi and Dawdi shuffled into the great room. Mammi wore a cozy flannel nightgown and a fuzzy purple knitted cap. Dawdi had donned his trousers and suspenders over an oversized nightshirt.

"Tyler," Dawdi said. "How nice to see you. Did you hurt yourself?"

Beth gave Mammi a swift hug. "I'm sorry. I hoped you'd sleep through all the commotion."

"What commotion?" Mammi asked as she let her eyes adjust to the light. "Felty feels a little cold coming on, and I thought I would make him some peppermint tea."

Mammi's mouth drooped into a puzzled frown as she looked at the mess Isaac had made when he'd shoved Beth's supplies off the table. "Oh, I see you've already cleared off the table."

"I'll make the tea, Mammi."

Tyler found a small frying pan and retrieved the take-out bag of cheese fries from the table. He must have deposited them there when he'd first come in. "Would you like some cheese fries?"

Dawdi pulled out a chair for Mammi. "Why not? I've already got heartburn."

Mammi took a good look at Tyler's face. "What happened to you?"

Tyler shared a secret smile with Beth. "I had a very bad date tonight."

"Oh, dear," Mammi said. "I told Beth it was a bad idea to try to find you a wife when I already made plans for you. I hope you'll stop all this nonsense before someone gets hurt."

Before someone gets hurt.

Jah, Tyler should stop all his nonsense before someone got hurt. Beth couldn't pull her eyes from his face as he stirred the cheese fries in the skillet. He was so handsome, so kind. How would she ever resist him?

Beth couldn't shake the uneasy feeling that if anyone was going to get hurt, it would be her.

Chapter Fourteen

Tyler folded up his coat collar and blew on his hands as he jumped from the buggy. Aden had told him there was something called global warming going on, but today, such a thing didn't seem possible. His breath hung in the air as he helped Dat unhitch the horse and lead it to the Shrocks' barn.

Mamm and Joe didn't wait, but headed for the warmth of the house. No one should be out for long on a day like this.

Dat would be joining Beth's brother and Mary Shrock in marriage today. Beth's brother, like many of Anna and Felty's posterity, was tall and lanky with pleasant features. The Helmuths had a reputation as a handsome family. Beth was the prettiest one of the bunch.

Tyler emerged from the barn with his dat as Anna and Felty drove up the lane. His heart clanked against his ribs. Beth would be with them.

Dat went into the house, and Tyler ran to help the Helmuths with their buggy. By the time Tyler got close enough to help, Anna had already jumped out. "Well, Tyler, dear," she said, giving him a firm pat on the arm, "that bump on your head is looking much better. And your lip isn't swollen at all. Did you use the helichrysum I gave you?"

Tyler reached into the buggy and took Toby from Beth's arms. "Jah. I rubbed it on my eyebrow every day."

"It did the trick."

Toby, bundled in a thick little coat and sporting a beanie likely knitted by Anna, grinned and revealed a mouth full of tiny white teeth. "Mommy," he said, before resting his head on Tyler's shoulder and getting comfortable there.

Beth looked stunning in her crisp white kapp with a gray and black fuzzy scarf around her throat. Tyler offered her his hand. She hopped out of the buggy and rewarded him with a dazzling smile and a glimpse of that dimple.

"Better get to the house," Tyler said, "or you'll catch your death of cold out here."

Anna reached into the buggy and pulled out a cake pan covered with tinfoil. "I know the groom's family isn't expected to help with the meal, but I wanted to bring a little treat to go along with dinner. It's a recipe I made up."

With some concern, Tyler glanced at Anna's pan. Anna didn't have much luck even when she used a recipe. The lack of a recipe might prove to be disastrous. She pulled back the tinfoil and let Tyler have a peek at her concoction. Grated carrots and bite-sized slices of dill pickles floated in a murky sea of green gelatin. "It looks delicious."

Her eyes sparkled. "I'll save a big helping for you."

Tyler swallowed hard. He'd have to eat at least three healthy servings to spare Anna's feelings.

Tyler transferred Toby to Beth's arms and slipped his hand under one of the straps securing the horse to the buggy. "You go in, Felty. I'll see he gets stabled."

Felty winked and worked his gnarled fingers under the strap. "A young fellow like you might need a little help."

Beth put Toby on the ground and took his hand. "*Cum*, Mammi. It's cold out here."

Once they unhitched the horse, Tyler walked alongside as Felty led the horse to the barn. Felty wore a neon-orange scarf the like of which Tyler had never seen. "That is quite the scarf," Tyler said.

Felty grinned and nodded. "I won't be shot by a deer hunter."

"That's for certain."

"It's a mite fancy, I know, but I didn't have the heart to tell Anna. She loves her knitting needles. She and Beth are two peas in a pod. Anna stayed up 'til all hours knitting scarves, and Beth kept her company finishing a dress. She's wearing herself mighty thin."

Tyler massaged the back of his neck. "I know."

Felty put out some oats for the horse. "She could use a gute man to take care of her."

Didn't he know it. "She's a little stubborn when it comes to talk of marriage."

"Stubborn like her mammi. Her best quality."

Tyler smiled to himself. Truer words were never spoken.

"That brother-in-law of hers won't let her be."

A knot formed right between Tyler's eyebrows. "Isaac? He's been back?"

"Nae, but he writes her letters. Three or four times a week. I've been tempted to feed them to the fire before Beth even sees them. They upset her something wonderful."

"What do they say?"

"Nothing that makes her happy, I expect."

Tyler forced himself to take a deep, calming breath even as he felt as if Felty's horse had kicked him in the chest. No doubt Isaac's letters pressured Beth to return to Nappanee. Who knew what cruel manipulation Isaac used on paper? Tyler's blood heated up as if he were standing in the center of a raging forest fire. How dare Isaac do anything to upset sweet, gentle Beth? Tyler would not allow it. Isaac could not be allowed to harass Beth while Tyler had the power to do something about it. Even if Beth didn't want his protection, he was determined to give it. He wouldn't stand for any harm to come to her or Toby. "Denki for telling me."

Felty slapped Tyler on the shoulder. "Don't tell Beth. She doesn't think I pay attention. I'd like to keep it that way."

They walked out of the barn, and Felty broke into a chorus of "Joy to the World" as he tromped toward the front door. Tyler immediately heard the sound of Toby's crying carried on the wind. He jogged around the side of the house and caught sight of Beth kneeling beside Toby as she struggled to disentangle him from a thorny rosebush. The spiky thorns had snagged his coat and the more he struggled to break free, the harder he stuck. He wailed in displeasure.

"Hold still," Beth cooed as she tried to free his coat and keep Toby from scratching his hands and face at the same time.

Tyler grabbed Toby's little hands and shielded his face from the unforgiving spikes as Beth pulled the branches away from his coat. The bare bushes finally released him, and Beth pulled him a few feet away to check for wounds. A small scratch on his hand and a tiny spot of blood on his ear were his only battle scars. She kissed his chubby cheek. "He took off running straight to the bush and ran even faster when I told him no. Then he started whacking at it just to spite me. If I tell him not to do something, it's the first thing he wants to try, as if he doesn't trust me to know where the trouble is. Last week he threw a tantrum because I wouldn't let him get run over by a car."

Tyler took out his handkerchief and dabbed at Toby's nose and then picked him up. "Sounds like he wants to learn things the hard way."

"He doesn't know that he'd really rather not get his finger sewn into one of my dresses."

Tyler couldn't resist brushing his fingers against the silky softness of Beth's scarf. "That yarn color is very pretty against your skin." Beth didn't like compliments, but her beauty begged to be noticed.

She blushed and smoothed a lock of hair from his forehead. He felt the sparks to the tips of his toes. "Your head looks a lot better. It's just a yellow bruise now, like a smear of mustard on your eyebrow."

"That is mustard. I'm a messy eater."

She giggled. "You and Toby should be best friends."

He wanted to stand there forever gazing into her eyes, except it was pretty cold out there and they'd be a pair of icicles if they stayed out much longer.

She broke eye contact first and cleared her throat as her smile faded. "So, are you ready for your next date?"

He tried not to frown. She'd think she had upset him. "After my string of disastrous experiences, I hoped you'd given up. Christmas is in a few weeks. Let's put the whole thing off until January."

"A wedding is the perfect time to meet a new girl. Erla Glick is expecting you to sit by her during the singing. Strike up a conversation and ask her on a date."

She had no inkling that his hopes for spending a sublime day with Beth had just burst like a hundred defective balloons. Erla Glick seemed like a nice girl. She lived in Tyler's district and had brown hair and had once gone cliff diving in the jungles of Mexico. He wasn't interested. "And what are you going to do while I'm having a gute time with Erla Glick?"

"Oh, I'll sit with the family and listen to *Onkel*

Perry tell the same jokes he tells every year. Maybe I'll even go home early and take a nap with Toby."

Tyler pressed his lips together. Weariness etched lines around Beth's usually bright eyes. "You're not getting enough sleep."

She brushed some imaginary lint off Toby's coat. "I have lots of orders. I'll rest after the Christmas rush."

He lifted his hand to caress her silky-soft cheek and thought better of it. She'd take it as a sign of pity or some other emotion that Tyler couldn't guess at. "Mamm and Dat can cover for me at the dairy. I could come over tomorrow and play with Toby so you can sew."

"I'll get it done. Mammi and Dawdi are watching out for me."

"Felty and Anna are in their eighties. They need someone to watch out for them."

"The four of us do just fine."

"You do better than fine, Beth. That's not the point."

She held up her hand. He shut his mouth. "I don't want to be your service project, Tyler."

"You need help."

"You think I'm helpless."

Tyler felt his temperature rise at her accusation. She was the most exasperating woman he'd ever locked horns with. "You're not helpless. You're stubborn as a mule, Beth Hostetler."

She widened her eyes in surprise and chuckled. Tyler wanted to kick himself. This was a serious conversation, but all he could think about at the moment was how much he loved the sound of her laughter.

"That's the first time you've ever fought back," she said. "I like it when you fight back. I don't feel so guilty for attacking you."

He stifled a smile and took a deep breath. "I'm sorry. I didn't mean to call you stubborn."

Her eyes twinkled. "Don't back down now. You were just getting warmed up."

Beth wanted to make light of it, but he couldn't let the moment go to waste. "Beth, you do the work of a mother and a father. I don't think you're helpless. I think you're wearing yourself out."

"Well, I don't need a husband, if that's what you're hinting at."

"I wouldn't dare hint at anything like that. I thought you might want me to come over and sweep something."

She huffed and bit her bottom lip. "I was tempted, you know."

"What?"

"When you asked me to marry you, I was tempted to accept. Marriage seems like such an easy way out of so many troubles. It's hard to raise a son alone." She sighed. "But a bad marriage is so much worse."

A sharp ache seized Tyler's chest. "You think I'd be a bad husband."

She sighed in resignation. "Nae. But I didn't think Amos would be a bad husband when I first met him either."

She might as well have slapped him across the face. "I am not Amos."

Her voice caught in her throat. "I'm sorry, Tyler. I've let my mouth run wild again."

He tried to catch his breath and give her a reassuring grin. It probably came out more like a wince.

She returned a fake smile and wrapped her fingers around his upper arm. With a gentle nudge, she led him toward the house. "I don't want to quarrel. This should be a joyous day. My brother is getting married, and you are going to be with Erla Glick. Let's go have fun."

Tyler tightened his arms around Toby and let Beth lead him into the house. He had never faced such a joyous occasion with such a heavy heart.

Tyler didn't hear one word of the sermon and didn't remember singing one hymn. The bride and groom didn't even make much of an impression. Beth filled his vision. She sat on the first row with some of her family, her hands folded in her lap, oblivious to the fact that every piece of Tyler's heart focused on her and only her. A slight movement of the stuffy air teased a wisp of hair at the nape of her neck, and Tyler thought he might go mad with the need to smooth it between his fingers.

Forcing his gaze in any direction but hers, he clenched his hands until his knuckles turned white and the sensation subsided. If he didn't look, the yearning wouldn't overpower him.

He peered down the row of girls. Beth's relatives,

girls from the district and elsewhere. One of them might be persuaded to marry him if he asked. He shoved his fingers through his hair as the lie he'd been telling himself untangled itself in his brain.

He didn't want just a companion. His experience with Lily had hurt enough that he had talked himself out of what he truly needed—what God surely wanted for him. He wanted a true wife—a woman he could love the way God wanted him to love. He wanted Beth. And only Beth.

He longed to share every breathless moment of every day with her. He wanted to sift his fingers through her hair and make her laugh and give her children. He wanted to hold her in his arms and show her that she need never be afraid again. And, yes, she'd be mad if she even knew he had the thought, but he wanted to rescue her, to help her be whole. To love her so well that she would willingly risk her heart again.

For a moment, the intense emotions swirling about him turned to rage as he thought of Amos Hostetler and what he had done to Beth. He had destroyed her trust in men and her faith on God.

It were better for him that a millstone were hanged about his neck, than that he should offend one of these little ones . . .

Tyler relaxed his fists and let the fury pass through him like wind through the bare trees. He had no right to judge Amos. His sins had most likely been inherited from his father and his father's father before him. Who knew what scars of abuse the generations had passed on to him?

Tyler would do everything in his power to see that Beth would not have to live with those scars.

Nae, not everything in *his* power. He had no power at all. It would have to be through God's power and grace.

Tyler bowed his head as the bride and groom stood to take their vows. Not knowing what else to ask for, he pled from his very soul. *Dear Heavenly Father, show me the way.*

He didn't multiply many words, for God would understand the depths of his longing.

When he opened his eyes, the entire service was over. The room seemed to explode into a beehive of activity as women and men rose to prepare for the wedding dinner. In a stupor, Tyler stood, and two men took the bench right out from under him.

"Tyler Yoder." A tall, slender girl held out her hand and expected him to take it.

He attempted a look of enthusiasm. "Erla Glick," he said. "Beth says we're supposed to get to know each other."

"Come on," she said. "I'll show you the way."

Green gelatin mixed with pickles tended to be watery. That didn't stop Tyler from helping himself to a liberal amount of Anna's concoction at dinner. No one else but Felty would eat it, and Tyler didn't want Anna to get her feelings hurt. After the meal, the gelatin sloshed around in his stomach as he and Erla Glick sat on one of the benches and sang with the rest of the young people. The bride's mother handed out pieces of moist pineapple upside-down cake, and Tyler felt compelled to take one, even though he thought he might explode.

"There are some New Order Amish building an orphanage in Mexico," Erla said, though Tyler barely listened. His gaze kept wandering to the kitchen, where he spied Beth sitting at the table with Toby in her lap, sharing a laugh and a piece of cake with one of her cousins. If she knew how much he suffered at this very moment, would she even care? Or would she stomp her foot and tell him to quit trying to rescue her?

She tapped her fork to her mouth. He wished he were that fork. What he wouldn't give for a taste of those lips. Tyler swiped his hand across his eyes and reined in his thoughts. No good taking them in that direction. He'd only drive himself crazy.

"There is so much need there," Erla said. "The poverty and crime are astounding."

"How long were you in Mexico?"

"Almost four months. I picked up enough Spanish to get by." Erla set her plate down and leaned back on her hands. "I love weddings," she said. "I love the way the groom looks at the bride like she is the only woman in the world."

"Jah. I like that too," Tyler said, massaging his forehead as he watched Beth take another bite of cake.

Erla sighed. "I want my groom to look at me the way you look at Beth Hostetler."

Tyler gawked at Erla even as he tried not to act surprised. "What . . . what did you say?"

Erla tilted her head and smiled sympathetically. "People are usually interested in my Mexico stories, but you don't seem to be aware that there is even such a country. It's like Beth is the only girl in the room. You're completely ignoring me."

A pit formed at the bottom of Tyler's gut. He had offended yet one more person today. He should give up and get out of here. "I'm really sorry. I didn't mean—"

She waved away his apology. "I've got a very thick skin, Tyler. And if you want to know the truth, I'm envious. If Menno Petersheim looked at me the way you look at Beth, I would be one very happy girl."

"Menno Petersheim?"

She pointed to a muscular, youthful-faced boy sitting in the corner all by himself. "He's so afraid to talk at gatherings that most of us girls have never heard his voice." She puckered her lips playfully. "But he'll talk to me, if I'm persistent."

"He's shy?"

Erla nodded. "Modest and humble. I wish I knew how to draw him out."

Tyler rubbed the back of his neck. He wished he knew how to tug Beth in. "Where does he work? What does he like to do? You could talk about things you have in common."

"His family owns a market in Shawano. They make bread and cheese and press apple cider."

"Maybe you could volunteer to do the shopping."

Erla flashed her teeth. "I already do." She turned her gaze in the direction of the kitchen. "What's your story with Beth? Doesn't she like you?"

Tyler masked his surprise by turning his face away. He wouldn't spill his guts to Erla just because she was nosy enough to ask.

She saw his frown. "I'm not trying to be rude, Tyler. I was never afraid to ask the impolite question." She nudged his shoulder with hers. "You look miserable. I want to help."

"I don't think you can help."

"Beth made specific arrangements for you and me to spend the day together." Erla lowered her voice in case anyone happened to listen in on their conversation. "Is she trying to get rid of you by matching you up with me?"

That thought felt like a knife right to the chest. "She wants to help me find a gute wife."

"But she doesn't want it to be her."

Another twist of the knife. "Nae."

"Then you've got a lot of work to do. Girls want to be courted, made to feel special."

Beth didn't. She wanted to be left alone so she could prove her independence to everyone.

Erla tapped her finger against her lips. "Since Beth thinks she's helping you find a wife, you'll have to sneak up on her, like a cat on a mouse, so she won't know what hit her until she finally realizes she's in love."

"What if she thinks I'm repulsive?"

Erla locked a firm gaze on him. "Not possible, Tyler. Any girl in Bonduel would be eager to catch you as a husband. Me excepted, of course. I mean, I think you are a wonderful-gute boy, but I've had my sights set on Menno for ages. He's got a mole on his cheek that I can't resist."

"I'm not going to paint moles or scars or cysts on my face to impress Beth."

"You have to be yourself to impress Beth. That will be enough."

It had to be enough. Tyler refused to be someone else to win Beth's heart. She had to want him for all his flaws, to love him because of all the things about him that annoyed her. He wouldn't stop trying to help her, even if she demanded it. He wasn't that type of person.

Erla's face glowed with excitement. "You could pretend to court me to throw her off the scent. She'll let her guard down if she's not suspicious of your motives."

"I'm not going to deceive Beth."

Erla rolled her eyes. "Use your imagination, Tyler. Beth will draw her own conclusions and be watching at the front while you sneak around to the back door."

"The back door?"

"Of her heart, Tyler. Try to keep up, will you?"

"Why do you want to help me?"

"Because any boy who likes a girl as much as you obviously like Beth deserves a chance with her. Especially you, Tyler. You have a reputation, you know, for being the kindest, most thoughtful person anybody has ever met. We all feel bad about what happened last autumn."

"I've gotten over it."

"Of course you have. Aden and Lily were meant

for each other, and we are all happy for them, but none of us liked seeing you hurt like that. You deserve a chance at Beth. And after what she's been through, she needs a boy like you."

A weak thread of hope pulsed through Tyler's veins. Beth needed him. Maybe he could find a way to convince her. "I . . . don't know what to do."

"Since you are without guile, you will have to leave everything to me."

"I'm not sure I like the sound of that."

Erla grinned. "You're smart to be wary."

Tyler glanced at Menno, sipping his punch in the corner. "I have been wanting to learn how to make cheese. I'll bet Menno Petersheim knows how to make cheese."

"He does."

Tyler cocked an eyebrow. "You've been wanting to learn how to make cheese, haven't you?"

Erla's eyes sparkled as she leaned closer. "More than anything."

"We'll find Menno's back door yet."

Chapter Fifteen

Beth crumpled the paper and shoved it into her pocket, disgusted that she couldn't keep her hands from trembling. Even though it wasn't warm in the kitchen, a bead of sweat trickled down her neck. Why did she let Isaac Hostetler frighten her like that? He was blowing smoke, the same as in every other letter he'd written.

Beth, it's my duty to marry you and your duty to give yourself in marriage to your late husband's brother.

Come home. You're needed here.

I'm sorry I lost my temper last time. I didn't mean to hurt anybody.

Mamm's health is failing. She needs you to take care of her. Repent of your bullheadedness and return to the bosom of our family.

Reconsider, Beth. I'll come fetch you if I have to. Don't think I won't.

Would Isaac really take her back to Nappanee by force? Maybe she should tell Tyler about Isaac's threat, in case she came up missing.

She pursed her lips. Isaac made his threats to scare her, in hopes of gaining her cooperation, but he still had his wits about him. He wasn't so desperate or so foolish as to think he could drag her back to Indiana against her will.

Blowing smoke. Isaac was just blowing smoke. Tyler need not be dragged into her troubles. Especially since he would want to fix everything for her. She didn't want his help.

Beth paused at the window. The snow had made down hard last night, and a glistening blanket of puffy, crunchy snow crystals covered Huckleberry Hill. She caught her breath as a flaming-red cardinal swooped from a nearby tree to nibble at the pinecone birdfeeder that she and Toby had hung on one of the bushes yesterday. They had made the birdfeeder from a jumbo pinecone smeared with peanut butter and rolled in birdfeed. Toby hadn't really appreciated that he would be feeding the birds, but he'd loved squishing the peanut butter between his fingers and licking it off his hands.

"Toby, Toby. Come look." Toby toddled to her, and Beth scooped him into her arms and held him up to the window. "Do you see the bird?"

Toby stared in awe as the cardinal pecked birdseed off the pinecone. "Ball. Ball," Toby said. He made a fist and knocked on the window. The cardinal retreated to the safety of the trees.

Beth's heart did a little flip-flop as a horse-drawn

sleigh appeared around the bend. Tyler, looking alarmingly handsome with one of Mammi's blue scarves wrapped around his neck, caught sight of her at the window, bloomed into a smile, and waved merrily.

Toby pounded on the window with his little fist. "Mommy, Mommy."

"That's Tyler. Can you say Tyler?"

More pounding. "Mommy."

Beth bit her bottom lip and attempted to temper her enthusiasm. Judging from the wild galloping of her heart, she was even more excited to see Tyler than Toby was. She turned away from the window. Of course she was eager to see him. She wanted a report on how things were going with Erla Glick. Tyler's courting adventures always made her laugh, and today, she needed a good laugh.

Mammi walked into the kitchen carrying three bolts of fabric. "I hope Tyler makes it up the hill. It looks like three feet of snow out there."

"He's here, Mammi."

"Gute. Right on time."

"I didn't know we were expecting him."

Mammi's eyes twinkled with the delight of a hundred secrets. Her lips formed into an O. "Maybe I didn't know either."

Beth eyed Mammi suspiciously. There was nothing wrong with Mammi's memory. Hearing Tyler's quick steps on the porch, she couldn't help herself. She put Toby down and smoothed the creases of her dress before checking to make sure her kapp sat in place.

Why he even bothered knocking anymore was anybody's guess, since he was practically a member of the family. Mammi opened the door to Tyler, who grinned from ear to ear. He didn't smile often, but when he did, the sight of it stole her breath.

Once he was inside, he laid a brown paper bag on the table before Toby raced into his arms.

"Ball, ball." Toby squealed and patted Tyler's cheeks. "Mommy, ball, side." Apparently Tyler now had three names. *Mommy, ball, and outside.* Toby's favorite things.

"Did you make it up the hill okay?" Mammi asked.

Tyler nodded. "That snow is so wet, a bucketful would weigh thirty pounds." He turned his eyes to Beth and almost blinded her with the warmth of his gaze. "Hello, Beth."

Why did she immediately feel self-conscious? "Hello."

Tyler put Toby on the floor, pointed out a ball for him to chase, and said to Beth, "I brought you a present."

She tried not to frown. He acted so happy. "I said I don't want presents."

"You'll like this one. It's for you and Anna and Felty." He unfolded the top of the bag and pulled out a white paper package about the size of one of Mammi's balls of yarn. He handed it to Beth. "Open it."

Beth folded back the paper to reveal a cream-colored ball of lumpy cheese.

"This is our third attempt," he said. "I fed the first two to the hogs."

She turned it over carefully in her hands. "You made this? It's wonderful."

His face glowed with warmth. "It might not be wonderful. You haven't tried it yet."

Beth pulled a knife from the block and cut a thick slice for each of them. The buttery, salty flavor danced on her tongue as the cheese seemed to melt in her mouth. She sighed with pleasure. "Oh, Tyler. It's wonderful-gute. What kind is it?"

"It's supposed to be mozzarella."

"Just like my mamm used to make," Mammi said.

Tyler's eyes danced. "It's quick and doesn't have to be aged. We made another white cheese that Menno said needs to sit for a couple of weeks. I don't know how it will taste, but at least it looks like cheese."

"Menno?"

Tyler suddenly seemed very interested in how Toby got along with his ball on the other side of the room. "After Thanksgiving, I asked Menno Petersheim to teach Erla and me how to make cheese."

Beth hadn't expected the profound disappointment that pounced on her and left her short of breath. "Oh. He's teaching you and Erla?"

"I think a man who has a dairy should know how to make cheese. It might come in handy."

Beth suddenly lost interest in Tyler's cheese endeavor. She went to the kitchen sink and picked up a rag. Maybe she could find something to wipe down.

Tyler cleared his throat and sat down at the table. "Beth, I need your help."

She found a grimy smudge on one of the cupboard doors and swiped at it. He probably wanted her to help him make a cheese for his precious Erla, but she really couldn't spare the time.

Again he turned his gaze from her. "There's a group of us going ice skating at one o'clock. I need you to come with me."

"What for?"

"I want you to see how things are coming along between me and Erla Glick."

She'd rather a horse stepped on her big toe. On both big toes. "You don't need me for that."

"I thought you might want to see how it's going."

She scrunched the dishrag into a soggy ball in her hands. "It's none of my business how it's going."

"Of course it is. You're the one who got us together." He smoothed his hand over the table, brushing off imaginary dust. "Please come ice skating, Beth. It will be lots of fun."

"It's too cold out for Toby."

It seemed Mammi was waiting for the perfect moment to pounce. "I'll stay with him. I'll put him down for a nap and catch up on my knitting."

Tyler winked at Mammi. "Denki, Anna."

Beth dropped the rag into the sink. "It doesn't matter. I don't have time." She pointed to a bolt of maroon fabric on the sofa that needed to be cut into a dress by tonight.

Mammi clicked her tongue. "*Sufficient unto the day is the evil thereof.*"

Beth regarded Mammi with puzzlement. How did that scripture apply to her situation?

"*Tomorrow will take thought for the things of itself,*" Mammi added.

The corner of Tyler's lip turned upward. "There will always be a dress to sew or a cow to milk. How many fine days do we get for ice skating?"

"I don't have any skates."

"I have a pair you can borrow," Mammi said. She seemed to have a ready answer for everything.

Beth resisted the urge to stick out her bottom lip. A woman of her maturity did not pout. But she couldn't think of anything she'd like to do less than watch Tyler and Erla Glick skate around the pond together. "I don't skate very well."

Tyler raised his eyebrows. "Let me be clear that I don't think you're helpless in any way, but I am a wonderful-gute skater. I will help you, if you want."

She smiled in spite of herself. "Maybe I don't want your help."

"But I really want yours."

All her excuses crumbled. She'd have to give in. "As long as you remember I'm not helpless."

"If I offend you," he said, reaching into his paper bag and pulling out a plastic sunflower, "you can give me a good whack with this."

Beth's insides did a little somersault. Who knew

she could take so much pleasure in his teasing? She giggled. "Don't think I won't."

Tyler probably thought he'd brought a lunatic along with him to the pond. Beth spent most of the sleigh ride waving her hands in the air and whooping and hollering to the sky. She loved the whooshing sound of the runners and the exhilaration of the icy breeze on her face as the horse pulled the sleigh swiftly across the snow. She'd been crouched over her sewing machine too long. Tyler hardly said a word the entire trip. He simply grinned at her with barely contained amusement.

Tyler put his strong hands around her waist and lifted her from the sleigh, a most unnecessary gesture, but one that Beth found quite pleasant, just the same. His hands lingered on her waist once she stood securely on her feet. "You need to get out more," he said, chuckling softly.

"I do not."

The skating pond, not much more than a grand puddle, sat a quarter mile from Erla Glick's farm. A lot of ice-skating went on there in the winter because it froze over right quick and was shallow enough that if someone happened to break through the ice, they wouldn't go in over their heads. Patches of brilliant blue sky peeked from behind the dull gray clouds, promising some sun for their outing. Seven or eight young people were already on the ice, some gliding deftly across the frozen pond, some shuffling awkwardly in hopes of staying on their feet. That was how Beth skated, as if she were in a contest to see if she or the ice would break first.

Erla Glick looked very appealing this afternoon. She wore a heavy black coat and gray sweatpants under her dress. A muted pink and yellow scarf covered her head, with enough length left over to wrap the scarf all the way around her neck. She trudged toward the sleigh, no doubt to lay claim to Tyler. A stocky young man followed close behind her.

Erla flashed that bright smile she was known for. Beth didn't like it one little bit. "I'm so glad to see you. Isn't this a gute day for skating?" Erla hooked her arm through the crook of the young man's elbow and pulled him forward. "This is Menno Petersheim. He has been teaching Tyler and me how to make cheese."

Menno had a manner about him that spoke of extreme shyness. "Hullo," he said, before lowering his eyes and stepping back a pace, content to let Erla do the talking.

"The ice is a little thin on the south end," Erla said, "but it froze nice and smooth."

Tyler reached into the sleigh and pulled out their skates. "We'll be careful. Come on, Beth. I don't mean to brag, but I'm going to amaze you with all the tricks I can do."

Beth glanced at Erla as tension tightened her throat.

She shouldn't have come. A cow on skis would fare better than she could. Tyler would feel obligated to help her when he'd rather be spending time with Erla. She'd only be in his way. That thought made her want to plop down in the snow and have a good cry.

"You and Erla go skate. I can sit by the fire and watch."

Erla swatted that suggestion away. "Menno and I are doing some cooking experiments. I'll skate later."

"We're making hot chocolate," Menno said.

Erla smiled. "And we're making hot chocolate." She gave Beth a little nudge with her elbow. "Go skate. It will be fun."

Beth looked from Erla to Tyler. What did Tyler want? He didn't seem bothered that Erla was so eager to tend to the fire. Without a second glance, he grinned playfully, took Beth by the elbow, and helped her through the snow to the edge of the pond. If Erla wouldn't skate with Tyler, the least Beth could do was try to help him have a good time so he didn't feel as if he'd wasted his day. Were his feelings hurt? She couldn't tell.

They sat on a sturdy wooden box at the edge of the pond that did duty as a bench and put on their ice skates.

"If you're laced up well, your ankles won't wobble," Tyler said. "Do you want me to tighten your laces for you?"

Beth arched an eyebrow. "You don't think I can lace my own skates?"

He clamped his mouth shut and held up his hands in surrender as his eyes danced. "Yes—I mean, no. I would not touch those laces for all the tea in China. Don't even ask."

"Gute, because I would hate it if you thought I couldn't even tie my own shoes."

"You are very gute at tying your own shoes."

Tyler stepped onto the ice and made an impressive figure eight. He held out a hand for Beth but pulled it back almost as soon as he had offered it. "Oh, I forgot. You don't want help."

Beth reached for him. "Ice skating was your idea, Tyler Yoder. I'll hold you responsible if I break my arm."

Grinning, he took both her hands and nudged her slowly onto the ice. With her fingers clamped around his, she took several baby steps and tried to avoid sliding at all. If she slid, she feared her feet would slip out from under her, and she would end up on her *hinnerdale*.

"Stop," Tyler said. "You're going to kill yourself skating like that." He let go of one of her hands so he could skate beside her.

"I'm afraid I'm going to kill myself either way."

He pointed to a bushy pine tree growing a hundred feet from the pond. "Focus your eyes on one point. It will help you get your balance. Now walk slowly around the edge with me so you get a feel for the ice."

"Don't let go."

"I wouldn't think of letting go," Tyler said. "It's a wonderful-gute excuse to hold your hand."

Beth tried to ignore the warmth that spread to the tips of her toes. She wouldn't let herself be distracted even when her hand felt so good nestled in his.

"Now, think of yourself as a graceful animal, moving through its natural habitat."

She grunted and jerked forward. He tightened his grip on her hand as she nearly lost her balance. "I'm thinking moose on roller skates. What are you thinking?"

He chuckled. "I see a beautiful dove floating lazily over the hill."

"You need glasses."

On her second time around the pond, her steps became less choppy, and she felt she might be making progress.

"Gute," Tyler said. "Now relax. Bend your knees a little and try a short glide."

Beth wondered if she'd drawn a breath since she got onto the ice. Still holding Tyler with the death grip, she relaxed her stiff back and concentrated on adding a little glide to her step. So far, so good.

"You're doing very well," Tyler said. "But not well enough for me to let go of your hand."

"I see that," she said, kind of hoping she wouldn't skate all that well today. "The first time my mamm and dat took me skating, we went to a huge rink in Green Bay. My parents made a day of it. They hired a driver and took me and my younger brothers and sisters out to lunch. It was a big to-do renting our equipment and getting all our skates on. The second I stepped onto the ice, my feet flew out from under me, and I fell flat on my back and got a concussion."

"Ouch."

"Five minutes after we got there, we turned in our

skates and left. They wouldn't give us our money back. I cried all the way home."

"Because you wanted to skate?"

"No, because me head hurt something wonderful."

Tyler moaned in sympathy. "I'm sorry."

"Well, I was only eight. I'm over it now."

"Oh, yes. I can see you're over it," Tyler teased. "How many times have you been skating since?"

She quirked the corners of her mouth upward and bumped her shoulder into his. "Never, smarty pants."

He made a slight bow. "I am honored that you would trust me to keep you from making a fool of yourself."

"I think you're secretly hoping I'll make a fool of myself."

He chuckled. "Absolutely not." He kept his gaze on her face. "I don't actually think it's possible for you to make a fool of yourself."

Beth caught her breath as she lost her concentration and nearly fell. Tyler whipped in front of her and wrapped his arm around her waist. "You okay?"

He was too close. She felt his warm breath on her cheek and thought she might melt into a puddle on the ice. "I'm okay."

Still holding her other hand, he quickly looked away, slid his arm from around her, and pulled her forward. "You almost made a fool of yourself," he said, with a playful smile.

Jah. She almost had.

Five or six more young people had joined the

group around the fire. Beth didn't know what they were cooking, but the faint smell of chocolate and citrus wafted their way. Die youngie around the campfire started singing Christmas carols.

"Music is my favorite thing about Christmas," Beth said. "Dawdi sings carols from sunup to sundown."

"I've never known Felty without a song on his lips."

"Toby has started singing with him. He doesn't really say any words, but when Dawdi breaks into song, Toby joins him with humming and oohing."

"I love hearing your dawdi sing. I can't carry a tune in a bucket."

"No, you can't."

Tyler widened his eyes in mock indignation. "You don't like the way I sing? I sing to the cows all the time."

"Oh, those poor creatures."

Her reply took him by surprise. He laughed until she thought he might not catch his breath. Then he growled and skated faster until she felt like she was tripping over her own feet to keep up. "Tyler, slow down this instant. Tyler, Tyler, slow down or I will be forced to pull out my sunflower."

He slowed down enough to let her regain her balance. She gripped his hand even tighter. "You are a wicked boy. I almost fell."

"You shouldn't insult the man who stands between you and a mouthful of ice."

When had his smile become so special to her? "When we first met, I thought you never smiled. But

I was wrong. You smile all the time. I just didn't notice it before."

His gaze made her already-wobbly legs feel like pudding. "Maybe I have so much more to smile about these days."

Out of the corner of her eye, Beth saw Erla and Menno each don a pair of skates and step onto the ice. She did her best to mask her disappointment. Tyler would want to skate with Erla now, and Beth would gracefully back away so she wouldn't make a pest of herself.

Both Erla and Menno acted as if they had been born on skates. Erla glided toward them like a bird in flight—the fluid motion that Beth had not been able to master. Erla held an orange in her mittens and presented it to Beth when she came close.

"Try this," Erla said. "It's Menno's invention."

Tyler let go of Beth's hand and wrapped his arm around her waist. There was no way she would fall while in his firm grasp. She took the orange and a plastic spoon from Erla.

"Blow on it," Erla said. "We hollowed out an orange and poured cake batter into it. You cook it over the coals for about ten minutes."

Beth scooped a spoonful of cake from the orange, blew on it, and took a bite. It tasted like an orange-cream sweet roll. "This must be what they eat in Heaven," she said. She held out a spoonful for Tyler. "Are you afraid of my germs?"

Tyler inclined his head. "I'll swap germs with you any day."

He took a bite, savored it, and sighed. "Very nice, Erla."

"How did you think of it?"

Erla squeezed Menno's arm. "Menno is always coming up with some new thing for the store. He showed us his own secret recipe for cheese yesterday."

Oh. Cheese.

Tyler and Erla made cheese together. Like a giant vacuum, that thought sucked all the fun out of the air. Beth handed Erla her orange. "I should probably get out of the way so you two can skate together."

Amusement danced in Erla's expression. "You two seem to be getting along so well. I don't want to ruin it."

"You're never going to get better without my help," Tyler said. "Ever."

Beth smirked at him. "Oh really?"

"Yep. You need me."

Erla was all smiles. "I'll skate with Menno. He likes to go fast."

Menno nodded.

They didn't even wait for Beth's agreement. Still holding her orange, Erla followed Menno as he took off around the pond. Beth caught her breath. They weaved in and out of other skaters with careless speed. She was impressed that they managed to stay on their feet.

"Aren't you glad Menno isn't helping you learn how to skate?" Tyler said.

"I see a broken collarbone in his future."

Tyler took her hand, and they glided around the edge of the pond, out of the way of anybody who wanted to go fast. "You'll never take me for granted again, will you?"

As they skated in comfortable silence, Beth watched Erla chase Menno around the pond. She seemed quite delighted when Menno changed directions and started chasing her.

Was Erla interested in Tyler at all? Surely she would have jumped at the chance to skate with him. Maybe she was playing a game, trying to excite Tyler's interest by seeming indifferent. Beth furrowed her brow. Erla might have gone cliff diving in Mexico, but she didn't seem the type to toy with someone's feelings like that. Gluing her gaze to Erla's face, Beth couldn't come to any other conclusion. Erla carried a torch for Menno, not Tyler.

Should she feel guilty for how happy this thought made her?

She nibbled on her bottom lip. Would Tyler's heart be broken when he found out? Even though Erla's indifference made Beth strangely giddy, she couldn't bear the thought of Tyler being hurt again. She had to tell him before he fell in love with Erla and ended up swearing off dating forever.

Maybe he wouldn't care. Truthfully, Beth would be quite relieved if Tyler hadn't been all that interested to begin with. Hadn't she been the one to push him to go out with Erla?

After they made one more pass around the

pond, Beth squeezed Tyler's hand, and he smiled at her. She tried to make her voice as low and soothing as possible. "Tyler, you wanted me to tell you what I think about Erla."

"And?"

"She's not interested."

His lips twitched as if he were holding back a smile. "She isn't?"

"No. She seems to be quite taken with Menno Petersheim."

She held her breath and studied his face carefully for any signs of disappointment. She saw something else entirely. His eyes seemed to dance as he rubbed the whiskers in his chin. "Maybe so. Menno is a nice boy."

She should have waited until they were off the ice. She wanted to look into his eyes and really see his heart, to determine if he was devastated or indifferent. "Are you . . . are you okay?"

"Are you sure? You told me I give up too easily."

"I'm sure. Look at them."

Tyler glanced at Menno and Erla. "They seem to be having a gute time together."

Beth slowed down and pulled on Tyler's arm. "Tyler, stop. Look at me." She took his face between her hands. "I never for one minute want you to be hurt. I'm sick that I matched you up with her."

He grew serious, pressed his mouth into a hard line, and stared at her lips. "I don't want to be hurt again." She hadn't perceived any movement, but they suddenly seemed to be mere inches from each other. He radiated heat like a cook stove. "I refuse to be cautious anymore. I'm not going to hold back just because there might be pain at the end of this." His eyes flashed with an emotion so deep, Beth almost cried out in sorrow. "I can deal with pain. I've done it before. Today, I'm ready to put my whole heart and soul into love."

In that breathless moment, Beth felt she might do anything to see that Tyler found all the happiness he deserved.

"Look out!"

A skinny young man with wobbly ankles and flailing limbs careened toward them. Tyler cried out, but his reaction came too late. The young man crashed into Beth and sent her sprawling onto the ice.

The young man launched into the snow at the edge of the pond for a much softer landing than Beth had on the unforgiving ice. She ended up on her backside with no hope of righting herself, much like an upside-down turtle. A ball of crumpled paper rolled from her pocket and came to rest a few feet out of reach. Even while caught up in the pain of a hard fall, Beth recognized Isaac's letter. She'd forgotten to throw it away.

Tyler knelt beside her on one knee. "Are you okay? Can you move? Where does it hurt?"

Beth managed to sit up with Tyler's help. "My pride is wounded, and I will probably have a very impressive bruise that I won't be able to show anybody."

The young man brushed the snow off his coat and bravely teetered back onto the ice. "I'm sorry," he said, holding out his hand for Beth. "I lost control."

Tyler and the young man each took one of her hands and helped her stand. "I think that's all the fun I can take for one day," she said.

Tyler knit his brows together. "Come on. Let's go by the fire." Wrapping his arm tightly around her waist, he said. "I won't let you fall again."

As he pulled her along, he nearly tripped on Isaac's balled-up letter. Her heart jumped as he bent over and retrieved it. "You must have dropped this," he said, turning it over in his hand and examining it. His frown cut deep lines into his face. "Is that . . . Beth, is that another letter from Isaac?"

She snatched it from his hand and stuffed it into her coat pocket. "It's not important."

He looked as if the world might come to an end. "Anything that upsets you is very important."

"How do you know about Isaac's letters?" And how did he know they upset her?

"He should be ashamed of himself."

"He just blows smoke. It doesn't bother me," she lied.

The muscles in Tyler's jaw tensed as he tightened his grip around her waist. "I warned him to stop. I guess I wasn't convincing enough."

Her dread grew like mold. "What do you mean?"

"He knows—*he knows*—you want him to leave you alone."

Beth halted their progress across the pond and turned to look him straight in the eye. "What do you mean you warned him to stop?"

"I wrote to him and told him to quit harassing you or I would talk to his bishop."

Beth felt like she'd crashed onto the ice for the second time. "You wrote a letter to Isaac?"

"I won't let him hurt you like that, Beth."

She couldn't breathe. Rage overwhelmed her as she pressed her palm into his chest. "No. No, Tyler. I won't allow you to think you have any right to deal with my family. *My* family. Isaac is my problem." She pushed him away from her. Dazed, he dropped his hands to his side and acted as if she'd thrown a stone at his head. "Do you understand how you've humiliated me? Isaac tells me constantly how helpless and stupid I am. Your meddling only makes things worse."

He could barely speak. "I didn't think it would—"

"You wanted to rescue me, because, like Isaac, you believe I'm helpless and stupid." It was a cruel thing to do, to compare him to Isaac, but her accusation found its target.

He stumbled backwards as if she had shoved him. "I don't think you're stupid," he stuttered.

"Leave me alone, Tyler." She turned away and haltingly made her way to the shore. He reached out a hand. She recoiled. "Don't touch me. Don't follow me, don't help me with my boots, don't even think about driving me home. I'll find my own way."

He stood frozen to the ice and watched her go.

Chapter Sixteen

She knew she'd have to arise mighty early. Tyler got up hours before the sun.

But it didn't matter. She hadn't been able to sleep anyway, so getting up at 4 AM. wasn't much of a hardship. She slipped her dress and apron and sweatpants on, kissed Toby while he slept, and tiptoed out the front door.

Her fingers already felt half-frozen as she clumsily saddled the horse. The buggy might not make it down the hill in all this snow, and she had to get to Yoders' immediately. She'd never felt such a profound sense of urgency.

The ride to Tyler's took almost half an hour. She'd covered every part of her body that might be exposed to the frosty air, except for the open folds of her scarf she left for her eyes. By the time the Yoders' two silos came into sight, she shivered with cold. A three-story white barn housed the family dairy. Two thick silos stood next to the barn, and snow-covered pastures surrounded it on three sides. The barn was built into a rise of earth that made up two walls of the first level.

Beth trudged up the incline through the snow and cracked open a door on the second floor of the barn. The loud hisses and clicks of the several milking machines attacked her ears. She slipped into the barn and closed the door behind her. It wasn't toasty—ice formed on the cement floor on the edges closest to the outside walls—but it was at least twenty degrees warmer than outside.

A dozen cows stood patiently while Tyler, his parents, and his brother tended to them in the well-coordinated effort of milking. Everyone seemed to have a job and few words were spoken, which turned out to be a good thing because the noise of the milking machines drowned out normal speech. Tyler and his brother Joe washed teats and hooked the animals up to milking machines. His mamm kept an eye on the knobs connected to the tubes and pipes running across the ceiling, while his dat sprayed the floor using a high-pressure sprayer.

Beth stepped timidly toward Tyler's mamm where she sat on her stool checking gauges. She caught sight of Beth, and a frown flitted across her face before giving way to a reserved half smile. "Nice to see you, Beth," she yelled above the din of the machines. "I hope you are feeling better today."

It was a good guess that Tyler's mamm had heard about Beth's blow-up at the pond yesterday, although his mamm most likely hadn't heard the news from Tyler. He never said anything bad about anybody, even when they deserved it. Even when they'd had no call to attack him.

By this time, Tyler's dat, Joe, and Tyler were all looking Beth's way. Joe and the bishop appeared mildly curious. Tyler acted as if he were torn between sprinting out the back door and ignoring Beth's presence altogether. His expression mirrored the one he'd worn on the first day she'd met him. Serious and contrite. Then, like yesterday, she had jumped down his throat for something he hadn't deserved.

She raised her voice. "I want to talk to Tyler, but I can wait until he's finished milking."

"That'll be near two hours," his mamm replied. "Better pull him away now."

Beth motioned for Tyler. He yelled something to Joe and handed his brother the milker he held.

As if he were going to a funeral, Tyler walked toward her with his earplugs still stuck in his ears. She kept her gaze glued to his face. He didn't seem angry.

Of course he wasn't angry with her, but he looked extremely unhappy.

He held up his arms as if to defend himself from an attack. He had to raise his voice to be heard above the noise of the machines. "I promise I only wrote one letter."

She couldn't have felt any worse if she'd been the mud on his boots. He wouldn't look her in the eye, and his face was etched with weariness. She'd hurt him badly this time. Feeling a hitch in her throat, she made a valiant effort to keep her voice steady. "No, Tyler. I didn't come here to . . ."

Furrowing his brow, he took a quick step forward and grabbed her hand. "Are you okay?"

She nodded but couldn't seem to form the words. She'd given him a good tongue-lashing, and he worried about her?

"Let's go outside," he yelled.

The other three members of the family stared unapologetically as Tyler escorted Beth out the door. They probably feared for his safety.

The door slammed behind them. Tyler blew into his hands. "Is it too cold out here for you? We could go to the house."

Shaking her head, Beth leaned against the side of the barn and slipped Tyler's plastic sunflower from beneath her coat. She handed it to him. "You can tear the petals off and throw them at me if you want."

He gave her a look of surprise; then the shadow of a grin played at his lips. "Why would I ever want to do that?"

"Because I was rude and mean, and I practically jumped down your throat and pulled your tonsils out with my bare hands."

"I'm glad you didn't really do that."

A sigh came from deep in her chest. "Yesterday, I acted horrible. Really horrible, and I'm sorry."

He lifted his brows. "You're not mad at me?"

"Of course I'm mad at you, but there is no excuse

for my behavior. I've never been so ugly before."
Why did the waterworks choose just now to turn on? Tears flowed down her cheeks, and she sniffed hard in a futile attempt to yank them back.

With the lines deepening around his mouth, he stuffed his hand into his pocket and pulled out a crisp white handkerchief.

She took it, blew her nose soundly, and mopped up her face. She tried to give it back, but he shook his head. "Consider it yours."

"I'm not usually a crier."

Tyler folded his arms. "Don't feel bad, Beth. I never should have sent that letter."

She sniffled louder. "You didn't mean any ill will by sending it. You definitely shouldn't have done it, but I didn't need to pounce on you like that." Her voice caught. "I have a very bad temper."

"It's one of my favorite things about you."

She dabbed at her nose. "Now you're just being nice."

"I'm not really all that nice."

She hiccupped weakly. "Now you're just being humble. I wouldn't blame you one little bit if you steered clear of me permanently. I've given you nothing but trouble."

He placed his hand on the wall of the barn a few inches above her head and leaned closer. "Can I come over tonight after milking?"

"What for?"

"Because if you think I'm going to steer clear of you, you're crazy."

A pleasant warmth tingled up her spine. "Well, yesterday, a lot of people probably thought I was crazy."

"Can I come over?"

It was the least she could do after the way she'd treated him. "Okay."

"Okay?"

"Jah, come over. Toby needs someone to play catch with him."

Tyler bloomed into a full-blown, this-is-the-best-day-of-my-life smile. "Okay."

She loved seeing him so happy, and Tyler, it seemed, couldn't be truly happy unless he helped someone. "But don't ever write to Isaac again."

"Never, ever again in a million years unless I want you to rip my tonsils out."

"Just so we understand one another."

"I'm really sorry I wrote that letter."

She tapped the sunflower against his chest. "Stop it right now, Tyler. Just stop."

He shook his head in resignation and chuckled.

A movement behind Tyler caught her eye. Erla Glick and Menno Petersheim tromped through the snow toward the barn. Erla waved enthusiastically. "Yoohoo."

Didn't Erla know that Tyler needed to do the milking? He didn't have time for a social call.

Tyler cleared his throat and stepped away from Beth. His eyes darted from Erla to Beth, and he fingered the buttons of his coat as if this meeting were the most awkward moment of his life.

"Hi, Beth," Erla said, her voice laced with high-fructose corn syrup. "I hope everything is okay after yesterday."

Beth wanted to growl. One very public display of her atrocious temper, and everybody suddenly worried about her sanity. Well, she was just fine, thank you very much. "Everything is gute."

Erla smiled as if she were thinking about a funny joke. "Look what we brought." From the grocery sack in Menno's hand, she produced a clear plastic bag full of a white powder. "It's starter culture. We're going to try cheddar cheese next."

"I've got to finish with the milking first."

Gute boy, Tyler. Send pretty Erla and her cheese ambitions away. You've got more important things to do.

"We know," Erla said. "Menno and I wanted to drop it off. He's on his way to work, and I'm riding with him into town. We hired a driver and everything. But we maybe wanted to take a look at that cheese we made last week. Do you have time to show us?"

"Oh, jah. It's in our cellar. I made a cave for it," Tyler said, motioning toward the house. "*Cum.* We can turn it."

Beth felt as if she were attending the meeting for a club that she didn't belong to. Cheese-making was something Tyler and Erla shared, and she had no part in it. Her heart sank as she eyed Tyler and then Erla. Maybe she had been wrong. Maybe Erla was interested in Tyler.

She folded her arms as she began to feel extraordinarily dull. She'd gotten up too early. The lack of sleep had caught up to her.

"Come on, Beth," Tyler said. "You can see what we've been up to."

"No," she said, more abruptly than she intended. She couldn't stomach the idea of sitting silently in the corner with Menno while Erla and Tyler laughed about their adventures with cheese curd. "I must get home to Toby."

Tyler gazed at her doubtfully. "Are you sure? It will be fun."

"I'm sure." Beth practically swaddled her face in her scarf before she marched down the little hill as fast as she could go.

"Beth," Tyler called, but she ignored him and made a beeline for her horse. She'd done what she had come here to do. No need to linger.

She didn't care for cheese all that much.

Chapter Seventeen

"Get out of my kitchen," Mamm said. "You're fidgeting."

Tyler quit pacing and folded his arms across his chest. "Am I? Sorry."

"Tell me again why you like this girl."

Tyler grinned. He felt alive with electric energy just thinking about Beth. "There are too many reasons to count."

"Lydia says she yelled at you something wonderful."

"She's feisty, Mamm. I did something I shouldn't have, and she took me to task for it."

"If she wants to win your love, she shouldn't yell at you."

He sank to a chair at the table as all his enthusiasm seemed to drain away. "She doesn't."

"Doesn't yell at you?"

"Doesn't want my love." He felt rotten saying it. Was he hitting his head against the wall?

Mamm narrowed her eyes and propped her

hands on her hips. "So, you're chasing a girl who doesn't want to be caught?"

"I don't know."

She sat next to him and placed her hand over his arm. "I refuse to watch you get hurt like last time."

"It was never right between me and Lily."

"This isn't Lily," Mamm said. "You're crazy about this one."

"You don't think I was crazy about Lily?"

"You liked her. She would have made a gute wife." Mamm waggled her finger at him. "But this one? This one makes my boy, who only smiles on special occasions, smile for no reason at all. This one's got you staring off into space when you should be paying attention to what your mamm tells you."

"It's almost impossible to think about anything else."

"So what's wrong with her?"

"Nothing."

"Any girl would have to be blind or out of her mind not to fall head over heels for you, Tyler Yoder."

"You're my mother. Of course you believe that."

"I have eyes, don't I? I swear a dozen girls breathed a sigh of relief when Lily married Aden instead of you."

Tyler traced his finger along a wavy crack in the table. "She's afraid."

"Of you?"

"Of getting married," Tyler said. Saying it out loud made that particular obstacle seem even bigger.

Mamm frowned. "I've heard the rumors. At the wedding, Amos Hostetler acted a little too cock-sure, if you ask me."

"He wasn't kind to Beth, that's for certain. And since we don't allow divorce, she was stuck with him for life. How can she trust anyone after something like that?"

"She must trust in God, without regard to you or anybody else. People will let you down. Only God's love is certain."

Tyler shifted in his chair. "My love is certain."

Mamm placed her hand on his cheek. "If she rejects you, I don't think I'll ever be able to smile again. I can't stand to see my children get hurt."

Tyler took her hand from his face and squeezed it. "I'm not giving up on Beth, even if it hurts worse than anything."

Mamm thought about that for a minute. "Then I'm going to have to see what I can do to make sure Beth falls in love with you, because my boy is not getting hurt."

"What are you going to do?"

"Oh, I know how to meddle in other people's lives."

Tyler groaned. "Promise me you won't do anything embarrassing."

Mamm's eyes twinkled mischievously. "What do you consider embarrassing?"

"Lawayne Burkholder's mamm went to gatherings and asked girls to ride home with him."

Mamm huffed derisively and pushed that suggestion away. "Too obvious."

"She wrote out questions for Lawayne so he would have something to talk about with the girl he took home."

"If you can't talk to a girl by now, then I'm a failure as a mother." She propped her elbows on the table. "Maybe I should sit by Beth at gmay. I could write your name on the back of her hand, like we used to do in primary school. I could make sugar cookies in the shape of your name and leave them on her front porch or sneak into her house at night and whisper nice things about you in her ear."

"Oh, jah. That wouldn't be embarrassing."

They both stood when they heard the knock at the door. "She's here," Mamm said. "Time to put my plan into action."

"Don't even think about it, Mamm."

She pulled a pen from the drawer. "Don't worry. Beth won't suspect a thing." She scribbled on her palm. "Will she think I'm odd if I want to shake hands?" She opened her hand.

Tyler is a good catch, she had written.

Tyler chuckled. "You are odd, Mamm. No escaping that."

Tyler's house was a split level, with the living room and kitchen upstairs and the bedrooms downstairs. He bounded down the steps, so happy to be seeing Beth he thought he might burst. The fact that he'd seen her every day this week did nothing to damper his excitement. If he could take Beth in with every breath, he would.

She carried a large canvas bag in one arm and Toby in the other. "Merry Christmas!" she said, beaming with enthusiasm. She had nice teeth. Tyler would have to put that on his very long list of things he liked about her.

He saw a little bit of Beth in Toby when the toddler smiled at him. "Mommy!" Toby squealed. With a grunt, he reached his mitten-covered hands out to Tyler.

Tyler took Toby and the bag from Beth. "Cum reu. It can't be more than twenty degrees out there."

She grinned. "Eighteen. I checked Dawdi's thermometer before I left."

After depositing Beth's bag on the step, Tyler gave Toby a big smack on the cheek and pulled the beanie off his head. His curly hair stood on end, and his cheeks glowed like bright red Christmas ornaments.

"Hat," Toby exclaimed.

Tyler smoothed Toby's hair. "Hat. A new word."

Beth shrugged off her coat. "He adds three or four every day. Although, he also calls Dawdi *hat* so I can't be altogether sure he knows what it means."

Beth helped Tyler with Toby's coat and mittens, which she hung on the hook by the door. "Denki for letting me come. I want the cake to be a surprise, and I couldn't go to my mamm's house. She's busy baking for the school program on Friday."

"I'm glad you came, although I feel bad I'm not going to be any help. I don't know how to boil water."

She raised an eyebrow. "Well, if you remember, I'm not so good at taking what help is offered, so it's probably just as well."

Tyler headed up the stairs. "And yet I keep trying."

Smiling, Beth picked up her bag and followed him. "You're so annoyingly persistent that way."

"I lie awake at night trying to come up with new ways to annoy you."

Her eyes twinkled with amusement. "That is quite obvious."

Grinning, Mamm stood in the kitchen with her fingers laced together in front of her, probably so the writing on her hand wouldn't show. "Beth Hostetler. It's so good to see you," she gushed. "And I can't believe how big Toby is getting." Tyler decided not to point out that Mamm had seen Toby three days ago at gmay.

She took Toby from Tyler's arms, and he settled into her embrace as if he recognized a seasoned mother when he saw one. "You are the cutest little guy," she said, bouncing Toby on her hip. "Can he have a cookie?"

Beth nodded.

Mamm retrieved a cookie from the cookie jar and handed it to Toby, who stuffed half of it into his little mouth.

Tyler smiled to himself. Mamm was trying too hard, but her effort wasn't overblown, so Beth probably didn't even notice. Of course, she didn't have to pretend with Toby. Mamm loved babies more than anything else in the world.

"Tyler tells me you're making a cake for your mammi."

"Jah, she turns eighty-three tomorrow. We're having a party for her and Toby at the same time. Their birthdays are a day apart."

"Toby is two yet?"

"Jah. It seems like he was born just yesterday."

Mamm gestured in the direction of the cupboards, being careful to keep her palm safely from Beth's view. Tyler had to bite his tongue to keep from laughing. "Feel free to use anything in our kitchen. Tyler can show you where everything is."

Beth lifted her bag. "I brought all my own ingredients so I wouldn't impose."

"You're not imposing at all. It's our pleasure. We'd love to see more of you around here."

"Denki."

"Tyler and his dat built this table for me, and you should see the bureau in my bedroom. Tyler built that himself. He's such a gute boy, everything a mother could ask for in a son. He'll make a fine husband someday."

Tyler felt the need to intervene. Mamm was getting too close to proposing to Beth on his behalf. "Okay, thanks, Mamm. Beth better get started."

Mamm tickled Toby's chin. "Is he hungry?"

"No, he just ate breakfast."

She put Toby down and took his hand. "Can I take him downstairs with me? It will be easier for the two of you if I keep him entertained while I make beds and start the laundry."

"Okay," said Beth. "That would be very nice. Oh, I almost forgot." She pulled two multicolored potholders from her bag. "Mammi told me to be sure to give these to you."

Mamm took them and set them on the counter. "How wonderful. Anna's potholders are famous."

Mamm and Toby walked out of the kitchen, with

Toby's hand securely in Mamm's. Acting as if he were going on a great adventure, Toby waved to Tyler and his mamm. "Bye, bye."

"Bye, bye, Toby." Tyler sat at one of the stools at the counter. "What kind of cake are you making?"

"Pineapple upside-down cake. It's Mammi's favorite, but it's kind of tricky. If you're not careful, the whole thing can fall apart when you turn it upside-down. But a lot of sins can be covered by a mountain of whipped cream. Amos didn't notice anything amiss if I buried my mistakes in whipped cream."

Tyler attempted a carefree laugh. He didn't want her to suspect that talk of Amos always made him angry enough to spit. She didn't say much about Amos in their normal conversation so it was a good sign that she felt comfortable at least mentioning her late husband in Tyler's presence.

"I would have preheated the oven, but Mamm suggested I wait so you could tell me the temperature you want," he said.

"Let's do about three hundred and fifty degrees. That should be perfect."

"That's one thing that always amazes me, how a gute cook can tell how hot she wants the oven just by guessing."

"Guessing is not the sign of a gute cook. It's the sign of a cook who doesn't know what she's doing."

Chuckling, Tyler turned the dial on the LP gas oven. "I don't even know how many degrees you need to bake a cake, so you're still more skilled than I am."

"Don't make that conclusion until you see how the cake turns out."

Tyler washed his hands. "While the oven heats up, do you want to take a look at the cheese I made yesterday?"

Beth's face fell, and Tyler felt that pang of guilt he always experienced when he thought about Erla Glick and her schemes with Beth. In giving Beth the impression that there was more between him and Erla than there was, he felt he deceived her.

The mere mention of Erla seemed to put Beth in a sour mood. Was she jealous? He didn't feel quite right toying with her feelings like that. If something he did upset Beth, he should quit, no matter how good of a plan Erla Glick thought it might be. Even if Tyler ended up finding the back door to Beth's heart.

When Beth hesitated, Tyler said, "I made it all by myself." He reached into a cupboard above the sink and pulled out four covered plastic containers. "These work pretty good as cheese caves," he said.

He opened the first container and gasped.

Beth peeked into the bowl. "I don't think it's supposed to look like that."

Tyler opened the other three containers. The mess inside each looked the same as the first. "It looks like an explosion of curds and whey," he said, almost laughing at the disastrous result.

The corner of Beth's mouth twitched. "Maybe it's not so bad. You should taste it."

"You taste it."

She giggled. "I'm not touching it. I'd rather not be in the hospital for Christmas."

"I was so proud of it." Tyler stuck his finger into one of the containers and pushed the white chunks around. "I never should have tried cooking anything without close supervision."

"I'm afraid even the hogs might not eat that. You probably cooked it too long, or it got too hot before you stirred it."

He regarded Beth curiously. "You know how to make cheese?"

"It's one thing I know how to make well. Treva refused to eat any cheese but mine."

He slapped his forehead with his palm. "I've been wasting all this time with Erla when you could have been teaching me?"

She lowered her eyes. "I wouldn't say you've wasted all that time."

"I would." He might as well be honest about it. "I'd rather spend my days with you and Toby than do anything else."

An attractive blush tinted her cheeks even as the corners of her mouth drooped. He'd been too honest. She wasn't ready for his confession of undying love.

"Erla is putting together goodie baskets to hand out when we go caroling to the shut-ins on Friday. I was in charge of the cheese. The baskets will be a failure."

"I wouldn't say failure. They'll just be without cheese."

A wonderful idea jumped into his head. He

couldn't have asked for a better opportunity if he had ruined the cheese on purpose. "Will you help me make more?"

She raised an eyebrow.

"Please. I really need your help."

"This is a switch, you needing my help for a change."

Tyler had the sudden, overwhelming urge to wrap her in his arms and tell her he desperately needed her help every day. He needed her help just to feel whole. He needed her to bring complete happiness into his life. Instead, he opted for an earnest gaze and a nod. "I'll help you make the cake—"

"I don't think so."

"And then you can help me make cheese while the cake bakes."

She nibbled on her bottom lip. "Erla is the one who helps you with cheese."

"She knows less about making cheese than I do. Besides, she and Menno are in Shawano today. I don't need Erla's help. I need you."

Looking pleased with herself, Beth backed away from him and pulled a green apron from her bag. "Of course I'll help. The shut-ins deserve a lovely goodie basket."

He couldn't contain a wide smile. "I'm so glad I ruined that batch."

Her blush deepened. "I can see right through your flattery, Tyler Yoder. It will not work on me. There's nothing stopping you from going to the market and buying four perfectly good blocks of cheese."

Tyler sat at the counter, and Beth told him funny stories while she stirred the cake batter. Her hands fascinated him; the way she moved them so gracefully made him think of a bird in flight. Who knew anyone could make stirring eggs and flour so enchanting? And he couldn't get enough of her mouth. Surely her lips were as soft as rose petals.

A powerful yearning clamped around his throat until he felt he couldn't breathe. He averted his eyes and studied his hands. His patience was slipping, along with his control. How much longer could he bear to go without her as his wife?

Unaware of the storm raging inside him, Beth meticulously arranged pineapple slices in the bottom of her pan and allowed Tyler to place a cherry in the center of each one. He'd never been so careful about anything in his life because he refused to be responsible for ruining Beth's pineapple upside-down cake.

When all was ready, he opened the door, and she held her breath as she slid the pan into the oven.

"It's going to be delicious," Tyler assured her. He could see how anxious she felt about it.

"There'll be plenty of whipped cream on hand, in any case." She set the timer and dusted off her hands. "Now, should we get started on the cheese?"

"I didn't even ask if you have time today. Cheese takes a few hours."

"Would your mamm mind if Toby took a nap here?"

"Have you got to get back to your sewing?"

She shrugged and smiled warmly. "I have four dresses to cut out tonight. It won't take long. I have a fancy new rotary cutter that makes cutting a breeze."

The roundabout expression of gratitude didn't escape Tyler's notice. His heart swelled as big as the sky. "A professional needs the right tools."

The glow in her face was unmistakable. He wanted to see that look every day of his life.

"I assume you have milk."

"Two gallons raw and unpasteurized ready in the mudroom."

He fetched the milk and the pot he'd bought especially for making cheese. Erla's plan for ensnaring both Menno and Beth had been expensive.

Beth set the cheese pot to boil on the stove. Tyler showed her where all the utensils were, and Beth placed them in the boiling water to sterilize.

"I never boiled anything before when I made cheese," Tyler said. "Is that what I did wrong?"

"There are really so many things you could have done wrong," Beth teased, "that it will make your brain hurt thinking about them."

"My brain already hurts."

"Do you have a thermometer?"

He pulled the cooking thermometer out of the drawer. "Of course. Erla and Menno made sure we had all the right equipment."

Once the utensils were sterilized, Beth poured the hot water into a larger pot and nested the cheese pot inside it. She grinned at Tyler as she measured out the right amount of milk and poured it into the pot. "It's very convenient to have your own dairy when you want to make cheese."

Tyler wiped some drops of milk from the counter and tried to be casual about his next question. "You say you used to make cheese for your mother-in-law?"

"Almost every week when she went through chemotherapy. The cheese had to be cheddar, made by me. And certainly not from the store."

"She sounds demanding."

Beth pressed her lips together and hooked the thermometer over the lip of the pan. "Sick people can be that way. Treva was terrified, and she took her fear out on the people around her." She busied herself stirring the milk that didn't need to be stirred. "I got another letter from Isaac," she added softly.

Tyler clenched his teeth and balled his hands into fists but quickly shoved them in his pockets. Beth mustn't see his anger. "How is he?"

"He says Treva is feeling poorly again, and she wants me to come back."

Tyler didn't miss the fear that traveled across her face.

Studying his expression, she leaned against the counter and folded her arms. "Would you still be my friend if I told you I don't want to go back, even if Treva is dying?"

His heart beat against his chest in indignation. "Why would you go back? They treated you like dirt. You don't have to justify yourself to anyone, Beth, least of all me. It would be terrible if you threw yourself back into that abuse. Terrible for you and bad for Toby."

"Treva says I'm selfish."

"She wants to make you feel guilty when you've done nothing wrong."

Her eyes filled with doubt. "Can you be certain I've done nothing wrong? Ruth refused to leave Naomi, and she's got her own book in the Bible."

"I imagine Naomi was a nice mother who never demanded cheddar cheese from her daughter-in-law."

Beth cracked a smile. "She seems that way." She checked the thermometer, then sprinkled the culture into the warm milk and put the lid on the pot. "It needs to ripen for half an hour." She wiped her hands down her apron. "I haven't told anyone else about the letters."

"I'm glad you trust me enough to share it."

"Isaac thinks I'm weak. I never put up a fight with Amos. It would have been wrong for me to go against my husband."

"I disagree."

"But it's why your letter upset me. To Isaac, it was more proof that I can't watch out for myself, that I need an abusive, controlling man to take care of me."

"I'm sorry."

She shook her head. "It doesn't matter. Nothing anyone can do or say will make Isaac think better of me. Even if I sold a million dresses and became president of my own factory, he'd still see me as a child who needs correction."

"I think he's despicable."

The ghost of a smile played at her mouth before she turned her face away. "He thinks he loves me because I'd be a manageable wife. But he doesn't realize how I've changed. I'm not so meek anymore. If I were his wife, I'd only frustrate and anger him. He doesn't realize I'm doing him a favor by refusing his proposal."

"I hate to think how bad it was for you there."

"At least Treva needed me. Nobody needs me in Bonduel. I'm more of a burden than anything else."

Tyler tried not to sound cross. "That's absurd, Beth. Anna and Felty need you. Toby couldn't live without you. Your family needs you." Dare he say it and risk scaring her away? "I need you."

Beth fell silent and made a show of measuring the salt for the third time. She looked at him and smiled playfully. "Jah, you need me all right. I am the only person who can save your gift baskets." She had decided to make light of it. He supposed it was better than getting mad and storming out of his house.

"I am grateful."

She swiped some crumbs off the counter. "I sound so whiny."

"Not at all."

"I shouldn't complain about my in-laws. What's in the past is better left in the past."

"What happened hurt you very deeply. Thank you for trusting me enough to talk about it."

They both jumped when the timer clanged like a fire engine. Beth opened the oven door and stuck a toothpick into the center of the cake. "It's done," she said, dread mixing with anticipation in her voice. She donned two heavy oven mitts and pulled her cake from the oven.

Tyler shut the door for her as she placed the cake on a trivet on the counter. "It smells delicious."

"It does, doesn't it?"

She hurried to her bag and pulled a rectangular dish from the bottom. "This is the most important part. We've got to turn the cake upside-down onto this plate. Everything depends on it."

"What can I do?"

She shaped her mouth into a teasing grin. "Maybe you should stand back."

He pressed his back against the wall.

With her mitts on, she laid the plate over the top of the cake. Keeping her thumbs against the bottom of the plate, she pressed the bottom of the cake pan with her outstretched fingers, lifted the cake, and turned the whole thing over in one fluid motion.

They both held their breath as she gave the pan a little tap and slowly lifted it away from the plate.

"Oh my," Beth said.

Breathing in the aroma rising from the steaming hot cake, Tyler marveled at the stunning pattern of pineapple circles and cherries. "It worked."

"No sunken middles or crumbly corners." Showing her irresistible dimple, Beth did a little hop and clapped her hands. "It looks like a picture from a recipe book."

"And I think the cherries look especially tasty."

"I had my doubts, but I decided to take a risk on you. I'm glad I did."

She was joking with him, of course, but Tyler's heart skipped a beat.

I decided to take a risk on you.

If only she would. He would make her the happiest woman alive. A smudge of flour dusted her cheek, and he had to clamp his arms around his waist to keep from brushing the white powder off that silky skin. His gut clenched. She hadn't given him any encouragement, and if he acted rashly, he'd scare her away. He wanted to marry Beth so badly, he could already taste the bitterness of rejection in his mouth.

He swallowed hard. "What now?"

"Now we let the cake cool while we finish the cheese. Rennet is next."

Tyler picked up the small bottle of liquid rennet and handed it to her. He should stick with the plan. Erla had a gute plan. "Will you come caroling with us Friday night?"

"Caroling is for the young people."

"I'm the same age as you, and I'm going."

"I feel years older," Beth said.

"Well, you're not. I really want you to come."

She raised an eyebrow. "Why?"

"It's a huge caroling party. Probably thirty of us are going. There'll be hot chocolate and cider and donuts."

"Why do you want me to come? Erla will be there."

"And Menno."

She furrowed her brow.

Tyler placed a hand on the counter and leaned toward her. Better to smell her enticing scent that way. "It won't be fun without you." As he stared at her mouth, the longing attacked him with renewed force. "And you're making the cheese. You should at least be there to help us give it away."

Her breathing became shallow as her gaze wandered to his mouth. That slight movement of her eyes sent the blood racing through his veins. "I see," she mumbled.

They stood like that for mere moments, but Tyler felt the yearning of a whole lifetime in her face.

She scooted away from him around the edge of the counter as if she needed to hold onto it to keep herself from falling. "It's time. . . . We're ready for the rennet."

Remembering to breathe, Tyler took a step back and handed her the bottle. "Is that a yes to the caroling?"

She seemed to regain her composure as she mixed a spoonful of rennet with some water. "Jah, I will come. Since I am a widow, I can act as a chaperone to any of die youngie bent on mischief."

"What if I'm bent on mischief?"

"Then you will get a scolding."

He smiled. "I've had a few of those."

She smiled back. "You've deserved every one. Here, take the lid off for me."

Tyler lifted the lid as she poured the rennet-water mixture into the milk. "I would be lost without you, Beth."

Her eyes twinkled merrily. "Not really. You can buy cheese at the store. But I'm glad I could help."

He lost his head and took her hand. "Nae. I mean it. I would be lost without you."

She looked into his eyes and quickly pulled her hand away. Clearing her throat, she said, "Don't thank me yet. We don't know how it's going to turn out."

No. He didn't know how things would turn out. He watched as Beth stirred the milk. He wanted her for his wife more than the desert wanted moisture. He would keep hoping and praying. Surely Heaven and Erla Glick would help him out.

Chapter Eighteen

Beth felt as old as a schoolmarm. Davy Miller, who had just turned sixteen, and his friend Junior had been kind enough to pick Beth up and drive her to the gathering. Davy possessed a baby face pocked with acne, and he had the habit of making moony eyes and laughing nervously when he spoke to her. Junior said hardly anything. As soon as Beth had climbed into the front seat of Davy's buggy, Junior, who was squished between them, had turned bright red, pulled out a fancy cell phone, and started playing games.

If the rest of the evening was as uncomfortable and awkward as her buggy ride, she might have to leave extremely early.

But still, she felt grateful for the lift. Tyler had offered to pick her up, but she couldn't rely on his kindness all the time. She must learn to take care of herself.

She caught her breath when she saw Tyler. He stood on his porch obviously waiting for something.

She loved how the fading light of dusk sharpened his solemn features, making his face seem as if it were carved in stone, like an ancient statue of a noble hero.

Davy maneuvered his buggy alongside the row of other buggies and sleighs in front of Tyler's house. "Denki for the ride," Beth said, leaping from the buggy as soon as it slowed enough for her to land safely on the ground without breaking an ankle. Lord willing, she could find another way home. She stumbled and regained her balance before anyone saw her; then she groaned. She'd left the blankets.

Tyler jogged to her. "Did they push you out?"

Beth grinned. "Nae. I escaped."

"Who brought you?"

"Davy Miller and Junior. I thought it would be convenient since the Millers are Mammi's closest neighbors. But I think Davy is scared of me, and Junior is fond of his Angry Birds."

"Davy's not scared of you," Tyler said. "I've seen him at gmay. He stares at you as if you were a warm brownie with double fudge sauce."

"He does not."

"I promise he does."

She huffed at such a ridiculous thought. "I'm seven years older than he is."

Tyler's eyes danced. "A fellow can dream, can't he?" He took her elbow and nudged her toward the house. "That's why you should have let me pick you up. I may stare at you like you're a thick slab of cherry pie, but at least I'm past the pimple stage."

A giggle tripped from her lips. "Could I be a huckleberry pie? And maybe not so thick?"

She finally made him smile. "Did you bring blankets? I've got extra if you need."

"Unfortunately, they are in Davy's buggy with my bag."

"I'll get them," he said, bolting from her before she had a chance to stop him. He soon returned with three thick quilts and her bag. "What's in here?"

"Mammi made potholders for the carolers. She's been knitting like crazy. And I almost forgot." She reached into the bag and pulled out a purple scarf. "This is for you," she said, standing on her tiptoes and wrapping it around his neck. The movement got her close enough to catch a whiff of his scent. Tonight he smelled of hickory smoke and pine needles. He'd been helping his mamm with the fire.

He stood like stone as she brushed her fingers against his neck and looped the scarf over itself in front.

"How did the cheese turn out?"

"We cut each block in half so Erla could stretch it to four baskets. I evened out one of the blocks with my knife and ate the scraps. It tasted delicious, thanks to you. Erla was thrilled."

Beth determined that, tonight, the mention of Erla's name would not sting like a hornet.

They stomped the snow off their shoes and went into Tyler's house. Beth must have been the last to arrive. The sound of loud and merry voices proved deafening as they walked up the stairs to the kitchen.

Probably two-dozen young people milled around Yoders' upstairs, drinking cocoa and visiting.

Tyler's mamm acted as if the three wise men had walked through her door. She gave Beth a hardy embrace and handed her a mug of hot cocoa with chunky marshmallows.

Erla, with Menno in tow, marched up to Beth and smothered her with an enthusiastic hug. "Denki for helping Tyler with the cheese."

"She didn't help me," Tyler insisted. "She did it all herself. I handed her utensils and tried to stay out of the way."

Erla gave Beth an extra squeeze before she let go. "Our plan is working so well." She looked from Beth to Tyler. "With the baskets. Our plan with the baskets. And Menno is going to show me how to make Swiss next week. Aren't you, Menno? He's so gute with cheese," she gushed.

The bishop, Tyler's dat, got everyone's attention by standing on a chair and whistling through his teeth. "We are going to four houses tonight. Don't jump off the wagon while it's moving. You'll get run over. That would ruin your Christmas."

Everyone laughed with all the anticipation of a wonderful-gute evening.

"Did everybody bring a blanket? It's going to be mighty cold. Okay, let's pray and load up."

They walked outside to where Freeman Zook waited with his four-horse team and wagon loaded with haystacks. Tyler jumped onto the wagon, reached out his hand, and pulled Beth up. "Let's sit toward the back," he said. "That way if you fall off, you won't get run over by the tires."

Beth smiled to herself. Tyler thought of things that didn't even cross her mind. "Do you really think I'm going to fall off?"

"You can never be too careful."

They found an empty hay bale, and Tyler wouldn't let her sit until he had spread a blanket over it. Bales were relatively comfortable seating, but a bit prickly on the backside. Tyler sat next to her, keeping a proper distance, and Beth unfolded one of her blankets over them. She couldn't figure out why Tyler wouldn't try to sit next to Erla, unless he could see that she was a lost cause. It was plain as day that she and Menno wanted to stick together. That was fine with Beth. Tyler was the best friend she had in Bonduel, and she had a feeling her evening would be much better if she spent it with him.

"Tyler, have you got an extra blanket?" someone behind them asked. "It's a lot colder in the open air than I thought."

Tyler jumped from the wagon. "I'll fetch one. Does anyone else want another blanket?"

Three or four people chimed in that they might need another blanket, and Tyler jogged to the house for more. He always seemed so happy to put others' needs before his own. And Beth had the good fortune of spending the entire evening with him.

It was never a gute thing to count her chickens before they hatched.

Vernon Schmucker, the one who had been so

eager to meet her at the bonfire several weeks ago, grunted forcefully as he heaved himself into the wagon and tromped over several bales to reach Beth. He eyed the space next to her, which unfortunately looked roomy enough for Vernon's wide girth. His face widened into a toothy smile, and he plopped himself next to her. "This is a gute night for cuddling," he said, pumping his brows up and down. He seemed to do that with some regularity.

"Oh, Vernon, I'm sorry. Tyler is sitting here. He went in to get some extra blankets."

Vernon had the nerve to help himself to the other half of Beth's blanket. "He'd better hurry if he doesn't want to be left behind."

"What I mean is, that is Tyler's spot. You'll have to find somewhere else to sit."

Vernon chuckled, or rather guffawed, as if she'd said something hilariously funny. "The way I see it, the early bird gets the worm, if you know what I mean."

"No, I don't know what you mean. Really, you'll have to move."

Vernon settled into the crunchy hay bale and folded his arms. "I love to go caroling. Everyone appreciates my bass voice. I can sing so low, I make windows rattle like a tornado was coming. It makes 'Joy to the World' extra nice for the old folks."

Beth huffed impatiently. How insistent would she need to be? She might have to resort to downright rudeness. "Vernon, go find another seat. Tyler is sitting here."

"He'll find somewhere else. There's plenty of room."

Tyler came bounding out of the house with an armload of blankets. He slowed considerably as he caught sight of Vernon making himself cozy under Beth's blanket. A deep line appeared between his brows, but other than that, his expression didn't alter from the serious one he always wore. He hopped onto the wagon and distributed the blankets while Beth followed his every move with her eager gaze. He seemed intent on keeping his eyes averted as he handed out blankets and asked several of the girls if they were warm enough.

Vernon made no sign of budging. She could wait to see where Tyler sat and go sit next him, but that would seem quite forward, wouldn't it? And what if Tyler ended up sitting next to Erla or some other young lady he had his eye on?

She could demand Vernon go elsewhere, but could she be forceful enough to convince him to move? Her heart stuck in her throat. It felt as if she were back in Nappanee, giving in to Amos's wishes because she was too timid to fight for herself. But what would she be fighting for? Tyler might not really care if he sat by her or not. She shouldn't make a big scene for nothing.

Once everyone got comfortable, Tyler glanced her way and then walked to the front of the wagon, sat on the bale used as the driver's seat, and started making stiff conversation with the driver, Freeman. Freeman snapped the reins, and the four-horse team seemed to come alive. The wagon lurched forward slowly. The start always proved most difficult for the horses.

Tyler remained on the front hay bale as if he were the navigator for the hayride. She longed to sit by him. She knew she could make that serious expression disappear from his face in an instant. Instead, she was stuck sharing a blanket with Vernon Schmucker, who carried the faint smell of sour milk.

"Do you know how to make *yummasetti*?" Vernon said. "I love yummasetti. I could come visiting Sunday if you want to make a special meal."

"I know how to make it, but my late husband told me my recipe tasted like dog food. You best not trust my cooking."

"Better yet, I could bring you a trout. You just cut up some onions and peppers and stuff them in the fish, then wrap it real tight in foil and set it in a pan of boiling water. Makes it nice and moist."

"I don't like fish."

"Everybody likes fish. I go two or three times a week in the summer and go ice fishing in the winter. Fly-fishing is my favorite. Last time, my waders sprung a leak, and I ain't been back since. I'll take you sometime. It's hard to get the knack of it, but a gute teacher stands right behind you and holds your hands tight in his. You can get real close while fly-fishing." Up and down went his eyebrows. Beth didn't know whether to laugh out loud or gag in disgust. She opted to ignore him.

Soon the wagonload of carolers broke into a

chorus of "O Come All Ye Faithful," and Beth was saved from more of Vernon's fish stories because they needed his low bass voice for the singing.

Beth didn't have the heart to sing as her eyes strayed to where Tyler sat, back ramrod straight, staring at the road ahead like a sentry watching for danger. He could have been carved out of ice.

A profound feeling of loneliness spread to her bones like fog rising from the forest floor. She was honest enough to admit that she didn't simply feel lonely. She was lonely for Tyler Yoder. She pushed the feeling away. She couldn't let herself be over-whelmed with loneliness. She had years to live on her own, years to raise her son and run her own life. Feelings of loneliness only led to a longing for something she didn't really want.

The wagon stopped at the first house, and Beth jumped off the hay bale as if it were on fire. Running from annoying men was becoming an unfor-tunate habit.

The young people walked en masse to the front door, with Erla and Menno and their basket of cheese and goodies leading the way. Beth hung back until she saw that Vernon dogged her every move. She deftly pushed her way to the front of the carolers and stood next to Erla and Menno. Tyler appeared at her side and gifted her with a smile like the sun. She couldn't help grinning stupidly back at him.

"Did you have a nice ride?" he whispered.

She groaned. "I tried to make him move, but he's quite persistent."

He winked at her and sent that familiar thrill skipping up her spine. "You looked like you were having a wonderful-gute time."

She breathed a sigh of relief that he wasn't mad at her for letting Vernon take his bale of hay. Why had she worried? Had she forgotten that Tyler didn't have an angry bone in his body? "I thought of shoving him off your spot, but I didn't think I'd be strong enough to manage it," she said.

"I would have come to help you. Vernon listens to men where he won't pay any heed to what women say. But you've given me strict instructions not to rescue you. I knew you could manage him without me."

"I did a horrible job of it."

"Don't be offended, but I'm not leaving your side for the rest of the night."

Although she knew she should have resisted everything about Tyler Yoder, she couldn't have been happier at that news. "That's quite a risk. You know how easily offended I am."

He put his lips close to her ear. "I wouldn't want you any other way."

It took her a few seconds before she could breathe again. Still, she sounded as if she'd run a race when she spoke. "It will be awfully hard to court Erla with another girl hanging on you like a burr all night."

"Do you still in your wildest imagination believe that I want to court Erla?" His whispering made her giddy.

"Maybe not," she stammered.

Menno knocked on the door, and the carolers burst into a rousing rendition of "Jingle Bells." Vernon pulled two sets of jingle bells from his pocket and shook them wildly. All heads turned to look at him, and everyone laughed in surprise. Instruments of any kind didn't usually make their way into an Amish gathering, but Vernon didn't seem to be one to go along with convention all that often.

Elderly Edna Mast answered the door, accepted her basket of goodies, and handed out candy canes. They wished her a merry Christmas and went back to the wagon.

True to his word, Tyler stuck to Beth like glue. Just in case Vernon decided that one particular bale was his territory, they retrieved Beth's blankets and sat on the other side of the wagon but still behind the tires, at Tyler's insistence.

Unfortunately, Vernon found them. He climbed onto the wagon and stared at Beth and Tyler as if trying to reason out a difficult arithmetic problem, probably involving fractions. Without a word, he stepped over Tyler's feet and plunked next to Beth on the four inches of hay to her right. Surprised amusement popped onto Tyler's face.

Beth slid closer to Tyler to give Vernon more room and bit her lip to keep from laughing. She was squished between Vernon's ample frame and Tyler's lean one.

Vernon balanced precariously on one side of his hinnerdale while propping his foot on the hay bale next to them to keep from falling over. "Tyler," he said. "Do you like to fish? Beth and I are going fly-fishing as soon as the weather warms up."

Tyler wrapped his arm around Beth and gently pushed her to stand. She stood, and he scooted along the hay bale behind her while nudging her to his right, effectively trading places with her. He squeezed himself as close to Vernon as he could, took Beth's arm, and directed her to sit. Grateful beyond words, all she could do was smile at him with her whole heart.

He winked at her as the wagon lurched forward and the carolers began to sing. Had he any idea of the butterflies he unleashed in her stomach when he behaved like that?

"What flies do you like to use?" Tyler asked, as if he hadn't just scrambled Vernon's plans like eggs.

"If it's late summer, I always fish with a Joe's Hopper. I tie my own." Vernon leaned forward, pushing harder against Tyler so he could talk to Beth. Tyler, as solid as an oak, held his ground. "Beth, if you come to my house tomorrow, I can show you how to tie any fly you want."

"Where do you like to fish?" Tyler asked.

"Oh, anywhere I can get to in a day. The best spot is the Kickapoo River, but I have to take a bus to go all the way out there. My cousin lives along the West Fork and lets me bunk with him for a week in the summer. I caught a brown trout there once. Three feet long."

"I don't get out much anymore with the dairy growing and the cows needing to be milked."

For the next fifteen minutes, Tyler listened attentively while Vernon told one fish story after another. Beth learned that the best way to catch a big trout was with a Yellow Zonker or a Muddler Minnow, whatever those were, and that Shawano Lake had good pike fishing. She marveled at Tyler's unfailingly kindness, even when listening to Vernon Schmucker drone on about fishing.

Vernon would have talked for another three hours if they hadn't pulled up to the Simons' house just off the main road.

The Simons were an old Englisch couple who lived in the heart of Bonduel. Len Simon, who used to be a doctor, was confined to a wheelchair and had lost most of his eyesight. The Simons had always been extremely kind to the Amish folk in Bonduel, giving them cheap medical care, delivering babies, and driving them to town in emergencies.

In an effort to avoid Vernon—there was a limit to even Tyler's patience—Tyler and Beth blended into the center of the crowd of carolers on the porch. Tyler's face glowed with warmth as he reached down, tugged Beth's glove off, and took her hand.

She stared at him with wide eyes. "What are you doing?" she whispered, not at all eager for him to pull away.

"There are so many people pressing in on us that no one will even notice." His eyes flashed mischievously. "And my fingers have been itching to touch yours ever since you climbed out of Davy Miller's buggy."

She laughed lightly. "You are an incorrigible tease."

"You're right," he said. "The itching started about three months ago."

His smile warmed the air a good ten degrees as the carolers started singing "Hark! The Herald Angels Sing." Tyler sang like Dawdi would have sung—at the top of his lungs. The only difference was that it was impossible for Tyler to sing one note on pitch. He didn't seem to care that his notes were sour. He sang as if his voice could soar to the sky and serenade the angels.

His eyes twinkled when he saw her laughing at him. "I know how much you like my voice," he said. "You let me hold your hand. I can't keep from singing."

She giggled, and he sang louder just to make her laugh. "Please, Tyler, sing softer or the Simons will ask us to stay away next Christmas."

Grinning, he lowered his voice so he wouldn't be heard over the other singers. Beth sighed. It was better that way.

Mrs. Simon threw the door wide open and clapped her hands. "Let me get Len. He'll want to hear you." She disappeared down the hall and reappeared pushing her husband in his wheelchair. Beth marveled at how he always seemed to be smiling, even though he couldn't walk or see.

"Come on in," Mrs. Simon said as she wheeled

her husband into the living room. "I'll make some hot chocolate."

Dr. Simon squinted, trying to make out the shapes of the people in his house. "Sing us one of your German carols. They take me right back to my days in the Army."

They filed into the house with Erla and Menno leading the way. The two dozen of them fit nicely into the Simons' spacious living room.

Tyler let go of Beth, but he cupped his hand over her elbow and led her to stand by the hearth, where a fire crackled merrily. "Is this too warm?" he said.

"Nae, it feels gute."

They sang three songs, all in German, and Dr. Simon sang along when he remembered the words. Tyler sang so softly that not even Beth could hear him, but he did it with a smile, so she knew he didn't mind.

Even though she longed for the feel of his hand again, Tyler couldn't very well hold her hand in plain sight of everybody, but he gazed at her with warmth to rival the fire. Pleasant goose bumps tickled her skin.

Mrs. Simon handed out hot chocolate with tiny marshmallows, and Erla, in turn, gave the Simons the goodie basket.

As they sipped their hot chocolate, Vernon pushed his way between Tyler and Beth and leaned over to warm his hands by the fire. "If you can't make yummasetti, I don't mind meatloaf and stuffing," he said.

Beth shook her head and laughed. What had Tyler said about Vernon? He was nothing if not persistent? "I'm really quite hopeless as a cook."

Tyler didn't smile, but his eyes flashed with amusement. "I make very gute pancakes and bacon."

Vernon wrinkled his forehead until it looked like a nicely plowed field. "Can you bake bread?"

"Amos said I make it too dry."

Clouds gathered on Tyler's face. "Amos mostly didn't know what he was talking about." After he drank the last of his hot chocolate, he said, "I'll be right back." He turned and walked away.

Beth almost screamed at him to come back. He'd promised to stick by her side, and he'd left her stranded with Vernon Schmucker, who was excessively preoccupied with food. And fishing.

"Do you know how to make pie? I love raisin pie."

Beth kept her gaze glued to Tyler as he made his way to Erla and whispered something in her ear. Beth didn't know what he was saying, but Erla seemed to grow increasingly irritated as he spoke. She folded her arms, glanced at Beth, and rolled her eyes.

Still talking, Tyler spread his arms as if he were asking for a hug. Erla cracked a smile and nodded. "Denki," Beth heard Tyler say.

The carolers began filing out the door, and Tyler returned to Beth as if she would disappear if he didn't hurry. Relief soaked her like rainwater.

Tyler took Beth's hand, right there in plain sight

of Vernon. "My mamm has a gute recipe for whoopie pies," Tyler said. "Do you like whoopie pies?"

At this point, Vernon probably felt quite annoyed. He couldn't get a word in edgewise without Tyler interrupting him. Beth hid a smile, partly because of the look on Vernon's face and partly because Tyler's hand felt so nice.

Walking against the tide, Menno parted the crowd of carolers parading out the door and gave Vernon a firm pat on the back. "Vernon," he said. "Erla needs you to be our *Vorsinger*. She's afraid everyone will run out of enthusiasm for the caroling unless you keep us going."

Menno, with his solid build and firm grip, pulled Vernon away from Beth and Tyler even as Vernon tried to protest.

"Erla won't take no for an answer," Menno added.

Vernon glanced at Beth in confusion, but apparently, Menno didn't take no for an answer either. They were soon out the door.

Tyler squeezed Beth's hand. "Sorry about leaving you with Vernon like that, but I had to make sure he wouldn't ruin the rest of our evening."

"What did you do?"

"I told Erla it was her turn to entertain him. He's been tagging along with us long enough. No offense to Vernon, but I don't want to share you with anybody tonight."

Maybe she should have been offended that Tyler acted as if he had a right to monopolize her or manipulate events to be with her. Instead, her heart fluttered, and she found herself smiling unintentionally.

They were the last two onto the wagon. Vernon stood at the front, leading the group in "Coventry Carol," which had a very nice bass part. Their blankets waited for them. Once they sat down, Tyler sidled close to her and wrapped the biggest blanket around Beth's shoulders. He didn't withdraw his arm.

She raised her eyebrows.

He smiled playfully. "I don't want you to get cold."

"I'm plenty warm."

"Because I've got my arm around you. Does this bother you? Because I think it must be what Heaven feels like."

She felt her face heat up. "I don't mind."

"And no one can see that I've got my arm around you under this blanket."

Beth giggled. "You just fell off the turnip truck if you believe no one can see us. You're too close not to attract attention."

Tyler's eyes danced as he squeezed her arm. "Gute. People are always happier if they have something to gossip about."

She leaned against him and let him enfold her in his arms. "I'd hate to disappoint anyone."

The clouds parted, and Beth glimpsed a sliver of moon surrounded by a patch of bright stars. Their breath hung in the air as the clip-clop of horse hooves echoed in the frosty evening above the singing. Beth didn't think she'd ever been so content. She glanced at Tyler. He studied her face with that endearing seriousness he wore like a favorite hat.

"Your eyes reflect the moonlight," he whispered.

"So do yours."

"Do you know what I see when I look in your eyes?"

His intensity unnerved her. Better to make him laugh. "Sheer exhaustion?"

He determined not to be distracted. "I see a thousand stories waiting to be told." He smoothed his finger down her cheek. "You're laughing in all of them."

She held absolutely still, savoring his touch as her surroundings seemed to disappear. They might have been the only people in the world. His soft, low voice lingered like the scent of cinnamon pinecones and caressed her with its deep longing. Beth could have closed her eyes and listened to it forever.

Vernon's bass part could be heard above all other singers. "*Away in a manger, no holding hands on the hayride.*"

Both Tyler and Beth glanced up in surprise to see Vernon glowering at them pointedly, as if he were the hayride enforcement officer.

Beth turned to Tyler. Amusement flashed in his eyes. Beth stifled her laughter by clapping her gloved hand over her mouth.

Some heads turned, but Tyler didn't show any inclination to put even a little space between them. If anything, he tightened his arm around her, without taking his eyes from her face. "You should always be laughing," he said.

The horses turned up the lane to Huckleberry Hill. Mammi and Dawdi were their last stop. Halfway up, they all jumped off the wagon and walked. The lane had become a little steep and too much of a burden for the team of horses pulling their weight. Tyler wasn't even subtle about it. He grabbed Beth's hand and trudged up the hill without the slightest sign that his actions were out of the ordinary or inappropriate.

When they reached the top of the hill, the carolers took a moment to catch their breath, and then Vernon led everybody in "Silent Night." She and Tyler fell to the back of the group as they ambled to the porch.

The music floated up among the tall, bare maples and echoed off the snowdrifts. Beth closed her eyes to savor the sweet sound of voices blended together to sing of Jesus's birth.

All is calm, all is bright.

A single pillar candle burned in the front window. The wreath on Mammi's front door was made from different size balls of red, green, and white yarn glued to a Styrofoam wreath. A pair of knitting needles stuck out of one of the green balls and added a festive touch to the front porch.

Mammi opened the door with Toby in her arms. Beaming like a lighthouse, she whispered in Toby's ear. Toby shaped his mouth into an O and listened spellbound as they finished their song. When the last strains of heavenly peace faded into the night, everyone paused momentarily in silent reverence. Even Toby stilled in Mammi's arms as a hush fell over the carolers.

Of course, Toby's wonderment was as short-lived as his attention span. The quiet came to an end when he clapped his hands and yelled at the singers. "Ball, ball."

Several people laughed. Beth smiled. Toby had a way of wheedling his way into people's affections.

"What a surprise this is," Mammi said. "I thought you only went caroling to the shut-ins and the elderly. Come in and sing for Felty."

One by one they stepped into Mammi's house, stomping their snow-covered boots and wiping their feet on the mat. Beth and Tyler were the last to enter. As soon as Toby saw them, he reached out his arms for Tyler. "Mommy," he said, rejoicing when Tyler opened his arms wide and enfolded Toby in a bear hug, complete with growling and tickling.

Beth's ironclad resistance almost melted. She had a soft spot for anyone who adored Toby.

She took a deep breath. What did she think she was doing? The Christmas music and the hot chocolate must have weakened her resolve.

She had promised herself she wouldn't let her heart be ambushed ever again, and here she stood, in the same place she had been four years ago, flirting and holding hands and making eyes at a boy. It must have been the miniature marshmallows that got to her. She loved miniature marshmallows.

A wall of warmth enveloped her as she walked

into the great room. Mammi had spent hours stringing popcorn and cranberries to hang at the windows with the long evergreen branches cut from pines in the woods. She had knit ten bright red bows, which she used to tie off the evergreen at the window corners. It definitely looked like Christmas at the Helmuth house.

Dawdi sat in his recliner, and Mammi fumbled through the fridge. "I've got some leftover rice. I'll cook up a batch of rice pudding while you sing to us." A saucepan clattered loudly as she set it on the cookstove. She poured the rice into the pan and waved her hand in their direction. "Go ahead and sing. Don't mind me."

Beth would have decamped as far from Tyler as she could, but he held Toby, and she couldn't very well abandon her son just to avoid Tyler. Tyler smiled at her while bouncing Toby on his hip. He seemed so natural, so content. He'd make a wonderful-gute father someday. But not Toby's father.

Beth would have to renew her search for a wife for Tyler. He deserved to have a gute woman by his side and children he could care for.

Vernon decided on "O Little Town of Bethlehem," and they sang all four verses.

How silently, how silently the wondrous gift is given. Thus God imparts to human hearts the blessings of His heaven. No ear may hear His coming, but in this world of sin, where meek souls will receive Him still, the dear Christ enters in.

That particular verse had always touched Beth. God's gifts were given so quietly that many people didn't even recognize blessings when they came.

She felt the familiar pang in her heart and folded her arms across her chest to keep the hurt from spilling out. She had seen nothing but sorrow for the last four years. Why hadn't God taken care of her? Why hadn't He stopped her from marrying Amos? Didn't He love her? Didn't He care how painful her marriage had been? Apparently He didn't. He had forgotten her. She must look after herself.

"There's another verse to that song," Dawdi said. Without further fanfare, he began to sing, "*O little Inn of Bethlehem, how like we are to you. Our lives are crowded to the brim with this and that to do. We're not unfriendly to the King, we mean well without doubt. We have no hostile feelings, we merely crowd Him out.*"

"A very gute message," Erla said.

Dawdi waved his hand in the air. "Sing another."

They sang "O Come All Ye Faithful," "Hark the Herald Angels Sing," and "It Came Upon the Midnight Clear," and then Mammi, still busy in the kitchen, announced that the pudding wasn't quite ready yet.

When they started "Jingle Bells," Toby wanted to get down. Tyler set him on his feet, and he danced around the room as they sang all the verses they knew and Vernon shook his bells with untempered enthusiasm. Tyler laughed when Toby bent over, tucked his head, and did an unintentional somersault. He sat up, not quite sure how he'd ended up on his backside. The laughter bubbled amidst the music.

"The pudding is ready," Mammi announced when they ended "Jingle Bells" with a loud "Hey!" Mammi stacked some plastic spoons and a tower of Styrofoam cups in the table. "Everybody get a cup and a spoon, and I will dish you some pudding."

Beth sensed a bit of foot dragging as one by one the carolers lined up for their share of rice pudding. Mammi had a widespread reputation as a bad cook. No one wanted to hurt her feelings, but few people looked forward to eating one of Anna Helmuth's concoctions.

Even Vernon, who apparently dreamed about food in his sleep, let several people go ahead of him. Was he hoping that if he stood at the back of the line, Mammi would run out of pudding before he got any?

Had Mammi passed on her cooking skills to Beth? Amos certainly would have said yes. She had never made him a meal he had enjoyed. Of course, Amos had always been at a loss for kind words, so she couldn't be sure. Since leaving Indiana and Amos's constant criticism, she had come to consider herself an adequate cook. Treva had liked it when she'd made cheese, and Tyler always devoured her cookies.

A lump stuck in her throat. Tyler devoured Mammi's cooking too. His eating habits didn't tell her anything.

Although she should have pulled back, she let

Tyler take her hand and lead her to the pudding line.

"You go first, Tyler," one of the young people said. "We know how you love rice pudding."

Tyler grinned at Beth and picked up two cups from the table. "Fill them to the brim, Anna," he said. "I'm starving."

With her eyes sparkling in delight, Mammi shook her finger. "Now, Tyler. You must save some for everybody else."

From the back of the line, Aaron Troyer called out. "Don't worry about us, Anna. Tyler's worked hard today to organize this hayride. He deserves the biggest helping."

Truly pleased that Tyler wanted two helpings, Mammi shrugged and filled his cups. Beth glanced at Mammi's pot. Tyler's selflessness wouldn't do much to help the rest of the carolers, even those in the back of the line. Mammi had made a generous batch.

Beth held out her cup, and Mammi poured her a ladleful of runny white pudding. At least it wasn't so thick that it would stick in her throat on the way down. No matter how unappetizing, runny was better. Beth studied her cup. The pudding had some sort of wrinkly red fruit floating in it. They might have been cranberries, but she decided it would be better not to ask.

They sat down on the sofa, and Tyler set one of his cups on the end table. Toby skipped to Tyler and wanted to be picked up. Tyler scooped

Toby onto his lap and offered him a spoonful of pudding. Toby opened his mouth and let Tyler feed him.

To Beth's surprise, Toby didn't spit the rice all over Tyler's shirt. "More," he said, smacking his lips and grinning with his whole face.

Tyler put the cup to Toby's lips and let him drink the pudding like a glass of milk. Toby gulped the pudding like it was his first nourishment in days.

Beth looked into her cup as if it held a perilous mystery. Doubtfully, she dipped her spoon and licked it. It wasn't horrible. In fact, Mammi's rice pudding tasted like nothing more than warm milk and sugar, with occasional lumps of rice and cranberries for texture. As long as she swallowed the cranberries whole, she could eat without cringing. Thankfully, no one would end up with a stomachache for having eaten it, and Tyler would not have to suffer for his thoughtfulness.

The other carolers discovered that the pudding was edible, and Beth could almost hear an audible sigh of relief as everyone sat down to enjoy their rice drink. Most abandoned their spoons and drank it down. Vernon went so far as to slurp, which was a sure sign that he enjoyed it.

Mammi handed Dawdi a cup, and he took a hearty bite. "This is the best rice pudding ever, Banannie. The queen of Africa never ate this well."

Toby drank Tyler's whole cup. "He likes it," Tyler said, glancing at Beth cautiously. She hadn't said a word since they'd arrived. The thoughts tumbled around in her head like pebbles in a swollen river. If she could stop her brain from spinning in circles, she might be able to make sense out of the confusion.

"Are you okay?" he asked.

"Jah. A little tired yet."

She could see by the set of his jaw and the agitation in his expression that he was already trying to figure out a way to make things easier for her without offending her. Part of her wanted to push him away and scold him for his annoying interference. A bigger part of her wanted to dissolve into his embrace and thank him for caring.

He looked too serious. The urge to kiss that frown right off his lips grew too great. She'd have to make him smile or else go crazy thinking about it. "Dodging Vernon is exhausting," she whispered.

He quirked the corners of his lips upward. "Unfortunately, it might be our turn to sit with him on the ride back. We can only ask so much of Erla and Menno."

"I won't be sitting with him at all. I'm already home."

Tyler looked sincerely disappointed as he bounced Toby on his knee. "I was afraid you'd realize that. I wanted one more chance to cuddle with you."

Beth turned her face away and willed herself not to blush. "You heard Vernon. *No holding hands on the hayride.* If I were going back, we'd have to follow the rules."

He chuckled. "Says who?"

Mammi walked around the room with a garbage bag in her hands, collecting cups and spoons.

"Denki," Tyler said as both his empty cups went into her bag.

Anna handed the bag to Felty and took Toby from Tyler's arms. "Tyler, there is something I want you and Beth to see in the barn."

"Should I come back tomorrow when it's light? We won't be able to see much out there tonight."

Mammi smiled sweetly. "You'll be able to see it well enough. Go out there and look up to the rafters."

"Are you sure? It's mighty cold yet."

"The barn is nice and warm. It will only take a minute." When neither Tyler nor Beth made any indication of moving, Mammi pursed her lips. "Please? It would make me so happy."

Tyler nodded. He would bend over backwards to make Mammi happy. He stood and offered Beth his hand. "Will you come?"

"What is this?" Beth asked.

Mammi took a tissue from her pocket and dabbed at Toby's face. "Dawdi and I did something special in the barn."

Beth pulled her gloves from her pocket. "Okay, but I need to get Toby to bed."

"Don't worry about that," Mammi said. "We'll get him ready and say prayers, and you can kiss him good night when you return. Now hurry so the wagon doesn't leave Tyler behind."

Tyler and Beth threaded their way through the crowd of young people, even avoiding Vernon by taking the long way around the kitchen table. They stepped out into the night. Tyler closed the door, muffling the voices inside. The scents of hickory smoke and pine, two of Beth's favorite Christmas-time smells, hung in the crisp, frosty air.

Tyler lifted the glowing lantern from its peg on the porch and took her hand. The cold seemed to disperse from the very air. Beth shivered with the pleasure of his warmth. When had Tyler wheedled his way into her heart like this, as if he belonged there, as if no one could fill the emptiness but him?

Her heart pounded like a drum in her chest, demanding her full attention. Did she love him? She could barely remember what giddy, head-over-heels love felt like.

She hesitated briefly as they stepped off the porch. At nineteen, she had thought she loved Amos. He had been charming and funny and given her a thrill every time he smiled at her. She couldn't let herself get carried away like that with Tyler—even when she had no desire to be sensible. His hand felt so gute.

They trudged to the barn, the snow crunching beneath their feet. The faint strains of another carol came from the house. Dawdi must have asked for one more song.

"What do you think your mammi wants us to discover?" Tyler said.

"I don't know, but I'm afraid my fingers will freeze before we find what we're looking for."

In response, Tyler wrapped his arm around her. "I'll keep you warm."

In the dimmest corner of her mind, she thought about resisting him but didn't have the will or the desire to do it. "Denki for humoring my mammi. She gets her heart set on things."

"I don't mind. It lets me spend a few more minutes with you. After this, all I get is Vernon Schmucker."

Beth giggled. "I'm envious. I won't get to see him again until the next gathering. That could be weeks away."

The well-greased hinges of the barn door opened quietly, and they heard the horse stir in the darkness. Tyler hung the lantern on a peg. The shadows danced in every direction around them as they gazed around the musty barn.

"See anything out of the ordinary?" Tyler asked.

"Mammi said to look up."

They turned their eyes upward at the same time. In Dawdi's barn, the rafters were only three feet over their heads.

A small sprig of green with white berries dangled from a string above them.

"Is that what Mammi wants us to see?" Beth said.

Tyler kept his gaze on that sprig as if it might disappear if he looked away. "Oh," he said.

"What is it?"

He slowly shifted his gaze to her face. "It's mistletoe."

"Why would Mammi hang mistletoe in the barn? It's not even an Amish tradition." Beth's puzzlement didn't last very long. Mammi had a full bag of tricks, and she obviously wasn't above using any and all of them. Dear Mammi proved more persistent than a spider in a waterspout. Beth almost laughed out loud until she noticed how intently Tyler stared at her. Or more specifically, her lips. He obviously took the mistletoe very seriously.

She fell silent as he moved closer. Close enough that, in the still of the barn, Beth could almost hear his heartbeat. "I wish your mammi hadn't done that," he whispered with that deep, smooth-as-chocolate voice, and the barn suddenly felt twenty degrees warmer. "I've resisted all evening, but now that the idea is in my head, I don't think I'm strong enough to put it out." He brushed his thumb down her cheek. "Please, can I kiss you?"

She should have refused him. He'd been entirely too fresh with her already. But when his thumb moved slowly along her jawline and then traced the outline of her lips, she lost the power of rational thought. "Uh-huh" was all she could muster.

Tyler wrapped his arms around her as if to protect her from harm. Then he lowered his head and brought his lips down on hers. A sigh bubbled up in her throat. Even though the temperature sat well below freezing, Tyler's kiss felt like a rare spring day when Beth could warm herself by turning her face to the sun. She almost sensed the balmy air caressing her cheeks while birdsong filled the meadow and wildflowers swayed in the breeze. She reached up to wrap her arms around his neck. This was where she wanted to stay forever.

He responded by squeezing her with those strong arms and leaving her breathless in a thousand different ways. "Beth, my Beth. I love you like crazy." She felt powerless to do anything but try to stay on her feet. She feared her knees might buckle at any second or she might float off the ground and never come down again. Had her heart ever beat such a wild rhythm before?

His mouth returned to hers, and his second kiss was filled with longing and tenderness so profound that Beth ached with compassion. How could she not love this man?

He pulled away from the kiss but still held her close. "Remember when I told you I didn't believe in love? I made a mistake. I've never felt anything like this before. I'm so far off the ground that I'm halfway to Heaven. I want to marry the woman I love. The woman I can't live without. I want to marry you, Beth. Please say yes."

With her hands still around his neck, Beth laced her fingers together to keep them from trembling. This did nothing to steady her ragged breathing. "I thought you didn't care about love."

He withdrew from their embrace and placed his hands on her shoulders. "If I were willing to settle for just anybody, you know I'd be married already. There are probably a dozen girls who'd say yes to me tomorrow if I asked. Lorene Zook, Millie Coblenz, even Eva Raber would probably say yes, if I could convince her to say anything. Don't you see, Beth? That's not what I want."

Beth took a step back. His words knocked her out of her romantic stupor and brought her crashing back to reality. The pain and heartache of three years with Amos assaulted her as the memories came flooding back. "Why did you say that?"

He stiffened and squared his shoulders as if readying for an attack. She'd done it to him too many times before. "I'm sorry if what I say upsets you, Beth. But I won't take it back. I love you."

How many times had Amos said he loved her before they were married? Tears of frustration sprang to her eyes. "Amos often told me he could have married any girl in our district. He'd point them out after gmay. *Look, Beth, there's Grace Martin. Look how pretty she is. She wanted to marry me. I could have had Wanda Weaver or Esther Miller, who actually knows how to cook. I could have had any girl I wanted, and I got stuck with you.*" She choked on the memory.

Pain and anger burned in Tyler's eyes. The raw emotion she saw there made her catch her breath. His words were slow and measured as if he kept his composure with great effort. "You're always saying you want me to fight back," he said, the muscles in his jaw tensing, "but I refuse to fight with a dead man. I am not Amos Hostetler, and if I haven't convinced you of that by now, I never will."

"Amos used to—"

His control almost crumbled. "I don't care what Amos used to do," he snapped, his eyes flashing with lightning.

Beth froze. In all the time she had known him, with all the abuse she had heaped upon him, she had never seen him truly angry before.

Taking a deep breath, Tyler turned his face from her and wiped his gloved hand across his mouth. When he spoke, his self-possession had returned. "You don't want to see the kind of man I really am, because you'd rather hold on to your pain like a security blanket. You can refuse to trust God because of what happened in the past, but I refuse to suffer because of it." He took a step toward her and reached out a hand but lowered it before she had time to decide if she wanted to take it. "I love you better than my own soul, Beth, but I'll not compete with a dead man for the rest of my life. You won't forgive Amos, and you're angry with God."

"What do you know?"

"Oh, you're angry all right. You've given God the cold shoulder ever since I've known you. You think you can manage your life all by yourself with no help from anyone, even Him."

"Because God abandoned me."

"You're wrong, Beth. If you were willing to open your eyes, you'd see His tender mercies everywhere. And you're fooling yourself if you think you don't need to be rescued. But I can't do it. Open your heart and let Jesus change you. Nothing else is good enough." Frowning with his entire body, he reached up and yanked the mistletoe from its string. "Please accept my apology for what I said about all those other girls. But I'm done explaining myself." He tromped out of the barn, leaving it a much more desolate place. Springtime had disappeared, and she felt as cold and empty as a starless winter night.

Chapter Nineteen

Beth should have been overjoyed, but she felt numb. She snipped the thread and held out the mint-green dress for a final look. Her last Christmas order and it was a whole nine days before Christmas. She'd made enough money to put away five hundred dollars and have a little leftover for some Christmas shopping for Toby and the rest of her family.

She glanced at Mammi, who was washing up the breakfast dishes. After last Friday night, Mammi hadn't exactly been cross with her, but she'd acted like an exasperated mother whose child wouldn't eat her broccoli. "My dear," she had cried when Beth told her about the mistletoe disaster, "how am I ever going to convince you that your mammi knows best?"

Toby sat on Dawdi's lap while Dawdi read him a book. With wide eyes, he bounced excitedly on his great-great-grandfather's lap with his finger in his mouth. Dawdi never actually got through a whole book. Toby just liked turning pages. Toby could use a new pair of shoes and another book for Christmas. And maybe a ball. Toby loved playing catch with Tyler.

Beth's heart grew heavier at the thought. Toby wouldn't be playing ball with Tyler again. The balls would be a waste of money.

Beth blinked back the unjustifiable tears. She would be fine. Just fine. Better to be sad over what might have been than to risk another miserable marriage.

Miserable marriage? Her heart rebelled at the thought that marriage to Tyler would be terrible. Tyler, who always put others before himself, couldn't be as bad as Amos. But how could she know for sure? She refused to take the risk. Better to be lonely than desperately unhappy.

But at the moment, she didn't feel merely lonely. Her heart had cracked into a million shards of glass. Could she live with that pain for the rest of her life?

Hearing a quick step on the porch, she smoothed her apron and willed her heart to slow to a gallop. Her reaction was silly. It wouldn't possibly be Tyler. He'd told her he was done explaining himself. He wouldn't be back.

Her cousin Aden poked his head into the great room. "Hello, everybody," he said, with the wide smile that seemed to be a permanent part of his face. Beth hadn't seen him without one since he'd married Lily Eicher. "We are here to finish that chest for Lily."

We? Beth held her breath. Tyler was surely with him.

"How nice to see you," Mammi said.

"Tyler made me promise to come." He glanced at Beth with a playful gleam in his eye. "Although I think he'd say he spent his time well on those days I didn't show up."

Beth couldn't muster any kind of smile. Aden obviously didn't yet know that Tyler had given up on her or that he would probably consider his hours on Huckleberry Hill a complete waste of time.

"Tyler's right behind me in his sleigh," Aden said. "Dawdi, do you want to come out and help us?"

"Sure do."

"I'll go out and get started," Aden said. He nearly shut the door before swinging it open again. "It's nice to see you, Beth. I'm sure Tyler will be in to say hello."

Nae, he wouldn't.

Dawdi closed the book and placed Toby on his feet. He rocked back and forth a few times to gather enough momentum to stand. He retrieved his heavy coat from the hook and pulled his gloves, hat, and scarf from three different pockets. When sufficiently bundled, he tromped out the door.

"Make sure Tyler comes in to see us before he leaves," Mammi said.

Beth's heart raced. She should have told Dawdi not to bother but couldn't bear to say it. She wanted to see Tyler in the worst way. Oy, anyhow.

The corner of Dawdi's mouth quirked upward.

"I ain't about to tell Tyler Yoder what to do. He's a man. He can make up his own mind."

Mammi raised her eyebrows as if Dawdi were the one who wouldn't eat his broccoli. "Do you really believe that, Felty?"

Dawdi chuckled, shook his head, and walked out. He started singing the minute the door closed behind him. "*Joy to the world, I love my Annie-banannie, but she should keep her nose out of other people's porridge.*" His lyrics didn't quite fit the rhythm of the original music, but he altered the tune somewhat to make it work out. Despite her low spirits, Beth smiled.

Mammi propped her wet hands on her hips. "I'm not fond of porridge. I prefer to stick my fingers in other people's pies."

Beth had the sudden overpowering need to jump from her chair at the sewing machine and race to the kitchen. She dropped the new mint-green dress on the table before stealing a peek out the window. She caught a glimpse of Tyler's leg before it disappeared into the barn with the rest of him. Her heart flip-flopped. It was a very good leg.

She turned to see Mammi staring at her with a loving scold on her lips. "I truly thought the mistletoe would work."

Beth pretended to be very interested in some fabric scraps on the table so Mammi wouldn't see the flash of pain in her eyes. "I already told you, Mammi. Tyler and I are just friends."

Mammi dried her hands on a towel, came around the counter, and wrapped her arms around

Beth's waist for a grandmotherly hug. "Dear Beth. Why do you want to be so miserable?"

"I don't. I want to be happy."

"Then why are you jogging down the road to unhappiness? No, not jogging. Sprinting. I'm trying to get you turned around, but you're not making it easy."

"I can't be so shortsighted as to trade my future, even for something I want wonderful-bad right now. That was my mistake with Amos."

"You don't think Tyler will make you happy?"

"He might, but I can't be sure. My first marriage cured me of any desire to marry again."

Mammi pulled out a chair and motioned for Beth to sit. Then she sat and reached under the table, where she kept a ready basket of knitting supplies. She took up a pair of needles already threaded with blue yarn and started knitting. It came as naturally as breathing to her. "I'm knitting a blanket for Suvilla Mast and Alvin Hoover's wedding in April, in case you wanted to know. Have you noticed how my matches always seem to work out?"

"Except for me, Mammi."

"You shouldn't let Amos ruin the rest of your life. He was a pill, but do you really want to give his memory that much power?"

Beth leaned her head on her hand. "It was so hard."

"Well, I can't help you there. Marriage is hard work. One time I made Felty so mad, he slept in the barn for a week. But our disagreements forced us to learn to get along. He would hurt my feelings, and I would make him so mad he couldn't spit straight, but he got tired of sleeping in the barn. We had to talk even when we couldn't stand to look at each other." She patted Beth's hand. "No person will make you as happy or as angry as your husband. But if you can't bear the sorrow, you'll never know the happiness."

"Amos never made me happy."

"Maybe you weren't married long enough."

"We were married too long."

Mammi shook her head. "In marriage, you have to give a little."

"To the point of losing myself?"

"To the point of becoming your best self and helping him become his best self." With yarn poised on her knitting needles, Mammi leaned in and whispered as if she were sharing some grand secret even though Toby was the only one around to hear. "Don't you see? You are strong, Beth. Amos might have learned eventually. You could have taught him how to be a gute husband."

Beth fell silent. She didn't know if she believed that. Would she have found the strength to insist that Amos be a better man? "What if he had refused to be better?"

"Then God would have told you to leave him and given you the strength to do it."

Beth drew back in surprise. "Leave him? I couldn't have left him. I would have been excommunicated."

Mammi shrugged. "There are some married Amish folks living apart, usually because one of them is too proud to change. It happens. We don't believe in divorce, but I am convinced that God would never want one of his children to be treated the way you were treated. He wants you to be happy."

"But He didn't stop me from marrying Amos in the first place."

Mammi's needles clicked in comforting rhythm. "God lets everyone make their own choices. Amos chose to be mean. God would have let him reap the consequences of those choices. You could have come back to Wisconsin to live with your folks. Or even left the church, if it came down to that. God would have shown you the way."

Beth shook her head. "He never did before."

Mammi's smile brimmed with patience. "Now, Beth, God never left you without help, even when you were with Amos. Especially when you were with Amos. But maybe you were too angry at Him to recognize it."

"I've been angry at God for a long time," she murmured.

"It's time to stop being angry and start listening instead of fighting Him."

Beth stood and looked out the window at the barn. She thought of Tyler, talking and laughing with Dawdi and Aden instead of her. Envy stabbed at her. She wanted to see his smile more than winter wanted to see spring.

"Tyler won't come back by wishing him to, and like as not, he won't return unless you mend a whole pasture of fences."

"I just . . . want him to be my friend."

Mammi smiled with her whole face. "A boy that scrambled in love doesn't want to be friends." Sighing plaintively, she leaned on the table and pushed herself to her feet. "Let's get labels on these jam jars," she said, as if she'd forgotten the entire conversation. "They need more huckleberry jam at the Christmas bazaar. They're going to sell out this year, Lord willing."

Beth bit her bottom lip. No matter how hard it would prove to be, she must patch up her friendship with Tyler. The thought of him out of her life left her gasping for air.

She helped Mammi bring the supplies to the table—two-dozen half-pints of jam plus pens and labels. They wrote out labels while Toby played on the rug, occasionally coming to Beth for a drink of "wadi" or a cracker. Beth hardly said a word. Her concentration centered on the inside of the barn, where Tyler stained a chest of drawers with her cousin Aden.

Dawdi opened the door and stomped the snow off his boots before stepping into the house.

"How's it going out there?" Beth asked, trying to keep her tone casual.

Dawdi hung up his coat and pulled a small brown bag from his pocket. Studying Beth's face, he said, "About as good as it's going in here, it would seem. You're looking as grim as an undertaker, and Tyler is trying to smile so hard his lips are bound to turn blue."

Things were worse than she'd thought. It wasn't like Tyler to pretend to anything. His solemn expression had always attested to his inner calm. He obviously wasn't feeling any peace at the moment if he grinned until his face hurt.

Dawdi placed the sack in her hand and cocked an eyebrow. "He asked me to give this to you, and he said not to be mad."

Her heart sank as she turned the bag upside-down and four thick spools of thread tumbled from it. She couldn't be mad. The hurt overtook every other emotion. He couldn't talk her into marrying him, but he still must have felt obligated to be nice.

She had turned into one of his service projects.

She didn't want to be one of his service projects. She wanted things to be the way they had been four days ago when they had shared a glorious evening on a hayride under the stars. She wanted it to be just like that but without the kissing or handholding. She only wanted to be friends. At this moment, Tyler's friendship felt more important to her than any other relationship in her entire life.

By the twentieth label, when her hand stiffened up, she quit debating with herself and determined to march out to the barn and persuade Tyler to talk to her, like they had always been able to talk with each other. She'd scold him for buying her thread, and he'd sprout that guilty grin he always got when he knew what he'd done had irritated her. She'd make him laugh at least three times. She could always make him laugh.

She hurriedly finished the labels for Mammi,

dashed to her room, and gathered Toby's hat, coat, and mittens. Toby's presence would ensure that Tyler would at least agree to talk to her. Even if Tyler wanted to avoid her, he couldn't resist Toby's big blue eyes and chubby cheeks.

Her limbs felt weak as she stepped out the door with Toby tightly in her arms. Why should she be so shaky? She'd seen Tyler four days ago. It wasn't as if they'd been apart for years and years. Still, she placed Toby on the ground and let him crunch through the snow as she held tightly to his hand. Unfortunately, he didn't like to be constrained. Pulling against her, he threw his head back and grunted his displeasure.

"Come on, Toby," she coaxed.

He pulled harder and flopped down in the snow.

She squatted and lifted him to his feet. "Toby, Toby," she said, as he struggled in her arms. "We're going to go find Tyler. Do you want to see Tyler?"

Toby's eyes lit up. "Mommy."

Toby let her take his hand and lead him to the barn. She swung open the door, and their footsteps echoed in the cold, dim space.

"Mommy," Toby called.

Tyler and Aden were gone. How had she not seen them leave from the kitchen window?

Her disappointment felt as palpable as if she were choking on a piece of stale bread. She needed to see Tyler. Why had he left without even a glance in her direction? Her eyes involuntarily traveled to the ceiling, where an empty string dangled from one of the rafters. Tyler had kissed her right here.

The mere memory sent a thrill dancing up her spine.

Why was she fighting this? Why did she struggle so hard to deny what lay in the very core of her soul—the thing that would make her deliriously happy and fill her life with purpose again?

Because if she admitted her true feelings, she would have to do something about them.

Suddenly, she couldn't breathe as the truth came rushing toward her and almost knocked her over. She loved Tyler so fiercely she thought her heart might burst with the intensity of it. But fear paralyzed her—the same fear that had been her constant companion since Amos died. It felt like a mountain impossible to climb.

Toby yanked his hand from her grasp and toddled toward the stalls.

"Toby, no. Toby, stop!"

He didn't heed her. At the sound of her voice, he ran as fast as his little legs would take him while she chased frantically after him. She saw it coming even as it was too late to stop it. He tripped on a crack in the floor, fell face first onto the cement, and cried out in pain.

In horror, Beth gasped and scooped him into her arms. He held his breath momentarily, then let out a scream that surely rattled the walls. A sickly purple goose egg already grew on his forehead and the skin on the tip of his nose was scraped raw and bleeding.

Beth clutched him to her breast even as she felt her heart would stop beating. "Oh, Toby. Oh, my little baby." She found the milking stool in the dim light and sat down with Toby bawling hysterically in her grasp. She pulled a tissue from her coat pocket and lightly patted the scrape on his nose. He screamed harder and swatted her hand away. Tears ran down her face. "Why didn't you listen to me? I told you not to run. You've got quit fighting me all the time, *heartzly.*"

She took in her breath sharply. Mammi's words came back to her as if they were flashing in bright letters in the sky.

It's time to stop being angry and start listening instead of fighting God all the time.

Toby's crying wound down as her agitation grew. Had she really been behaving like a two-year-old? Toby fought every effort to guide him. He threw tantrums when she tried to change his diaper. He became ferociously angry when she held his hand to cross the street. She tried to watch over him, and all he could do was be mad about it. She remembered the look on his face when she'd taken him to the doctor to get shots. He'd acted as if she'd betrayed him, even though the immunizations were for his own good.

Oh.

Had some good come out of her marriage to Amos? Had she been mad at God all this time for sending blessings she had been too stubborn to recognize?

Toby's wails died down to whimpers, and she dabbed the tissue to his nose once again. Not a lot of blood, but it would sure be sore for a few days.

She took off one of her gloves and softly pressed her cold hand to his goose egg hoping to make it feel better. He grunted and nudged her hand away. *Never mind.*

"There, there. It's okay. Everything is going to be okay."

Was it? How could she reassure Toby when she wasn't even convinced of it herself?

Pressing her lips against Toby's cheek, she bowed her head and prayed with silent fervor. "Dear Heavenly Father, after what happened with Amos, I was mad at you."

The thought seemed so silly. God already knew her heart. She wanted Him to change it.

"I want to trust you again, to see your hand in my life and recognize the good that came out of three years with Amos, if there was any. Please show me the way."

Behind her she heard the snow crunching underneath someone's feet and turned to see Dawdi making his way across the yard. "Your mammi said you came out to see Tyler. I should have told you he and Aden left about ten minutes ago." When he came closer, he noticed the tears in her eyes and the sorry condition of Toby's face. "Oh, *sis yuscht!* There's been some sort of kerfuffle."

"He fell" was all she could muster.

Dawdi reached for Toby and took him into his arms. "You was running away, wasn't you? You don't like to stay still." He brushed his hand lightly across the giant purple goose egg on Toby's forehead. "Let me see your eyes," he instructed.

"Eye," Toby repeated.

Dawdi walked out of the barn, into the sunlight muted by gray, and examined Toby's eyes. He shaded Toby's face and then pulled his hand away, exposing Toby's pupils to the brighter light. He repeated his examination three times. "His eyes look like they're working okay. I don't think he has a concussion."

Beth exhaled in relief. "He hit pretty hard."

"Jah, I can see he did." Dawdi took the tissue from Beth and dabbed around the scrape on Toby's nose. "One of your mammi's ointments will have you as good as new in no time." He kissed the top of Toby's head and tousled his curly red hair. "He's the spitting image of Amos Hostetler."

Beth had never liked hearing that. It meant she would never be free of Amos's memory. But today she thought of her son instead of her son's father. She couldn't even imagine her life without Toby. She remembered laughing in delight at that shock of bright red hair on a tiny, perfect baby just minutes after his birth. When the nurse had laid Toby in her arms, Beth had thought she would burst. She'd never experienced such indescribable love for another human being before. Her feelings had overflowed and coursed through every cell in her body.

That love had never subsided. She imagined it must be a small taste of the love that Jesus felt for her. It had to be. He had died for her. And for her son.

Without Amos, I wouldn't have Toby. The best gift God has ever given me.

How could she ever be mad at God for such grace?

With Toby in his arms, Dawdi turned and hiked to the house. "Let's have Mammi take a look at that nose."

Before following them, Beth paused for a moment and looked to the sky. "Thank you, Heavenly Father, for my Toby. He is the best thing in my life. And thank you for Amos for giving my baby to me." Her voice cracked. Not since the first month of her marriage had she thanked God for her husband.

A warm sensation radiated from the center of her heart to the tips of her toes and fingers. She felt as if a burden had been lifted from her shoulders. She smiled to herself. God would show her the way. She just had to listen.

And quit fighting.

Chapter Twenty

Toby did not want to sit, so Beth ended up following him around the large warehouse while Dawdi pushed the empty stroller. Every December, Kessler's warehouse was home to the annual Christmas bazaar, where Amish and Englisch alike set up booths and sold their merchandise for Christmas treasure seekers. The Kings sold Mammi and Dawdi's huckleberry jam in their booth of specialty Amish foods. Yost Bieler sold clever wooden toys and gadgets, and even Vernon Schmucker had a booth where he peddled his Yellow Zonker and grasshopper pattern fishing flies.

Toby tromped around the warehouse, dodging people and booths, sporting a scab on the tip of his nose and a fine bruise that covered the right half of his forehead. He paused occasionally to let passersby ooh and aah at him, but he didn't stay still for long. He marched along, oblivious to his mother, who followed his every step and made sure he didn't steer into any trouble.

Very much like God did with her, Beth thought. How truly unaware had she been that Heavenly Father continually watched over her? Since Tuesday she'd been assembling a list of tender mercies she had ignored in the last four years. It was becoming quite lengthy. Near the top of that list she noted the night that Tyler Yoder had taken a beating from Isaac. Beth had no doubt who had brought Tyler to her door at that very moment. It was nothing short of a miracle, and she had only just recognized it.

Her eyes scanned the crowds for any sign of Tyler. Although it wasn't likely he'd be here, she kept a lookout. She had to talk to him, and since he'd probably determined to never set foot on Huckleberry Hill again, she would need to go to him.

But she didn't know how she would patch things up once she did talk to him. "Please be patient with me" sounded selfish after all she'd already put him through. "I need more time" seemed like a weak excuse. He probably wouldn't believe "I love you," even though the feeling was as real as the warmth of the sun streaming through the clouds on a stormy day. He had every reason to reject her. He was ready, and she wasn't. With every fiber of her soul, she wanted to be ready to open her heart to him and trust her life to God. She couldn't give herself fully to Tyler until she could give herself fully to God.

She was working on trust. God was working on her heart.

Toby picked up his pace and ran recklessly toward one of the corner booths. Her heart somersaulted when she saw where he was headed. Tyler stood

near the candy booth with that solemn look on his
face Beth had come to cherish. With his arms
folded casually across his chest, he talked with one
of the ministers in the district.

The brightly colored candy sitting in open bins was
not what had attracted Toby's attention. "Mommy,
mommy!" he cried as he pumped his little legs with
all his might and ran headlong on a crash course
for Tyler.

Hearing his nickname, Tyler turned, caught
Toby in his arms, and tossed him into the air. Toby
squealed in pure delight, and Tyler's serious face
bloomed into a genuine smile.

Beth finally caught up with her escapee, her
heart pounding like a window-rattling bass drum.
Tyler barely glanced at her, but she saw him stiffen
at her presence. The drum played double time.

Tyler anchored Toby securely in his arms and
examined his face. "Oh, no, Toby. What happened?"
He looked sincerely stricken. "Have you been running from your mother again?"

"He fell in the barn. On the cement." Why
couldn't she speak to Tyler without panting for air?
"I didn't hold his hand tight enough. I feel like a
horrible mother."

He regarded her with those achingly beautiful
eyes before quickly looking away, as if gazing at her
too long would be dangerous. "You are a wonderful-gute mother," he said, his frown etched on every
line of his face. "Toby is two, unsteady on his feet,
and independent." He nudged a lock of hair from

the bruise. "He is determined to learn things the hard way."

Toby leaned his head on Tyler's shoulder and tapped Tyler's chest with his chubby hand. Tyler was his favorite person in the world. In turn, Tyler nuzzled his chin against the top of Toby's head and patted his back in a slow, easy rhythm.

Beth took a deep breath. "Tyler, can we have a talk?"

Tyler pressed his lips together and refused to look her in the eye. She could see his desire to be nice warring with his resolve to keep away from her. He turned and pointed to the bins of candy. "Could Toby have a sucker? They've got root beer."

Her heart sank. He seemed determined not to let her break through his defenses. "Jah, he can have a sucker."

Tyler quickly picked a sucker from the bin, paid a quarter for it, and gave it to Toby.

Doubt paralyzed her. What could she say to him to tear down that seven-foot wall he had built between them? "Can . . . can you come over tonight?" She tried for a playful grin. "The floors need sweeping."

He persistently looked anywhere but at her and forced a smile that could have been pressed into his face by an iron. Like Dawdi had said, he was smiling so hard his lips were going to turn blue. "I can't. We're having a Christmas get-together with some of the aunts and uncles."

Beth winced. She couldn't bear that fake smile. She never wanted Tyler to pretend anything with her. She should have held her tongue, but she couldn't help it. Couldn't he see how hard she tried? "Don't smile like that."

His lips didn't move from their unnatural position. "Like what?"

"Like you're barely tolerating me," she snapped.

He didn't fight back. Of course he didn't fight back, but at least he wiped the grimace off his face and finally met her gaze. "I'm sorry I offended you, Beth. The last thing I want to do is hurt your feelings."

Don't apologize, she wanted to scream. *I don't want your apologies. I want you to wait for me. I want you to love me.*

Instead, she turned her anger inward, where it belonged. Her stubbornness hadn't allowed God into her life or love into her heart. She had pushed Tyler away and had no one to blame for his behavior but herself.

She slumped her shoulders and tried to keep a sob from escaping her lips. "I'm sorry, Tyler."

Surprise flitted across his features before he put up that wall again "It's no use, Beth. It's no use." He said it with such an air of finality that she almost lost her composure. She frantically blinked back the tears that already brimmed in her eyes.

Tyler pretended not to notice. He transferred Toby into her arms while Toby protested loudly and reached for him. "Have a merry Christmas, Beth." He caressed Toby's cheek with his large hand. "You be a gute boy for your mamm. And no more falling."

Toby screamed as Tyler ambled away from them, but Tyler didn't look back. Beth wanted to scream too. Her head throbbed with questions even as her chest ached with the panicked feeling that she'd lost him for good. She kept her eyes glued to Tyler until he disappeared out the far door. The pain slapped her in the chest. What could she do?

"Mommy," Toby moaned as he watched Tyler go.

With Toby in her arms, Beth squeezed behind one of the booths. She'd rather not let the entire population of Bonduel see her cry. She put Toby down. He sat on the floor eating his sucker while Beth wiped her nose and cleared the tears from her eyes.

Please, Heavenly Father, please show me the way.

She saw a foot and recognized that someone was squeezing his way behind the booths just as she had done. Her heart jumped to attention at the thought that it might be Tyler, coming back in answer to her prayer. He'd done it before. Instead, Isaac Hostetler appeared, smiling and acting as if his presence were the most normal thing in the world.

Dread crawled up her back. Isaac certainly was not the answer to her anxious prayer. She immediately scooped Toby into her arms and turned her body to hold Toby as far from her brother-in-law as possible.

Isaac lost his smile. "I hoped I'd find you here. You always liked the bazaar. I didn't mean to startle you."

Beth looked at him in puzzlement. Isaac had none of the arrogant swagger that usually followed him like a foul odor.

He held out his hands and studied her face. "Beth, I'm really sorry for hitting that boy. I got upset and was afraid I'd lost you. I didn't think straight. It would make me sick if you hated me because of that one mistake."

Beth knit her brows together. Astonishingly, he seemed sincere. Still, she couldn't relax. He certainly hadn't come all this way to apologize for hurting Tyler.

"Is he your boyfriend?" Isaac's stance looked casual, but there was a certain intensity to his eyes.

Beth pictured Tyler's expression right before he had turned away from her. "Nae, he is not my boyfriend," she said reluctantly. Tyler might not even consider her a friend anymore.

Isaac grinned a bit too wide. "Nobody wants to marry a widow with a baby. They're a nuisance."

Beth clutched Toby closer. Isaac got a look at his face. "What happened to him?"

"He fell."

"Looks like it hurt."

Beth stroked Toby's cheek as if to comfort him, when she was really the one who needed reassurance. "What do you want, Isaac?"

"Mamm's cancer has come back."

An invisible hand grabbed at her throat. "Oh."

"It would mean everything to her if you could spend Christmas with us one last time. For her sake. You and Toby are all she has left of Amos."

Beth's mind raced. Was this one of Isaac's tricks to get her out of Bonduel? Did he think if he could lure her back to Indiana, she'd never leave? She pictured that oppressive little house with low ceilings and walls that converged to suffocate her. She imagined Treva lying helpless in her bed, with no one to care for her unless Beth showed some compassion. Beth found it impossible to breathe as she anticipated how Treva's cancer would linger for years and compel Beth to give up her own life to care for the mother of her dead husband.

"Mammi and Dawdi are planning on me for Christmas."

To her relief, Isaac did not lash out as he usually did. "*Cum*, Beth. Can't you find it in your heart to have pity on my mamm? She loves you like a daughter. You could bring so much happiness to the last days of her life."

Beth hesitated. How much would it cost her to show Treva a little kindness? She thought of Tyler, who never had a selfish impulse in his life. What would he do? But if she left, would she come back, or would Treva and Amos find a way to hold her there forever?

"A driver is ready to take us home," Isaac said. "He will be at Huckleberry Hill at nine o'clock tomorrow morning."

Unable to move a muscle, Beth felt as if she stood at a crossroads and that her choice at this moment would determine the course of the rest of her life. She had pled with God to help her learn to trust Him again. This was a test of that fragile trust.

She closed her eyes. *Heavenly Father, what would you have me do?*

Swallowing hard, she formed the next words in her mind. *I will do anything you want me to do. I want you to change my heart.*

Almost instantly, she knew what she must do as her heart seemed to radiate its own heat. Isaac had been the answer to her prayers after all. Fear pawed at her like a desperate wild animal, but she squared her shoulders, determined to obey the message she had received.

Isaac stared at her expectantly.

She nodded. "I will come."

Chapter Twenty-One

Isaac offered to carry Toby into the dawdi house. He had fallen asleep as they'd passed through Walkerton, and Beth didn't have the heart to wake him. His schedule would be completely messed up, but the poor little boy hadn't slept a wink the whole day. Unlike most babies, Toby seldom slept in the car. He'd fussed all day, and Beth had worked very hard to keep him happy while they traveled. She fed him crackers and cheese and read him books. Three hours into the trip, the driver had stopped at a convenience store, and they had bought Toby a slushy. Drinking through a straw had kept him happy for almost twenty minutes.

In spite of Toby's agitation, Isaac remained calm throughout the entire six-hour car trip. Beth tried not to let her surprise show on her face. She'd never seen Isaac so eager to please and so slow to anger. She knew what he wanted from her, but in the past he hadn't had the good sense to realize that he could catch more flies with honey than with vinegar.

She didn't expect his good behavior to endure for long, but she would enjoy it while it lasted.

Beth opened the door to the dawdi house, and Isaac carried Toby up the stairs to the nursery, where his crib sat in the same place by the window. Isaac laid him in the crib, and Beth tucked a thick blanket around his chin.

"I'll go fire up the stove," Isaac whispered. He tiptoed down the stairs.

Feeling like a stranger in an unfamiliar place, Beth took her bag to her old room and laid it on the bed. She opened the nightstand drawer and found the matches where she'd always kept them. Even though it was only four in the afternoon, she lit the lantern on the nightstand and the other one sitting on the bureau drawer. On this overcast day, she needed some bright light to help cheer her up.

Wrapping her arms around her waist, she sat on the bed that used to be hers and looked around the room. Nothing had been moved since she had left, as if they'd been expecting her return.

She shivered. Even though Mammi had tried to talk her out of coming, Beth still felt right about being here. God wanted her here for a reason. She only hoped she would be strong enough to do whatever He required of her. This whole trust-in-the-Lord thing had never been easy for her. Today, He seemed to be making it extra difficult in order to test her resolve.

Isaac trudged up the stairs and came into her room. "Do you like it?"

Beth wasn't sure what to say. The room looked exactly the same.

"I painted the walls blue," he said, grinning with satisfaction. "Blue is your favorite color. I wanted you to be happy to be back."

Beth hadn't even noticed the walls—the only thing that had changed in her absence. "Denki. They look very nice."

"I left the quilt on the bed. The one you made. It looks real pretty next to the blue walls."

"Jah."

Isaac stared at her while shifting his weight from one foot to the other. After a few minutes of awkward silence, he said, "You probably want to unpack and such. I'll go and tell Mamm you're home. When you're ready, walk right into the house. Don't even knock or nothing."

Beth took a deep breath and nodded. As much as she disliked Isaac, she dreaded a reunion with Treva even more. Treva had the uncanny power to make Beth feel about three inches tall. She wondered if the driver was still here. Could she get him to take her back to Wisconsin?

Trust in the Lord with all thine heart and lean not unto thine own understanding.

A lump formed in her throat. Tyler had rejected her. Maybe God had brought her here to care for her mother-in-law, like Ruth had with Naomi, to truly give her life over to the service of another person. Was that the kind of sacrifice He required?

She didn't know if she was strong enough or humble enough to do it.

A muffled sob escaped her lips as she thought of what she had already lost. How could she have been so foolish? With her tiresome self-pity, she had pushed Tyler away every time he'd tried to get close. She'd scolded him, lectured him, yelled at him. Her stomach seized in pain. She had dealt him a harsh and undeserved blow when she'd accused him of being like Amos. It was a wonder he had stuck with her as long as he had.

He must have really loved her.

That thought gave her no comfort today. It only succeeded in magnifying her sense of loss and the oppressive feeling of despair. Tyler would have been the best husband a girl could ask for, and she had been too blind to see it.

She deserved every unkind word Treva would hurl at her. Her heart sank to her toes. Deserved or not, she dreaded facing her mother-in-law. As despondent as she felt about Tyler, one word from Treva might reduce her to tears.

Dear Lord, I don't know for what purpose, but you've asked me to come. Will you help me withstand Treva's sharp tongue?

And bless Tyler to find happiness in spite of what I've done to him.

Thy will be done. Amen.

She looked in on Toby before descending the stairs and crossing the five feet of porch between the dawdi house and the main house. Pausing at the door, she said another prayer and squared her shoulders. With the perspective of four months' absence and Tyler's encouragement, she resolved to let Treva's criticisms slide off her like water off a duck's back. How long her resolve would last was another question, but she determined to think of Tyler and do her best.

A scripture leaped into her mind.

For God has not given us the spirit of fear, but of power and of love, and of a sound mind.

She stood taller still. Heavenly Father did not want her to be a victim. He had given her power to change her circumstances, a brain to think it through, and His love to accomplish it. She never stood alone because God would never leave her.

She opened the door and the stale, sharp smell of aging accosted her nose. If she must stay here more than a day or two, she'd need to wipe down the rooms top to bottom.

With her legs elevated, Treva sat in the lumpy, ample recliner she seldom abandoned. Like a queen on her throne, she could direct all the household functions from that one place. She wore a kapp, but her disheveled salt-and-pepper hair escaped from underneath it as if she hadn't tended to it for days. "Beth," she said, frowning and motioning broadly with her arm. "Come in and shut the door. Do you want me to catch my death of cold? It's bad enough I've got this cursed C disease. Do you want to kill me with a virus yet?"

Treva never gave voice to her cancer. She had

this notion that if she called it "the C disease," it didn't have the power to hurt her.

Isaac sat on the threadbare sofa, his arm draped casually over the back. He smiled and winked at her, as if he were sure of his success in finally convincing her to be his wife. Beth bit her bottom lip and looked away. He'd persuaded her to come this far, hadn't he?

She quickly crossed the threshold and closed the door behind her. Aside from the smell, the room was much as it always had been. The walls stood bare with no hint of Christmas anywhere except for a small, red candle glowing on the kitchen counter. The kitchen sat off to Beth's left. Unlike in Mammi and Dawdi's house, Treva's kitchen had barely enough room for two people to work at the same time. The long counter made the small space seem like an animal pen.

With great effort, Beth kept the disgust from showing on her face. The floor of cream-colored linoleum squares looked unrecognizably filthy. Had it been mopped since Beth left four months ago? A mound of unwashed dishes sat in the sink as water from the leaky faucet dripped rhythmically onto one of Treva's dirty dinner plates. Beth stiffened. How long had they been waiting for her to come back and take over the chores?

She took a deep breath, but not too deep—the smell would have made her gag—and told herself everything would be okay. God was tutoring her, teaching her through experience to trust Him.

But why did His lessons have to be so hard?

For God has not given us the spirit of fear, but of power and of love, and of a sound mind.

Treva waved her arm again. "Come over and let me take a look at you."

Pushing back her reluctance, Beth marched to Treva's chair and let her mother-in-law take stock of her.

"Doesn't she look pretty, Mamm?" Isaac asked.

"Beth was always real pretty."

Beth stared at Treva with wide eyes. Had she ever said a nice thing about Beth before?

Treva squinted, as if getting a better look. "Still too skinny, but your cheeks have a nice glow to them. Peaches-and-cream complexion, my dat used to call it."

"Denki," Beth murmured before she remembered her resolve to be brave. She sat on the folding chair next to the recliner and took Treva's hand.

Treva reacted as if she'd eaten a whole lemon with a mug of vinegar, but she didn't pull away.

"Isaac tells me the cancer has come back. What did the doctor say?" Beth asked, making her voice clear and confident, as if she were a person who could competently take charge of any situation.

Treva waved her hand in the air as if she were swatting a fly. "Oh, that doctor wants me to start chemo and then maybe surgery. I can't hardly understand what he's talking about. He looks like he's fifteen years old." Treva's voice shook like that of a much older woman, and for the first time ever, Beth recognized the fear hiding behind her prickly exterior.

"Everything is going to be okay, Lord willing."

Treva ripped her hand from Beth's grasp. "What do you know about it? You didn't even care to stay and look out for me, the mother of your dead husband. As if losing Amos wasn't bad enough, you couldn't wait to get away from your dying mother-in-law. You were always selfish like that. If I'd gotten more rest, it wouldn't have come back."

Her words found their mark, and Beth reeled as if she'd been smacked in the mouth. She told herself not to pay heed to Treva's words, not to let the accusations have power over her, but guilt squeezed all the breath out of her.

Ruth stayed with Naomi. Shouldn't I love my mother-in-law more than I love myself?

Beth paused long enough to let the air seep back into her lungs. *Heavenly Father, what would You have me do?*

That timid little girl crept back into her voice. "When do you start chemo?"

"He said to wait until after the New Year, but it doesn't matter. My Christmas is ruined anyway." She eyed Beth with disdain. "I had to do all the canning myself. You think that didn't make things worse?"

Beth asked a question she already knew the answer to. "What about Susannah and Martha? And Priscilla? Surely they offered to help with the canning."

Susannah, Martha, and Priscilla were Treva's daughters, all married with families of their own. They seldom spared time for their mother. Isaac and Amos had always been her favorites.

Treva scowled. "They're like strangers. I ain't seen

Priscilla for three weeks. Martha comes by to deliver eggs, and that's it. They're cut out of the same cloth as you. You never wrote once while you were away. Not once."

The guilt tugged at Beth again, but she tried to let it pass like water through a colander. What was done was done. She studied the lines on Treva's tortured face. Beth had no power to change the past. A determination grew inside her that she would not let the past hold her hostage or decide her future.

"Now that you're here, I'll stay off my feet. The doctor says I need my rest. Though I don't know how I'll get much rest with you in the kitchen. I've got to watch everything you do, or we'll end up eating charred potatoes and burned bread for the rest of our lives."

For the rest of our lives.

That sounded like such a long time.

Could Beth endure it? More importantly, could she ask Toby to endure it?

Treva clapped her hands together and came as close to a smile as she ever did. "Now, Isaac, go and wake my grandson. He's the only thing I have left of Amos, and Beth hasn't let me see him for four months."

"He should sleep a little longer," Beth said, "or he'll be ornery the rest of the night."

"It'll mess up his whole schedule if you let him sleep. You do have him on a schedule, don't you?" Treva shook her finger in Beth's direction. "I won't let you pamper my grandson like your mamm pampered you. If she'd been stricter, you would have learned how to cook and keep house, and the rest of us wouldn't have to suffer for it. Isaac, go get Toby and I'll play with him while Beth fixes dinner."

Beth clenched her teeth until she felt like one of them might crack. She was willing to endure the abuse heaped upon her, but she would not allow Treva to think she had a right to raise her son, or even think she had a right to an opinion about how he was to be raised. Treva had raised Amos. Beth refused to let Toby turn out like his father.

"He's dead tired," she forced out, trying not to sound angry. "I'm going to let him sleep until five."

Treva narrowed her eyes but did not argue. The resolve in Beth's voice must have silenced her opposition.

"He was a real pain on the drive," Isaac said. "He whined the whole way."

Treva glanced at Beth with a smug twist to her lips. "So. You've spoiled him rotten. My children got the switch for whining."

Surely Beth's teeth would crack any minute now. She stared at Treva and bit her tongue on the words pushing against her throat. Neither Treva nor Isaac would be allowed to use the switch on her son. Ever.

"A real pain," Isaac repeated. "I wished I'd had earplugs."

"We didn't have to come," Beth said quietly.

Isaac clamped his mouth shut.

Beth sighed in resignation and stood. If Toby was to eat dinner, she would have to be the one to fix it. Treva wouldn't expect anything else. And despite how Treva protested, Beth was an adequate cook.

She'd never be as good as Moses's wife, Lia, but she usually had more success than Mammi did. Most of what she made was edible. Her son would never go hungry, and that was all she cared about.

First she'd have to make the kitchen fit to eat in. She pushed up her sleeves and cleared the dishes from the sink.

"Don't use the yellow soap for the dishes," Treva said from the comfort of her recliner.

Beth nodded as if Treva had given her a piece of very helpful advice, even though Treva had given her the same instructions every day after Amos died. She also knew what came next. *And don't use too much of the green dish soap.*

"And you don't need to use a lot of the green soap. It's concentrated."

Beth had to smile, but her back was turned so Treva couldn't wonder about it. Poor Treva. The minute details of life were all she had left to hold on to. Beth tried to have pity on her mother-in-law. Her lonely life was much of her own making. Her daughters seldom visited her because she was petulant and critical when they came. Isaac rarely helped around the house because he'd been indulged as a child. Treva had no friends because she was so wrapped up in her own misfortunes.

The dishes were soon taken care of with the help of a constant stream of instructions from Treva. Isaac lounged on the sofa reading *The Budget* as if the floors weren't in need of a good scrubbing or the furniture didn't require a thorough dusting. Was it any use to give him a little training?

"Isaac, will you dry the dishes for me," she said, adding a little sweetness to the tone of her voice.

He flipped the paper down so he could see her over the top of it and considered her request.

"Jethro didn't do one dish in his whole life," Treva said, with indignant pride. Jethro, Treva's husband, had died when Amos and Isaac were sixteen.

"My dawdi does dishes all the time," Beth said. "He says a gute husband should be willing to help his wife around the house."

This didn't seem to impress Isaac. His frown deepened.

"We've got to redd up this kitchen before I fix dinner. You're hungry, aren't you?"

Isaac slowly set his paper aside. "All right then." He stood with a groan. "Give me a towel."

Once the dishes were put away, Isaac ambled back to his sofa and plopped himself down as if he'd done something really hard. Beth wiped the cupboards and set some water to boil. Then she peeled potatoes and chopped onions and carrots. Corn chowder was quick and easy, and Treva had everything in her cupboards that Beth needed for the recipe. While the potatoes boiled, Beth whipped up a batch of cornbread. The floors would have to wait until later. The family needed to be fed.

Treva made sure Beth did not ignore her. "What are you doing in there?"

"Are you using red potatoes? Don't be careless and let them sit without stirring or they'll burn."

"That's the wrong spoon. You'll scratch my pan."

"I could use a glass of water. No ice. You always forget I don't like ice."

"I want one with ice," Isaac said.

Beth brought Treva her water, but Isaac would have to go thirsty. He had two good legs. Beth would insist that he use them.

At three minutes after five, Beth pulled the cornbread out of the oven. "Isaac, I am going to wake Toby. Please set the table."

"I'll fetch Toby," Isaac said. That probably sounded like the easier job.

Beth raised an eyebrow. "And change his diaper?"

Isaac scowled as if Beth had tricked him into something. "I'll set." His expression would have made her laugh if there hadn't been menacing anger behind it.

Toby was understandably grumpy and disoriented when she woke him. He fussed and grunted his displeasure as she carried him into the main house.

Treva's eyes grew wide. "What happened to his face?"

The warmth traveled up Beth's neck. If Treva needed a shred of evidence that she was a bad mother, this was it. "He fell," she said without offering any other explanation.

Treva frowned. "You're careless. I always told Amos you're careless. My poor grandbaby," she cooed, spreading her arms to hold him.

Beth reluctantly set Toby on his mammi's lap. He wouldn't be happy about it, but Treva couldn't have been more pleased. "This could be twenty-two years ago, he looks that much like his dat."

As Beth expected, Toby struggled in Treva's arms as she tried to kiss him and force him to hold still. "Sit and let Mammi look at you," Treva insisted, but the more she tightened her grip around his waist, the more violently Toby tried to break free.

Beth finally snatched Toby from her and bounced him up and down while patting his back. He wouldn't let Beth console him either as he went right on fussing in her arms. She set him on the floor, and he sank to his hands and knees, then rolled over onto his back and cried as if his heart would break. It had been a very long day.

With a sneer on her lips, Treva stared at him as the lines of her face deepened into gullies. "What have you done to my grandson? You've ruined him." She glared at Toby. "Stop it, you little brat."

Beth felt the mother bear come alive, and her insides roiled around like waves on a stormy lake. Taking a deep breath, she pushed the anger back. What else would she have expected from Treva?

Let it pass.

Tyler had said she was a gute mother. The memory of him cradling Toby in his arms calmed her. Tyler would never belittle her son. Oh, how she longed to see him again!

"It's okay, Treva. Sometimes, he just has to cry it out." Sitting on the floor next to her inconsolable son, she began gently stroking his back and whispering words of comfort. "It's okay, Toby. Hush. Mamma is here. Hush now."

The tantrum slowly wound itself down. Toby didn't have the energy to put up a ferocious fight. Whimpering, he stood and wrapped his arms around Beth's neck. She hugged him and kissed him on the cheek. "It's okay, Toby." She retrieved a tissue from her apron pocket and wiped his face.

"Nose," Toby said, sniffling as she wiped it again for good measure.

Isaac and Treva stared at her as if she were doing it all wrong. She didn't care as long as they didn't interfere. When she finished, she picked up her son and cheerfully gazed at her in-laws. "Shall we eat?"

With Toby propped on her hip, she brought each dish to the table one by one. Isaac sat down and didn't budge from his spot, even if it meant a delay in dinner, because Beth had to set everything on the table herself.

They had no high chair or booster seat, so Beth pulled a large saucepan from the cupboard and turned it upside for Toby to sit on.

"Would you like to eat over there?" Beth asked Treva.

Treva made quite a show of getting to her feet. "No, I'll sit at the table. I want to be close to my grandson."

Once Treva sat down, they bowed their heads for silent prayer. Even Toby knew how to do that.

Beth served Toby his chowder last so she could blow on it before he ate it. He liked to try to feed himself, so Beth gave him a fork to skewer his potatoes. Food only ended up on the ground when he ate with a spoon. Between bites of potato, she fed him the broth with a spoon.

Treva drenched her cornbread in honey. "You didn't add enough baking soda," she said between hearty bites. Beth didn't feel too bad. Treva seemed to be enjoying it fine.

Toby became the favorite grandchild once again. Treva watched him manage to stab a potato with his fork and put it in his mouth. "Oh, look how smart you are," she said, in baby talk that sounded more like gibberish than any recognizable language. "He is Amos's boy for sure. Both Amos and Isaac had that curly hair. And I think he's got a dimple right where Amos's dimple was. Amos was such a handsome man."

Pretty is as pretty does, Beth thought.

Real sorrow flashed in Treva's face. "I miss that boy," she said. She cupped her hand to Isaac's cheek. "At least I got you with me still."

"Will you have more corn chowder, Treva?"

Treva held out her bowl and let Beth give her another ladleful. "It's not bad even if it's too salty."

Beth grabbed Toby's arm before he could throw a potato at Isaac. He must have been finished eating.

Treva pointed her spoon at Toby. "Oh, he's a Hostetler, all right, no argument about it. No one could guess who his mother is if they didn't know."

Of all the things Treva could have said, this might have stung the most. Toby was as much a Beachy as he was a Hostetler. That first day at Huckleberry Hill, Tyler had said that Toby had Beth's eyes.

"When he gets a little older, I'll take him hunting," Isaac said.

Beth rebelled against that notion. She didn't

want Isaac taking her son anywhere, as if he had a right to. As if he wanted to be a substitute father. Her mouth tasted like chalk dust. Unless that was God's plan. She took a gulp of water. Would she ever be able to stomach such an idea?

After supper, Beth did the dishes, making sure not to use the yellow soap, while Toby opened every cupboard he could reach to see what was inside.

Treva wasn't as interested in Beth's activities as before dinner. She sat upright in her recliner as she and Isaac leaned their heads together and spoke to each other in hushed tones. Eagerness animated their features, as if whatever they discussed caused them great excitement.

As Beth tidied the kitchen, their conversation became an oppressive weight on her shoulders. No doubt, they were planning her future, but she wasn't as sure of her future as they seemed to be. Right now, she couldn't bear to think beyond getting Toby to bed and scrubbing the kitchen floor. She trusted God to handle the details.

Treva leaned back in her chair so that she was nearly horizontal. Isaac laid an afghan over her legs, and she thanked him by patting him on the arm as if she lacked the strength to speak. "Beth," she called feebly, "come here."

Beth wasn't fooled. Treva often used the dramatics of illness to her advantage. To be sure, she hadn't suddenly grown weak from criticizing Beth all afternoon.

Beth picked up Toby and unenthusiastically trudged to Treva's chair. Isaac stood on the opposite side of the chair and faced Beth as if they were standing before a bishop about to take vows.

"Put Toby down," Treva said.

Though Beth wouldn't have obeyed merely to please Treva, she knew it would be better to get this over with without Toby wiggling in her arms. She placed Toby on the sofa and pulled three books from his *keavli*, or diaper bag. They wouldn't occupy him for long, but they would have to do.

Treva took Isaac's hand. "Give me your hand, Beth."

Beth reached out her hand as if Treva might bite it off. Treva took her hand and placed it into Isaac's. Isaac smiled bashfully and held on tight. Beth had never seen that particular expression on Isaac's face before. It was definitely an act.

Beth wanted to snatch her hand away as if she'd touched a snake. But she willed her skin to quit crawling and decided to let Treva have her moment. Resistance would only aggravate both Treva and Isaac.

"This is my second Christmas without my dear Amos," Treva said, her voice catching at the mention of her son. She wrapped her fingers around the hands clasped in front of her. "This is my balm of Gilead, seeing you two together like this. Amos would not have begrudged your relationship. He would have wanted Isaac to carry on in his place."

Beth pressed her lips together to keep a sharp denial from escaping her throat. *Let Treva have her say.*

Isaac increased his pressure on her hand. She winced. Was he trying to make her cry *uncle*?

He frowned at Beth as if daring her to argue. "Amos would have wanted us to be together. He wouldn't have wanted Toby to grow up without a *fater*."

Tears trickled down Treva's cheeks. Unlike Isaac's insincerity, Treva's pain was real. Beth couldn't imagine what it must have felt like to lose a son. "Beth, you cannot be so heartless as to refuse my dying wish. Even you must agree that I deserve a little happiness before I pass from this life."

Instead of arguing, as she would have done with Tyler, or letting the guilt paralyze her, as she had always done with Treva and Amos, Beth said a silent prayer.

What would You have me do?

Isaac squeezed still harder. "I deserve a little happiness too," he said.

Do I deserve a little happiness as well?

Beth felt a spark inside her as if someone had lit a match.

Studying the lines of Treva's face, Beth thought of her own son and how she loved him, and she felt as if she were seeing Treva for the first time. She recognized an old woman, unloved and frightened, grasping at anything she thought might possibly be within her reach.

A flicker of sympathy glowed in Beth's heart until it flamed into an overpowering feeling of love. Afraid of showing weakness, Treva had found it impossible to give and receive love from her family. She had pushed them away from her, until her own actions had molded her lonely life. After losing her husband, she had let the grief rule her until she couldn't see God's love through the bitterness festering in her heart.

Most importantly, Beth could finally see that through it all, God had not abandoned Treva. She was his daughter. He loved her.

Beth felt as if she glowed with the fervent heat of understanding. God loved her as much as He loved Treva, and she knew without a doubt that He wanted her to be happy.

She saw Tyler in her mind's eye. If she could talk him into marrying her, he would make her laugh everyday, and she would make him smile. She would get irritated and argue with him, and he would shrug his shoulders and apologize but never change his ways. He would always insist on protecting her, and she would give in and let him. He would cook bacon pancakes, and she would sew shirts and trousers. And God would smile upon them and open the windows of Heaven and pour out blessings.

Just as she knew in her very bones that she loved Tyler, she knew that God wanted her to be deliriously, overwhelmingly happy. Wasn't that what every parent wanted for his child? But must she ensure her happiness at the expense of Treva's? Was only one of them allowed to be happy at a time?

With sudden insight, Beth knew what to do. Her spirit soared to the ceiling, and she laughed out loud at the pure joy of God's tender mercies.

Isaac eyed her suspiciously. "What's so funny?"

"I'm so happy." The look on Isaac's face could

have curdled cottage cheese. Trying to subdue her
mirth for Isaac's sake, she pried her hand from his
and laid an affectionate kiss on Treva's forehead.
She'd never done that before. The corners of
Treva's mouth drooped glumly while the irritation
on Isaac's face grew.

"I love you, Mamm Hostetler," she said and meant
it. "I don't want you to worry. All things work together for good to those who love God. All things."
Feeling as if she'd shrugged a heavy load off her
shoulders, she said, "And I really believe that now."

Mammi had been right. She had become a
better person, a stronger person, because of Amos.
Her sorrows had forced her to seek God. She lifted
Toby from the sofa. "I must put Toby to bed now."

She was halfway out the door before Isaac recovered from his surprise enough to speak. "Beth,
what do you say? About you and me?"

She tried to let him down easy, even though he
had never wanted to accept her refusal, subtle or
blunt. "You must not expect it, Isaac."

He clenched his teeth as the anger that came
naturally to him flared in his face. "You're so ungrateful, Beth. After all we've done for you, and
you're still thinking of what you can get out of us.
We let you stay in the dawdi house without paying
rent. I painted your walls blue."

Treva reached out and squeezed Isaac's wrist.
"Hold your tongue, Isaac. She said everything
would work out for us."

Isaac's rage simmered to irritation as he pursed

his lips and knitted his brows together. "Think about it, Beth. Just promise me you'll think about it."

Beth gave him a tired, indulgent smile. Too exhausted to argue with him tonight, she said, "I will give you an answer next week."

And then she'd go home for good.

Chapter Twenty-Two

Beth lit the red pillar candle on the table and adjusted the greenery centerpiece. On Saturday, the day after she and Toby had arrived in Nappanee, she had bundled Toby in his snowsuit and taken him with her to cut pine boughs and other greenery for the house. She had dragged him on the sled behind her, and he had pointed out every bird and squirrel he saw. Four-footed animals were "dogs" or "dahs," as Toby said it, and he had started referring to birds as "up-up." She had cut enough pine boughs to decorate the dawdi house as well as the main house.

Beth's mamm draped pine branches over the doorframes and around the banisters every Christmas. The smells of pine and cinnamon always reminded Beth of Christmastime spent with her family, making cookies, exchanging gifts, and attending school Christmas programs.

Treva's house had needed a little sprucing up, and when Beth hung her boughs on Saturday afternoon, she'd hoped the smell of fresh pine would invoke good memories for Treva and inspire thoughts of the babe in a manger who had come to save His people. Perhaps the festive touches would help Treva feel more kindly towards the whole world. If there was anything the Hostetler house needed, it was some Christmas cheer.

Now, Beth glanced at the bird clock in her little kitchen in the dawdi house. She had timed Toby's nap so that he would be asleep when Amos's sisters came. They should be here any minute. Of course, Martha never showed up on time for anything, and all three of the sisters had acted a little suspicious when Beth had invited them to a Monday afternoon Christmas tea.

She pulled the miniature muffins out of the oven and tapped the top of one with her finger. They seemed done. She turned the tin upside-down, and the muffins tumbled into a wicker basket lined with a red napkin.

Today, everything had to be perfect. She did not want to give Amos's sisters an opportunity to find fault with anything. She hoped for their cooperation, not their resistance. Beth lined the teacups on the counter next to the stove and placed an herbal tea bag in each one. She'd chosen peppermint. It was Christmassy and had the added benefit of clearing out the lungs if anyone had a cold.

It had been a trick to convince Isaac to take her to the store this morning, but he was still on his best behavior and more easily persuaded than usual. She was able to buy everything she needed with the sewing money she'd brought with her. Her purchases had eaten up all her Christmas budget, but that didn't matter. The sisters had to be convinced of her resolve, and the Christmas tea seemed a wonderful-gute way to get their attention.

Beth clasped her hands together and surveyed the table. A small bowl of raspberry jam and a plate of store-bought cranberry scones sat on one side of the candle and a plate of colorful fruit sat on the other. A charming pat of butter waited on each plate, and she had accented the white stoneware with red and green plaid napkins.

She remembered the day Tyler had proposed to her. He'd worked so hard with those carefully folded napkins and the sunflower in a vase. It was a nice gesture, even if she'd practically snarled at him like a dog protecting its territory. She smiled at the memory. Tyler had been thrown completely off-kilter. She liked that she had the power to do that to him.

Even though she'd been expecting it, Beth jumped when she heard the knock. She hurried to the door and found Susannah and Priscilla standing on her porch.

The eldest Hostetler sibling, Susannah, was thirty-three years old and had four children. She often wore a sensible frown that had given rise to premature wrinkles around her mouth. Susannah was tall and thin but sturdy all the same, like a woman who worked hard all day but didn't have much time to spare in eating. Her dark auburn hair accented the myriad freckles that covered her face.

Priscilla, the sister just older than Amos and Isaac, stood almost six inches shorter than Susannah. Over the four years Beth had known her, Priscilla smiled less and less often. She'd given birth to a daughter seven years ago and hadn't been able to conceive again. Beth studied Priscilla's face. Bitterness had taken root there like a weed. She took pity on her sister-in-law because she understood all too well how bitterness could choke faith.

Priscilla and Susannah regarded Beth suspiciously, as if she were going to pounce on them the minute they entered her kitchen. "Cum reu," Beth said. "I'm very glad you could make it."

Amos's sisters practically tiptoed into the room.

"Oh, the table looks very nice," Susannah said. She'd always been kind, even though she kept herself fairly detached from the family.

"Jah," Priscilla said, remembering her manners. "Like a Christmas card."

The teakettle whistled, and Beth hurried to the stove. "Please sit down. I'll bring the tea over."

The two sisters looked at the chairs as if deciding where to sit was the most taxing thing they'd done all day. Oh dear, softening them up would be more difficult than Beth had imagined.

They heard a tap on the door, and Martha let herself in before Beth even had a chance to set down the teakettle.

Beth thought that Martha might have been beautiful once. Her strawberry-blond hair and shocking blue eyes combined with her silky skin for a look that should have turned the boys' heads. But her eyes often flashed with scorn, and she pursed her lips as if she always had a bad taste in her mouth. She had an air about her that made Beth feel she was constantly being judged and found wanting.

Beth's heart did a little flip, and she squared her shoulders. She resolved not to let Martha intimidate her today.

I can do all things through Christ which strengtheneth me.

"Martha, it's so gute to see you." She placed the teacups on the table. "Please, everybody, come and sit."

"This better not take too long," Martha said, sliding into the chair opposite Beth. "Danny was none too happy about staying with the kinner while I went off to tea."

"Denki for coming," Beth said. "I know how busy everyone is this time of year."

They said a silent prayer. Beth forgot to ask a blessing on her food. She had other, more pressing needs.

After praying, the three sisters lifted their heads and stared at Beth. She picked up the basket. "Would everyone like a muffin?"

Martha examined her knife and then polished it against her sleeve. "Are they good? You never did know how to cook well. Amos used to sneak to my house whenever we had fried chicken. He said he was losing weight being married to you."

Beth bit her lip and let the pain subside. She tried not to give Amos's memory the power to hurt her. She wanted to be stronger than that—at least someday.

Susannah cleared her throat and gave Martha a pointedly irritated look. Then she smiled at Beth. "This is so nice, Beth."

Priscilla snickered. "Nice without Mamm."

Susannah did her best to make up for both of her sisters' behavior. "We're so glad you're back, Beth. We've missed you."

"You ran off so fast, we didn't even have a chance to say good-bye," Priscilla added.

Martha smirked. "All those old men chased her away. They sure came courting once Amos died."

Priscilla spread jam on her muffin. "You should have married Isaac. Then you wouldn't have needed to run off. We feared you'd gone for good, but Isaac assured me you'd come back once you heard about Mamm's cancer."

"Jah," said Susannah. "You always took such gute care of Mamm, even though she didn't have a nice thing to say to you. You have a tender heart to agree to come back and care for her again."

Priscilla nodded, a little too eagerly. "We appreciate that you would put up with her."

"You're an answer to our prayers," Susannah said. She took a sip of her tea. "Peppermint. I love peppermint."

Beth steeled herself against their reaction to what she would say next. "You prayed that I would come back so that none of you would have to take care of her."

All three sisters froze and stared at Beth as if she had eaten her napkin.

She stared right back. "Isn't that the truth?"

Susannah pursed her lips and gazed at her plate. Martha propped her chin in her hand and glared in Beth's direction.

Seeing that her sisters weren't inclined to say anything, Priscilla defended herself. "I can't care for Mamm. I have my own family, and Perry's sewing machine business is just getting off the ground. I help him keep his books."

Beth shouldn't have put them on the defensive. That wasn't how she wanted to win their cooperation. She smiled. "That is wonderful about Perry's business. I love sewing machines. I too have a family to care for and a business to run."

Martha shook her finger as if scolding a child. "You're making that up. You don't have any way to support yourself. You care for Mamm, and she pays for a roof over your head and food on your table."

"You should marry Isaac," Susannah said, sincerely trying to be helpful. "It's plain he loves you. Then you wouldn't feel like you're a burden on anyone."

Priscilla raised her eyebrows. "That's a gute idea. You can't just live here for free."

Beth sighed in exasperation. "I don't want to live here for free. I don't want to live here at all. I want to go back to Wisconsin, where people love me."

Another prolonged silence.

"We love you," Susannah murmured, not all that convincingly.

Beth didn't want them to feel defensive or guilty. "It's all right. I'm not upset about it anymore. We don't really know each other. After I married Amos, the three of you didn't come around very often."

"Because Amos and Isaac are Mamm's favorites. She doesn't want to see us," said Martha. "And we don't want to see her. She's grumpy and bitter, and we can't stand her." Beth wondered if Martha ever looked in the mirror.

"I know how she is," Beth said. "I took care of her for a whole year."

Susannah dunked her tea bag up and down in her water. "We thought you didn't mind."

Beth laid a hand over Susannah's forearm. "You never asked."

"But . . . but you were married to Amos," Priscilla protested, as if this were the most convincing argument of all.

Martha wasn't above using guilt as a weapon. "Amos was Mamm's favorite. It's your Christian duty to take care of her now that Amos is gone."

Beth met Martha's eyes with a determined gaze. "Why isn't it yours?"

The tea turned cold and the muffins sat uneaten. At this point, none of the sisters would look Beth in the eye.

Beth broke the silence. "She is your mother. The woman who gave you life."

"She gave Amos life too," Priscilla said weakly.

Beth's throat constricted when she thought of Tyler. "There is a boy in Wisconsin," she whispered. Her relationship with Tyler felt too precious to share with her sisters-in-law, but she wanted them to know. "I love him. He is everything that Amos wasn't. Do you understand how unhappy I was here before and after Amos died?"

Susannah finally quit studying her plate and looked Beth in the eye. "Amos was a hard man." She cleared her throat. "I'm sorry for how he treated you. And for how Mamm treated you."

The tears sneaked up on Beth. "I want to be happy again, and I believe that God wants me to be happy. Will you begrudge me that?"

The lines deepened around Martha's eyes, but she wasn't scowling anymore. Priscilla looked genuinely worried, as if she were being forced to surrender the best years of her life.

Susannah breathed out a long sigh as if resigned to her fate. "Mamm has made herself so unpleasant, none of us want to take care of her."

Martha crossed her arms over her chest. "She's made her bed. We should make her lie in it."

"She is our *mater*," Susannah said. "The good Lord has commanded us to honor her."

Priscilla's high-pitched voice confirmed her distress. "But I have Rosie to take care of and all the sewing machines."

Beth took Priscilla's hand and squeezed it tightly. "I have been doing a lot of praying about this, and I believe your mamm does not want to be a burden to anyone."

"She likes to complain enough about it."

"Yes, she wants to be a burden," Martha insisted. "When she suffers, she thinks everyone else should suffer with her."

"Do you remember what the good Samaritan did when he found the man beaten alongside the road?" Beth asked. "He bound up his wounds, put him on his own beast, and took him to an inn. But the Samaritan did not stay at the inn. The next day, he went on his way and paid the host at the inn to care for the injured man."

"So, you're saying we should pay someone to care for Mamm?"

"I'm saying that there are many ways to make sure Mamm gets the care she needs, and we don't have to feel guilty because we look at other options." She turned to Priscilla. "You wouldn't want guilt to be the reason your daughter cares for you when you get older, would you?"

"Nae."

"I want to help her," Beth said. "Will you help me?" Priscilla nodded.

"Yes," Susannah said. "Of course."

"I'll help," Martha said. "But not cheerfully."

"We wouldn't have expected that," Susannah said.

Feeling generous, Beth served each of her sisters-in-law a scone. She gave Martha two scones.

"Denki," Beth said. "I have a plan."

Chapter Twenty-Three

Tyler felt like a sardine packed in a can. Felty sat to his left, Aden sat to his right, and Tyler was crammed in the middle of the backseat of the car. Though he had shrunk a little over the years, Felty had always been a tall man. And Aden, at six feet a hundred inches, took up more than his share of space. Tyler wasn't as tall as either of his companions, but his wide shoulders and muscular arms didn't fit so well between them. He groaned inwardly. They were going all the way to Green Bay like this. On the way home, he'd opt to sit in the front with Max Bonham, their driver.

Felty should have been sitting in the front right now. Tyler couldn't begin to guess why he had chosen to squeeze next to Tyler and Aden in the back.

Felty pried his arm from between them and pulled his small wire-bound notebook out of his pocket. "I'm glad you came with me. Annie is baking Christmas goodies and couldn't spare the time, and

I've got to see what I can do about finding the rest of my license plates. I've got Hawaii, Delaware, Nevada, and Rhode Island left to find."

Despite the heaviness in his chest, Tyler felt like laughing. Only Felty would pay the money to hire a driver to take him to Green Bay so he could scout license plates. On December 23.

Tyler thought it unlikely that they'd find Hawaii in the dead of winter in frigid Green Bay, Wisconsin, but they'd definitely see more license plates there than passed through Bonduel all year.

Aden propped his elbow on the small ledge next to the window. "Lily wanted me out of the house. I think she's planning a surprise for Christmas."

"Three pairs of eyes are better than one. Especially since I need glasses to see past the end of my nose." Felty nudged Tyler's squished arm. "To tell the honest truth, Anna asked me to bring you. She thinks looking for license plates will bring you some cheer. You smile like you've got heartburn."

Tyler let his smile droop. He should have known better than to try to fake happiness. Grinning stupidly was anything but natural for him—except when he spent time with Beth. He couldn't help but smile around her.

That was, until a week and a half ago. Now he felt lower than a fat beetle crawling across the floor. Finding Delaware wouldn't improve his mood one bit. Even Hawaii had no power to make him happy. He wanted to marry Beth in the worst way, and she wouldn't have him.

Aden shook his head in resignation. "I'll say it again, Tyler. Go talk to her."

"Every time I say something, she gets mad. I've apologized so many times my throat is raw."

Felty tapped his pencil on his notebook. "You told me stubbornness is her best quality."

Tyler wiggled his arms out from between Felty and Aden and folded them across his chest. "She's holding on to her past with white knuckles. It's not my place to pry her away."

"It's not like you to give up so easy," Aden said.

The weight pressing on his chest grew unbearably heavy. "Easy? I made her bacon-grease pancakes. I bought her a rotary cutter and asked her to marry me. I kissed her twice." The memory rendered him momentarily unable to speak. Those kisses would stay with him forever.

"Only twice?"

"Did you hear that part about asking her to marry me? I've done everything I can."

Aden lifted an eyebrow. "I got arrested, the elders had me shunned, and I stole your fiancée. You didn't give up on me."

He looked away from Aden's intense gaze. "She thinks I'll turn into Amos."

Felty turned from the window long enough to give Tyler a sympathetic glance. "I don't think even Annie has an answer for that."

Aden sneered. "That's insulting." He rubbed the new beard on his chin. "Those three years with Amos damaged her spirit. She came home unable to trust men and unwilling to trust in God. But if anyone can make her believe again, it's you."

Tyler clenched his fists. The thought of Amos's treatment of Beth still angered him as nothing else did. He leaned forward, rested his elbows on his knees, and buried his face in his hands. "It hurts too much. I don't want it anymore."

"It's love, Tyler," Aden said, placing a hand on his shoulder. "Love is a messy jumble of heartbreak and anger and happiness beyond your wildest dreams."

"The pain is going to suffocate me."

"She's worth fighting for."

Of course she was worth it. She had become more important to him than sunshine or rain. Her smile shined brighter than a thousand kerosene lanterns and put off more heat than a forest fire. The sound of her laughter still teased him in his sleep and the feel of her skin lingered on the tips of his fingers even now.

But he could also remember, in vivid detail, the pain that sliced through him when she had accused him of being like Amos, as if the four months they'd known each other didn't matter. As if all the kindness and affection he'd felt for her meant nothing, and nothing he could do would ever convince her of his faithfulness.

He ached at the thought of giving up, and he ached at the thought of trying again.

But as he sat there by Beth's cousin and grandfather, he knew without a doubt he must try again. The thought of losing Beth knocked the wind right out of him. "I'll . . . I'll go talk to her, as soon as we get home."

"That's no use," Felty said. "She's gone to Indiana with Isaac Hostetler."

Tyler thought his tongue might dry up and fall out of his mouth. "What?"

"Last Friday morning. He somehow managed to convince her to go back with him. Annie spent an hour trying to talk her out of it."

"Did she say why?"

"She told Annie it was something she needed to do, and she wouldn't be persuaded otherwise, so Annie sent her with some potholders just in case they would help."

The news punched Tyler in the gut. Only the direst circumstances would convince Beth to return to that pack of wolves. What in the world had compelled her to go?

Another punch to the gut. He knew what had compelled her to get away from Bonduel. He'd been short with her, almost harsh, when he'd met her at the bazaar. Ignoring the sorrow in her eyes, he had turned his back on her because he hadn't wanted to compound his own pain. Had he driven her into Isaac's arms?

There was no other explanation.

What had he done?

He smacked the back of the driver's seat. "Turn around," he said. Then, louder: "Stop the car. We have to go back."

In alarm, Max pulled to the side of the road into

a drift of gravel mixed with snow. "What's the matter?"

Tyler leaned forward. "Can you take them back to Bonduel, and then drive me to Nappanee?"

Max furrowed his brow in puzzlement. "Nappanee, Indiana? That's a six-hour drive."

"Please, Max. It's an emergency."

"It's two days before Christmas."

"I'll pay anything you want."

Aden asked the logical question. "Have you gone crazy?"

"Beth's in trouble. I don't know what he said to persuade her or if it was something I said, but she needs my help. You don't know what power those people have over her."

"Are you sure?"

"They insult her and criticize her and make her feel guilty and helpless, and I've got to save her." His sense of urgency increased as he spoke. He didn't care if she didn't want to be rescued. He would rescue her anyway. Let her be mad at him for the rest of her life. Let her destroy every sunflower on Huckleberry Hill. He couldn't bear it if those people hurt her again.

He turned to Felty. "I'm sorry. I know you need those license plates, but I've got to bring Beth back."

Felty shrugged and slid the notebook back into his pocket. "I had hoped to finish my list this year, but Annie would never forgive me if I made you come to Green Bay when you should be in Nappanee wooing our great-granddaughter."

"Max?" Tyler said.

Max glanced in his rearview mirror and made a hard U-turn. "Why not? I never could resist young love."

Tyler thought he might pass out with gratitude. Or desperation. She'd been gone four days already. If he had wings, he'd fly to Nappanee. He could only pray that she'd be all right until he got there.

Hang on, Beth. Don't lose hope. I'm coming.

Chapter Twenty-Four

Isaac lifted his spoon laden with stiff potatoes and let it fall to his plate with a heavy *kerplunk*. "How does anyone mess up mashed potatoes? Beth, you're the worst cook I've ever seen."

She'd been in Nappanee four days, and Isaac's criticisms had become more frequent every hour. He delivered his insults with a smile, which in his mind must have seemed teasing and playful instead of hurtful.

They didn't amuse Beth.

She was still puzzled as to why Isaac was so eager to marry someone he considered lacking in every way. It made no sense. His complaints made it seem as if he would be happy to get rid of her as soon as possible.

Treva took a small taste and smacked her lips, testing the consistency of her potatoes. "If you whip them too long, they get starchy." She discarded her spoon as if giving up on the whole dinner. "They taste like glue."

Beth shouldn't have expected anything more from the two of them. She'd cooked every meal since the day she'd walked into this house, and Treva and Isaac had seldom commented on the food except to find it overcooked or undercooked, too soft, too hard, too sweet, or too salty. In an attempt to please her relatives, Beth had spent the better part of the day preparing tonight's meal, because even though Treva didn't know it, it would be Beth's last in this house.

She'd found a nice little ham at the market, perfect for the three of them and Toby, and spent half an hour making a honey glaze. Beth took a bite. It hadn't turned out half bad. In truth, she'd be proud to serve this ham to Tyler. Tyler wouldn't even have to pretend to like it.

"The ham is dry," Treva complained. "You'll have to do better than that if I'm going to let you cook for me."

Toby seemed to be enjoying his meal. He'd dipped all his fingers in the potatoes and licked his hands hungrily. He alternated bites of potato and ham with handfuls of corn. The corn that didn't make it into his mouth stuck to the pasty mashed potatoes on his face. He would need a bath that Beth wouldn't have time to give him.

Beth glanced at the clock even though it was only one minute later than the last time she'd looked. Her driver couldn't be here until six. If she could have found a way to get out of here earlier, she would have taken it, but her driver options were limited the day before Christmas Eve. She felt grateful that anyone could drive her at all. Six o'clock would be early enough.

She still had to make explanations to Treva and Isaac and thought it might be better to spring the news on them right before she walked—or ran— out the door. Her suitcase and Toby's car seat and keavli sat on the porch, strategically placed for a quick getaway. She didn't want to take the time later to gather their things.

As far as Beth was concerned, she couldn't leave soon enough. In four days, Isaac had become insufferable, as he had last summer when he wouldn't leave her be. He tried to corner her when they were alone or steal a kiss when Treva wasn't looking, although it was plain that Treva knew exactly what went on. She had no reservations about Isaac forcing himself on Beth. Her mother-in-law wanted Beth to stay in Indiana. A marriage to Isaac was the best way to ensure that.

Toby picked up a handful of corn and threw it on the floor.

"No, Toby," Treva snapped as she smacked his hand.

Toby let out a wail as if his mammi had broken his tender heart.

Beth leaped from her chair and lifted Toby into her arms. Anger tore through her chest though her voice remained calm and rational. "Treva, I'll ask you not to strike my son, as I've asked you before."

"You spoil him," Treva protested. "I never let my babies throw food on the floor. They got the switch. He should feel glad I only tapped his hand."

Isaac pointed his fork at Toby. "Things will be different when I'm his dat."

A chill ran up Beth's spine. Less than an hour to go. Oh, how wonderful to be leaving!

She took Toby to the sink and washed his face and hands. Keeping him firmly in her embrace, she cleared the dishes, set the table with smaller plates, and brought dessert to the table.

"What's this?" Isaac asked, gazing suspiciously at the brownie-like cake.

"It's gingerbread with rum butter sauce. My mamm's recipe. She makes it every Christmas." It wasn't really Christmas without Mamm's gingerbread, and even though Isaac and Treva wouldn't appreciate it, Beth had been trying to be thoughtful when she made it.

She cut each of them a piece, spooned sauce over the top, and gave each piece a dollop of whipped cream. Not daring to let Toby out of the safety of her arms, she held him on her lap and fed him from her plate. She took a bite. Delicious. Sometimes recipes worked out okay for her.

Neither Treva nor Isaac commented on the dessert. Beth took that as a very good sign that they loved it. Isaac finished his portion in about four bites and served himself another piece.

Beth took one last bite and swallowed hard. There was no ignoring the boulder-sized lump in her throat and no avoiding the words she must say. "Treva and Isaac, I want to talk to you about my plans for the future."

It was incomprehensible that Isaac could be expecting a yes to his proposal, but his face brightened when she mentioned her future, and he leaned closer to her across the table. That lump felt like a bus lodged in her throat.

"First, Isaac, I'm flattered that you want to marry me. Amos always told me how you two could have your pick of any girl in the county. But I have to decline your offer. I am going back to Wisconsin."

Isaac turned to cold, hard stone.

She moved on. Better to get this all out before Isaac started shouting.

Treva beat him to it. "What are you going to do, leave me to die?" She stood, and Beth flinched when she pounded on the table. "Don't you dare. Don't you dare, you heartless girl."

Beth clutched Toby closer to her bosom and answered meekly. "Treva, will you sit down so I can tell you the plan?"

"No. You can't tell me anything, you ungrateful little snake."

"Priscilla, Martha, and Susannah have each agreed to take care of you."

"They hate me."

Beth ran her hand along Toby's arm as he started to cry. "They will each spend one day a week with you while you go through chemotherapy. We have all agreed to pitch in for a girl to care for you three days a week. Isaac will take care of you on Sundays, and I will come two weeks every summer."

"You're going to let a stranger come into my

home and do the job an ungrateful daughter-in-law should be doing?"

"Yes," Beth said, not even trying to defend herself. Treva was beyond reasoning with.

"And what about Isaac? He loves you. I'm not going to let you do this to him, to break his heart like that. Don't you care about his feelings? Don't you care that he feels a solemn responsibility to care for his brother's wife and child?"

"I release him of any responsibility. He is free to choose another wife."

Isaac finally spoke, and she could see the rage bubbling inside him like a geyser waiting to erupt. "Why don't you want me, Beth? I'm just like Amos. You loved Amos."

The lump traveled to the pit of her stomach. She didn't want him to think he could persuade her. Despite the risk, she would be completely honest. "The honest truth is, I was miserable being married to Amos. After the first few months, he never had a kind word to say to me."

Treva hissed. "Of course not. He tried to improve you. When he gave you suggestions about your cooking, he hoped to make you work harder in the kitchen. Everything he said was meant to help you turn into a better wife. He suffered through three years of bad food and shoddy housekeeping. He is the one who was miserable. You should thank his memory for that instead of holding a grudge."

"I have forgiven him. And you're right. I learned many things from Amos, but I hadn't realized it until a few days ago. Living with Amos helped me find my strength after he died. I'm grateful for that." She looked to the ceiling as if talking to God. "And I couldn't have said that a week ago."

Isaac scowled like she wasn't making any sense. "You should be grateful I'm willing to take you, Beth. You should be down on your knees thanking me for my generosity. Most widows don't get another chance."

Beth sighed. "Treva says Amos was miserable being married to me. Why do you want a wife who can't make you happy, Isaac?"

His agitation seemed to subside momentarily. "Because I love you. I loved you from the day I saw you."

"Why?"

His sputtering proved he wasn't used to saying nice things to Beth. "Because . . . you're pretty . . . and you smile at me."

Surely Isaac could find a pretty girl in Nappanee to smile at him once in a while. Maybe not. Maybe they all knew what he was really like.

She held her breath as he glided toward her and slid his hands around her waist. With Toby in her arms, she couldn't move fast enough to dodge him.

Refusing to look him in the eye, she said, "Please get away from me, Isaac."

"I want you to love me," he said.

"Stop it, Isaac," Treva growled.

"Get away." Beth shuddered as she felt his breath on her cheek.

"Your boyfriend isn't here this time."

Toby struggled in her arms as Isaac pressed himself closer.

She knew how much her next words would provoke him, but they had to be said. Her heart thumped anxiously against her chest. "I don't love you. I will never love you, and nothing you do will ever convince me to marry you."

Boiling with fury, Isaac shoved Beth away from him. She almost lost her balance but managed to stay on her feet. With Toby tightly in her grasp, she backed away until the sofa stopped her retreat. Her first concern was Toby's protection.

Yelling obscenities, Isaac swept his hands across the table and sent dishes and silverware crashing to the floor. Terrified, Toby wailed in alarm while Beth did her best to comfort him even while trying to quell her own rising panic.

Treva screamed at the top of her lungs. "What are you doing? Get a hold of yourself, Isaac."

Isaac pointed to Toby and then glared at his mamm. "Shut up, Toby! Shut up, Mamm."

Toby screamed as if he'd been stung by a wasp.

The front door swung open, and an angel stormed into the room. Apparently, angels didn't bother to knock. And he could have been the avenging angel for the dark look in his eyes.

Isaac froze where he stood. Treva clapped her mouth shut.

Beth's relief was as tangible as the comfort of a warm blanket as Tyler, tall and straight, surveyed the room as if he had come to conquer it. He strode to Beth's side and placed his strong hands on her shoulders. "Are you all right?"

Too breathless to answer, Beth looked into those stormy eyes and nodded.

Still bawling in Beth's arms, Toby struggled to reach Tyler. "Mommy," he cried.

Tyler ran his hand along the top of Toby's head but made no move to take him. "Go outside and wait in the car."

"Get out!" Isaac yelled. "Get out of my house!"

Tyler snapped his head around to look at Isaac. "Go, Beth."

She couldn't move fast enough. Instinct took her halfway to the door before a wave of awareness plowed into her and she realized what she had to do. She turned back and foisted Toby into Tyler's arms.

The shock on his face soon gave way to a look of sheer urgency. "Beth, take Toby and go."

Isaac hurled a plate at the floor. "You can't just walk in here. Get out!"

"Isaac, stop throwing things," Treva yelled. "You're acting like an animal."

Isaac yelled back. He and his mamm screamed insults at each other while Beth's mind raced.

She nudged Tyler toward the door. "I will not let him hurt you again."

"Better me than you," Tyler said, trying to give Toby back. She wouldn't take him.

"Tyler." She willed him to see the terror and the determination in her eyes. "I know what you are prepared to suffer for me, but if I can't fight for myself, I will never deserve you."

"That's not true."

"Tyler, look at me," she whispered.

He paused his protest long enough to let her take his face in her hands.

"I don't want you to rescue me," she said, pleading with her eyes. "Please. Let me do this."

His frown slashed deep lines into his handsome features. Breathing heavily, he stared at her for what seemed like an anxious eternity. With a look of stricken helplessness, he nodded almost imperceptibly and stepped back.

"Take Toby outside," she said, turning to face Isaac.

"I'm not going anywhere."

Isaac came toward them, no doubt to throw Tyler out of his house, as Beth stepped forward. "Don't touch him," she said.

"He's got no right to be here. I want him out."

Beth stood her ground as Isaac looked like he might bowl her over in an effort to get to Tyler. She put some force behind her voice. "Stop. You're going to hurt Toby."

Isaac paused long enough to shake his head. "Get him out."

Beth yelled so Isaac would have no trouble hearing what she said next. "Isaac, if you want to hurt my family, you'll have to go through me first."

He halted in his tracks.

"Go ahead. I know you've been wanting to for a long time."

Isaac stumbled back as if he'd been smacked in the forehead with a rock. "Wha . . . what did you say?"

She stood ramrod straight with her hands

clenched at her sides. "But know this. If you strike me, I will never set foot in this house again."

"No, Beth," Tyler said, the panic in his voice slicing the air like a bitter frost.

She held up a hand to stop Tyler from doing what he surely was considering doing at that very moment.

Isaac backed against a chair behind him. "I would never hit you."

"You're mad at me. Probably madder than you've ever been. I know you want to lash out at someone, and it shouldn't be Tyler. He's done nothing to deserve it. I am the one who made you mad. If you think it will make you feel better, strike me and get it over with. I'm tired of being afraid of it."

Isaac's knuckles turned white clutching the back of the chair. "No," he wailed in protest. "Why are you afraid of me? I would never hurt you."

"You hit Tyler."

"I'm not like that. I wasn't thinking straight that night. Love makes you do terrible things."

"Real love never seeks to destroy. Love is meek and kind and patient."

Her words doused the fire in Isaac's eyes. He sat on one of the chairs at the table, buried his face in his hands, and started sobbing. "I wouldn't ever hit you. I love you."

Breathing as if she'd hiked up a mountain, Beth held perfectly still and stared at her brother-in-law. A feeling larger than the sky and lighter than the air swelled inside her as the weight of four long years tumbled off her shoulders. She wasn't afraid of Isaac or Amos anymore. Never again would she allow Amos's memory to cripple her future.

Why had she been holding on to the fear for so long when all she had to do was open her hands and let it go, open her heart and hand her pain to God? She'd been so angry with God that she had pushed Him away without realizing He was the one she needed the most.

Four days ago, she'd believed God brought her to Indiana to settle things with Treva, to make sure she would be taken care of, but now she knew that God had led her here to find this part of herself—the part big enough and brave enough to step into the darkness and take God's hand.

She turned to gaze at Tyler, who patted Toby's back and whispered comforting words into his ear. The love of a gute man and the joy of a beautiful child were her most precious gifts. She'd never be afraid of anything ever again as long as she clung to her faith that God would walk her through any trial.

Beth tiptoed over the plates scattered over the floor. She saw Tyler stiffen as she laid a hand on Isaac's shoulder. Isaac did not lift his head. "Goodbye, Isaac. Take care of your mamm."

Treva still stood at the table as if unsure of what had happened. Beth went to the counter and pulled four of Mammi's potholders from the drawer where she had stored them the first day she came to Nappanee. Then she put her arm around Treva. "My mammi wanted you to have these."

Treva stared at the potholders. Beth laid them on the table. "You don't need to worry, Treva. Your family will watch out for you. I will write every week and come next summer, Lord willing. God will take care of you, no matter what."

Treva didn't respond. Beth hadn't expected her to. She couldn't very well start yelling again while Isaac bawled like a baby in her kitchen.

Beth glanced at Tyler. He regarded her with such tenderness in his eyes that she thought she might melt. She couldn't return to his side fast enough. With Toby firmly wrapped in one arm, he held out his hand, and she took it. His touch felt like walking into a cozy house after a night spent in the icy wind.

Her legs felt weak and her breathing sounded as ragged as his. "Will you take me home?"

"*Now* you want my help?"

"Now and forever."

That deep furrow between his eyebrows disappeared as his expression relaxed. "I can live with that."

Chapter Twenty-Five

They tiptoed into Mammi and Dawdi's house at one in the morning. It was officially Christmas Eve. Beth cradled Toby in her arms, and Tyler carried the bags and the car seat. Beth felt the urge to kneel down and kiss the floor, she was so glad to be home.

Once they'd left the Hostetlers', it had only taken a few minutes to calm Toby down. Tyler had fed him fruit snacks and read him books until he miraculously fell asleep, and he hadn't made a peep the rest of the trip. Once Tyler had taken care of Toby, he'd turned his attention to Beth, who never would have admitted she needed taking care of but had found Tyler's presence the only thing that kept her from bursting into tears.

He hadn't said much as he had reached across Toby's car seat and taken Beth's hand. He had interlaced his fingers with hers and caressed the back of her hand with his thumb. "Is this okay?" he had said.

Okay? She'd never wanted it to end.

He'd held on to her for the rest of the ride.

Without lighting a lantern, they went to Toby's room, where Tyler deposited the bags and seat and Beth placed Toby in his crib. He barely moved a muscle as she tucked the blanket around his ears like he liked it.

She straightened to find Tyler standing beside her, watching Toby. "He's had a hard day, poor little guy," he said.

"Jah, he's glad to be in his own bed."

The soft moonlight streaming through the window fell on Tyler's face, and his gaze made her tremble. Without taking his eyes off her lips, he slipped his arms around her waist. When he brought his mouth down on hers, a sigh came from deep in her throat as she let him kiss her to heaven. Her heart pounded wildly as it struggled to keep pace with her happiness. She felt as if she were a completely different person standing on the threshold of the rest of her life. She'd traveled thousands of miles in one short week. One part of her story had ended, and something wonderful was about to begin.

He left her panting for air when he pulled away. With his lips within an inch of hers, he said, "I am so mad at you right now."

She snapped her head back and drew away in shock. "You are?"

"Jah," he said, pulling her back into his embrace. "Don't you ever do anything like that again."

A giggle burst from her lips. "Like kiss you?"

His arms tightened around her. "Don't pretend

you don't know what I mean. When Felty told me you had gone to Indiana with Isaac, I think I sweat off ten pounds worrying about you. I know what they did to you. I would have done anything to save you from that pain again."

"God led me to Indiana."

"I wished He'd told me about that."

Beth smoothed a lock of hair from Tyler's forehead. "I needed to finish things, to stand up to my past and everybody in it."

"It was torture watching you put yourself in danger like that."

"But you did."

"Because you asked me to."

She rose on her tiptoes and brushed her lips across his. He held his breath. "Thank you for trusting me."

He softened his stern frown and gave her a swift kiss of his own. "I didn't want you poking me with one of your sunflowers."

"You believed I was strong enough."

"I've always known you were strong enough. You didn't have to prove anything to me."

"I had to prove it to myself," Beth said. "If you had stepped in to rescue me, like you have a very bad habit of doing, I wouldn't have known how strong I could be, and I wouldn't have learned to put my trust in God."

"How did you know Isaac would back down?"

"I didn't."

Tyler shuddered and laid three kisses on her cheek. "I didn't want to know that."

"But I knew God would take care of me, no matter what, even if I had ended up in the hospital."

He kissed her on the other cheek. "Don't make me think about it."

"If Isaac had hurt me, God would have made good come from it. Imagine how it would have changed Isaac."

Tyler shook his head. "I don't care. It would have been unbearable to me. So please, don't ever think about doing something like that again."

"I won't promise anything. You know how stubborn I am."

He growled and squeezed the stuffing out of her. "I was afraid you'd say that." He lowered his head and kissed her again, giving her the feeling of floating off the ground. She'd never grow tired of this.

When he withdrew, he swayed back and forth, and she could tell he felt as bewildered as she.

"This could get very dangerous," he said, not letting go for a second. "I can't promise we won't have our hard times. Considering our history, I have no doubt there are going to be times when I make you mad. And considering how I feel right at this moment, there are going to be times when I'll be furious with you." He tempered his scold with a grin. "No doubt this will annoy you, but I'm asking you to take a leap of faith. Will you marry me? I love you so bad I can't hardly breathe. I know you've refused me twice already. Some people would say

I can't take a hint, but I'm asking again, and I'll probably keep asking until you are forced to move to Florida to be rid of me."

"Tyler," she groaned, in mock irritation. "Stop talking. Just stop talking."

"Sorry."

"Don't you dare apologize." Standing on her tip-toes, she wrapped her arms around his neck, pulled him as close as she possibly could, and kissed him soundly. "Who am I to refuse a man who is willing to put up with me?"

Even in the dead of winter, his smile could have set three forests on fire.

"I love you," she whispered, when she really wanted to shout.

He kissed her again as if drinking her in, and she abandoned herself to the pure emotion.

They parted quickly as a ribbon of light illuminated the hallway. Dawdi appeared in his nightshirt, carrying a lantern and squinting into the darkness of Toby's room. "Tyler and Beth," he said as if he often encountered amorous great-grandchildren at one in the morning. "Merry Christmas Eve."

"Merry Christmas Eve, Dawdi."

Without another word, Dawdi turned and shuffled back down the hall.

It was fortunate their quiet laughter didn't wake Toby.

Tyler groaned and pulled himself farther away

from her. "I'd better go before we disturb the entire household."

"You mean Mammi?"

"I'd rather not give her a heart attack." He walked backwards slowly, as if it were painful to part from her. "Can I see you on Christmas morning?"

"Why not Christmas Eve morning?"

"I've got some shopping to do."

She cocked her eyebrow. "Don't buy me anything. You know how offended I get about gifts."

"I wouldn't dream of offending you."

"I'll be at my mamm's house."

He smiled. "So will I."

Felty doused the lantern and climbed back into bed.

Anna rolled over. "Was it a mouse?"

"Nope. Tyler and Beth spooning."

Anna sat straight up. "Is that so?" She nudged Felty's shoulder, "I was right about them. I knew I was right."

"I'd never argue with you about that."

Anna lay down, scooted close to her husband, and draped an arm over him. "Did they look happy, Felty? Really happy?"

"Tyler was kissing our pretty granddaughter. Of course he looked happy."

"All young people should be so happy. Don't you agree?"

Sensing a trap, Felty rolled over and tried to

make out his wife's face in the darkness. "What trouble are we in if I agree?"

"Now, Felty. I'm just saying that if we can bring sunshine into a young person's life, then we should do it."

"Are you thinking of anyone in particular?"

"Of course not. It's a good rule to live by."

Felty relaxed into his pillow. As long as Anna wasn't thinking about another one of her matches, everything would be right as rain. "Jah, a gute rule to live by."

Anna gathered the covers around her chin. "We need to think of a way to get our grandson Ben back to Bonduel."

"Annie-banannie, I knew you were scheming."

Anna grinned. "It will take something special to lure him here."

"He lives in Florida. What boy in his right mind would trade Florida for Wisconsin?"

"A boy in love." She patted his hand. "You might have to break your leg."

"Break my leg?"

"If he thought you needed his help on the farm, he'd come back."

"I'd rather not break any bones for your romantic notions, Annie."

Anna pursed her lips. In the dimness, Felty could see the wheels turning in her head. "Hmmm. I bet he'd come back for asthma. Or a serious case of shingles."

"Maybe *you* should get the shingles."

"Well, Felty, I don't see any other way around it.

We won't be able to persuade Emma Nelson to go to Florida."

Felty wrinkled his forehead. "Emma Nelson? She's the reason he went to Florida."

"And she's the reason he'll come back."

"I thought you said he'd come back if I broke my leg."

"Oh, thank you, Felty. Would you really?"

Chapter Twenty-Six

On Christmas morning, Mamm's house burst at the seams. Beth's entire immediate family was there, including Aaron Junior with his new wife and all the younger siblings. Aunt Ruth Anne and Uncle Matthias's family came, along with Uncle Tim's family. Three of Uncle Titus's ten children were there with five of his grandchildren. One of Beth's favorite cousins, Ben, was gone because he'd moved to Florida last summer.

Beth and Toby had slept at Mammi and Dawdi's last night as usual. Early this morning, the four of them had come to Mamm and Dat's to be a part of the Christmas morning festivities. The children always did a little Christmas play for the grownups, and then they would exchange gifts and cook a giant Christmas breakfast.

Beth's head was so full of Tyler Yoder, she was sure she'd be useless in the kitchen until she saw him again. Would he come early or wait until later this afternoon? He'd have to do the milking first, so she might not see him for several hours. The thought dampened her Christmas spirit.

Mamm had hung evergreen boughs over every window and tied them up with cheery red bows. A saucepan of cinnamon sticks and cloves simmered on the stove every day in December, so the house always smelled like Christmas.

The family crowded into Mamm's great room and listened as Beth's brothers and the younger cousins recited poems they had learned for the school Christmas pageant. Then Beth's brother Menno supervised the children in a reenactment of the Nativity scene. Since he was the youngest child there, Toby got to be the baby Jesus. He didn't really appreciate the honor. He pulled at the blanket they wrapped around him and draped it over his head, trying to get someone to play peek-a-boo.

Beth giggled with the others while keeping an eye turned to the front window, hoping by sheer will to bring Tyler to her. Now that he was truly hers, the minutes they spent apart seemed like eternities.

Everyone laughed as Toby took Uriah's shepherd's staff, a broom, and began dragging it across the floor as if he were cleaning up.

The loud, determined knock on the door surprised even Beth. Her heart did more somersaults than a tumbler in the circus, and she leaped to her feet. She wanted to be the first to greet Tyler on Christmas morning.

He stood on the porch with that solemn look on his face that she had grown to adore, holding a fistful of sunflowers. Real sunflowers. How had he managed that in the dead of winter?

She laughed at the sheer joy of seeing him. "You came."

He cocked an eyebrow. "Was there any doubt in your mind that I would? A thousand unmilked cows couldn't have kept me away." He leaned close and whispered, "Yesterday about killed me. I never want to be separated again."

For a moment, he stared at her lips, and she thought he might kiss her right there. She found herself wanting it even though her family would die of shock.

Mamm broke the connection when she called out, "Invite him in, Beth. It's cold out there."

Tyler stepped inside and handed the sunflowers to Beth. "I brought you a gift."

Beth took the flowers and giggled. "You're quite brave to give me such an irresistible weapon."

"They're not too much, are they?" he said, his eyes twinkling with amusement as he took off his coat. "I didn't want to offend you."

"They're wonderful. Denki."

It was then Beth realized that the entire room had fallen silent, and all her relatives stared at them with eager curiosity. Tyler shrugged his shoulders and wrapped his arm possessively around Beth. Beth looked at the flabbergasted faces of most of the adults in the room and couldn't keep a giggle from escaping her lips. Her relatives seemed to take a collective breath before they exploded into laughter.

She shivered with pleasure when Tyler put his

mouth close to her ear. "Do you want to tell them, or should I?"

"My parents might die of shock," she whispered back.

He sprouted a quirky grin. "They already gave me their blessing."

"Really?"

Tyler glanced at Beth's sunflowers as if they might be a threat. "About three months ago."

"What?"

"Mommy!" Toby squealed from across the room. He ran into Tyler's arms and made himself comfortable there.

"I don't know about anyone else," said Uncle Titus with a good-natured growl, "but I'd like to know what's going on here."

Tyler smiled with his whole body as he bounced Toby on his hip. "We're engaged."

The whole family clapped and cheered as if Tyler had won a race. Tears brimmed in Dat's eyes as he and Mamm embraced. Mamm remained dry-eyed. She had always been too sensible for tears.

Beth stared at Tyler in disbelief. "Three months?"

He took a step back and didn't lose that smile. "Try not to destroy the whole bouquet at once."

More puzzled than annoyed, she gave him a scolding twist of her lips and lowered the flowers as a token of peace.

Tyler chuckled. With his free hand, he hung his coat on one of the hooks inside the front door and retrieved a can of bright yellow tennis balls from the pocket. "Merry Christmas, Toby."

Toby clapped his hands. "Ball, ball."

Tyler put Toby down, sat on the floor next to him, and looked at Beth's mamm. "Is it okay if I open these? Or would you rather I not? Balls will fly everywhere."

"Pshaw," Mamm said. "What's Christmas morning without a little chaos?"

The can made a cheerful pop as Tyler broke the seal. Toby watched with wide eyes and breathless anticipation as Tyler handed him a ball. He reached out his other hand for the second ball. Not about to settle for two-thirds of his gift, he stretched out his arms, with a ball in either hand. Tyler balanced the last ball in the cradle of Toby's elbows.

"Ball," Toby said as he toddled away, determined not to let his balls tumble.

Beth laughed. The balls would be bouncing all around the great room soon enough.

"I want to hear the whole story of how you got together," said Aunt Sally Mae.

"You can thank Felty," Mammi said. "He agreed to let Beth come and live with us."

Dawdi's eyes twinkled as he stroked his beard. "Don't you start, Banannie. Don't you start."

"It was out of sheer persistence," Tyler said "I ask her to marry me three times. I think she said yes just to shut me up."

Uncle Titus raised both eyebrows. "No woman can resist a man who makes a pest of himself."

A sharp knock made them all jump. The younger children raced to the door. There was nothing like the excitement of an unexpected visitor.

Uriah reached the knob first, and he opened the door. At his feet sat a medium-sized box wrapped in white paper and tied with a red bow.

"What is it, son?" asked Aunt Ruth Anne.

Uriah picked it up and brought it into the house. "It says it's for Beth."

Beth glanced suspiciously at Tyler, who didn't make eye contact and didn't betray even a hint of a smile on his face. After handing him the sunflowers, Beth sat on the sofa, and Uriah gave her the present. Ten pairs of eyes watched as she pulled back the paper and reached into the box.

She pulled out a beautiful stainless steel saucepan, complete with a steamer and double boiler. The small card accompanying the pan said, *A wonderful-gute cook and cheesemaker needs the right tools.* She couldn't suppress the warm glow that seemed to envelop her with every breath she took. Surely Tyler didn't really believe she was a good cook, did he?

"Who's it from?" Uriah asked.

"It doesn't say." Beth looked sideways at Tyler and twisted her mouth just so, indicating she knew exactly where it came from.

His lips twitched ever so slightly, but she could see he was determined to play dumb. He sat next to her on the sofa and examined the pan as if he'd never seen it before.

"That's a real nice pan," Mamm said. "They say if you steam your broccoli, it has more vitamins."

Another knock at the door turned their attention. Another mass exodus by the children. Uriah seemed to have dibs on the doorknob. Again he opened the door to nobody, but a tall, bulky package stood on the porch.

Beth set her first gift aside. "Tyler," she warned, scolding him with her eyes.

He tried very hard not to smile. "What are you looking at me for?"

Uriah and three or four other children stepped outside to survey the package. Little Evie covered her mouth with her hands and giggled.

"Oh ho ho, Matthias," Uriah said. "I need your help."

Uriah's eleven-year-old brother, Matthias Junior, joined him on the porch. Matthias lifted the bottom of the package, tilting it until Uriah could catch the top end. Matthias turned and walked backwards into the house. The new package had to be at least five feet tall.

Beth lifted her eyebrows and nudged Tyler with her elbow. What did he think he was doing? He swiped his hand across his mouth as if wiping off a smile.

Uriah and Matthias set the package in front of her as the children gathered around in enthusiastic curiosity.

"Open it," said little Evie, practically squealing. A gift always held so much excitement for children. Okay, Beth admitted, at the moment, she felt pretty excited herself.

But she tried to act annoyed. Tyler should never have spent so much money on her.

She stood and started at the top, ripping the

paper right down the middle. Uriah and Matthias pulled the thick folds of paper from both ends. "Oh my," said Beth.

"It's a girl with no head," Evie exclaimed.

Beth grinned. "It's a dress form. I can put dresses on it to make sure they are the right size when I am sewing them."

A small note was taped to the front. *A good seamstress needs her own model.*

Beth ran her hand along the fabric that covered the dress form at the shoulders. This was not a casual, spur-of-the-moment gift. She looked up at Tyler. He studied her with those icy blue eyes that could have melted the North Pole. She formed the words on her lips without speaking them out loud. "Thank you."

He shrugged and jiggled the bouquet as if he had no idea what she was talking about.

Choking back the tears that threatened to turn her into a Christmas Day spectacle, she climbed back onto the sofa and moved as close to Tyler as she dared without raising Mamm's eyebrows. She didn't deserve this, but her heart swelled at the thought that Tyler believed she did.

Her eyes almost bugged out when another knock came at the door, and she looked at Tyler as if he'd played a naughty practical joke. He looked away, suddenly very interested in who was at that door.

Uriah and Matthias and the other children crowded around as if a pile of candy waited on the other side. Uriah opened the door, and the cousins stuck their heads out and looked to their right.

From where she sat, Beth couldn't see any presents on the porch, but when the children jumped up and down and screamed in delight, she knew it had to be big.

Her little cousins disappeared, and it wasn't too long before they heard Uriah call, "Dat, Uncle Titus, we need your help."

Titus trudged out the door with Uncle Matthias. "Soon there won't be room enough in this house for the people," Titus grumbled.

Beth caught herself holding her breath. Whatever it was, he shouldn't have.

Titus and Matthias each carried one end of the package wrapped in silver paper with the biggest Christmas bow Beth had ever seen. The bow itself had to be two feet in diameter. The way they moved, whatever hid inside must have been heavy. It looked almost like a small table.

Oh no.

Of all the outrageous things to do!

She gasped for air as her heart skipped several beats. She couldn't accept this. It was too much. He was too wonderful for words.

Her hands trembled as she reached out and fingered the bow.

"Are you going to open it?" her cousin Rose asked.

Uriah stepped around the dress form and gazed curiously at Beth. "Do you want us to open it for you?"

Rendered speechless, all she could do was nod.

Rose carefully detached the spectacular bow;

then six pairs of hands ripped at the paper to reveal a brand new battery-powered sewing machine complete with its own cabinet.

The female relatives sighed collectively at such a wonderful sight.

The tears trickled down Beth's face as if from a leaky faucet. Not in her wildest dreams had she ever hoped for a Bernina. She stood and ran her fingers across the top, admiring the smooth lines and crisp white knobs. She turned the handwheel just to see how smoothly it moved. The needle bobbed up and down effortlessly and without a sound. How many dresses could she make in a week with a machine like this?

She cherished the sight of it even as she grieved for its loss. She knew she couldn't keep it. She could never accept something so extravagant. No matter how he protested, she would put her foot down and make Tyler take it back.

A small note sat underneath the presser foot. *An expert seamstress needs a fine machine. You should find a place to put it, because I refuse to take it back.* And then a postscript: *The sunflowers are in case you're irritated.*

No wonder he'd brought an entire bouquet.

"That's quite a machine," said Mamm, whose practical side was her only side. "Does it cook pancakes and iron your clothes too?"

"Oh, Sarah," said Aunt Ruth Anne. "Don't be such a spoilsport."

Beth wiped her eyes and glanced at Tyler. The way he smiled, as if he knew he was going to get his way, left her feeling all jumbled and annoyed. She snatched the bouquet from his grasp, took him by the hand, and pulled him outside where they could have a little privacy.

"Are there more presents?" she heard Uriah say as she shut the door.

She turned to Tyler, ready to deliver an impressive lecture on the follies of giving his fiancée expensive gifts. "Tyler Yoder, you are in trouble."

He put up both hands as if stopping traffic. "Wait, wait. Use your flowers." With a patient grin, he slipped one from her bouquet. "I am in trouble because . . . ?" He popped the head off the flower and tossed it out into the snow.

She huffed in exasperation. "You're in trouble because you bought me a sewing machine."

His blue eyes danced as he selected another flower. "The sewing machine is beautiful, but you can't keep it because . . . ?" He decapitated that flower too.

She watched as the poor flower head fell to the ground. "Because it cost too much and . . . and nobody should get such a big gift at Christmas."

Before she could move the flowers out of his reach, he snatched another one from her hand and plucked all its petals off. They fell onto the porch like snowflakes. His grin got wider. "I've milked cows for twenty years so that when the time came I could buy the woman I love a sewing machine, and she obviously can't see how bad I want to give it to her because . . . ?"

"I don't deserve it."

"The woman who stays up all night sewing dresses so she can care for her son doesn't think she deserves a new sewing machine because . . . ?" Another poor flower lost its head.

Beth giggled. "Stop this, right now. You are ruining a perfectly good bouquet of sunflowers."

"I'm doing all the work here," he said. "There's plenty of flowers left for you to smash."

He tried to grab another flower. Beth stretched her arm away from him so he couldn't reach them. He pressed in on her, and she moved backwards until the porch railing stopped her progress. They laughed like children.

She held the flowers close to her face and let the petals tickle her cheek. "Okay, okay. I'll keep the sewing machine."

She probably could have counted his teeth, he grinned so wide.

"But only because I'd rather not see another sunflower die needlessly."

Crushing the bouquet between them, Tyler took the opportunity to wrap his arms around her and kiss her tenderly on the lips. She had no choice but to kiss back. He was too irresistible.

One kiss left her breathless. "This isn't fair," Beth said. "You caught me in a moment of weakness."

His mouth was a whisper away from hers. "I've never seen you in a moment of weakness."

"You're seeing it now."

"What weakness is that?"

With the bouquet in one hand, she slid her arms around his neck. "The weakness that I'm so out of my head in love with you that I am not thinking straight." She used her kiss as an exclamation point.

He closed his eyes and smiled. "Hmm. I hope you have that problem for a very long time."

"For as long as I live, Lord willing."

Smiling jubilantly, he bent his head and kissed her again. Beth wished she could bottle this feeling and preserve it always.

"Denki for the sewing machine. It is truly a wonderful-gute gift."

"My pleasure."

Strains of "Hark! The Herald Angels Sing" wafted from the house. The door opened, and Dawdi stuck his head out. It was the second time he'd caught them kissing, and he seemed as unruffled as ever. "Merry Christmas," he said.

"Merry Christmas, Dawdi."

Dawdi looked to the inside of the house. "He's been asking for his mamm."

A tennis ball flew out the door and bounced off the porch, followed by Toby with another ball held tightly in his fist. "Mommy," he said.

Dawdi disappeared into the house and shut the door behind him. He'd probably seen enough kissing to last him a lifetime.

Tyler hefted Toby in one arm and put the other arm around Beth in a three-way hug. He kissed Toby on the cheek. "My darling family." He brought his lips down on Beth's and kissed her until she heard angels sing.

She felt something brush against her cheek. Toby had managed to pull a sunflower from her bouquet, and he was tapping it against her cheek. "No, no," he said.

Beth covered her mouth to stifle her giggle. "You're in for it now, Tyler, from both of us."

Tyler eyed Toby in surprise, took his arm from around Beth, and buried half his face in his hand. "Oh, no."

Chapter Twenty-Seven

Three days after Christmas, the sale seekers still flocked to the stores hunting for goodies. A perfect day to haunt parking lots looking for license plates.

Tyler sat in the backseat of the car with his arm firmly around Beth. He'd been through a lot to get her to agree to marry him. He wasn't about to let go. Felty sat in the front with Max, the driver, where he could have a better view of every car they passed.

"I hear if you go to Yellowstone, in one hour you will see every license plate in the country," Max said, as he steered the car down another row in the parking lot of the Mayfair Mall in Milwaukee. Tyler and Felty had decided that Green Bay wasn't a big enough place in which to find the five rare and elusive plates Felty needed to win his game. So Mammi had agreed to care for Toby for the day so they could come all the way to Milwaukee. With only three days left to find license plates, it was an emergency.

"Next year, we should plan a trip to Yellowstone,"

Felty said gripping his pen and notebook like a detective working on a case.

"Only two left to find, Dawdi," Beth said, grinning and squeezing Tyler's hand. It was gute Felty was looking so hard, because Tyler had been too fascinated by the beautiful woman sitting next to him to care much about license plates, even on this special trip to Milwaukee.

They had already found two of the four plates Felty needed to complete his collection. Delaware drove by them on the highway between Oshkosh and Fond Du Lac, and Hawaii sat in the parking lot of Wal-Mart on West Hope Avenue. Nevada and Rhode Island were proving difficult.

"Denki again for paying for the driver to get us down here yet," Felty said.

Tyler shrugged. "You sacrificed finding your plates so I could fetch Beth from Indiana. It's the least I could do." He planted a kiss on Beth's cheek. "I wouldn't have my Beth if it wasn't for you."

"Thank Annie-banannie for that. I try to stay out of the goings-on at our house. But I know you're glad for the opportunity to make googly eyes at my great-granddaughter today."

"Very glad," Tyler said.

Max checked his rearview mirror. "I think we've looked at every car in this parking lot. I'm not seeing Nevada or Rhode Island."

"We've been to every mall and McDonald's in the city," Beth said. "Where else can we look?"

"Let's drive to California." Tyler scooted closer to his fiancée. "More time for cuddling."

Beth giggled and nudged him away slightly. "Behave yourself."

"I have an idea," Max said, pulling the car back onto the main intersection. "There is another place we might find a lot of plates."

Even with heavy traffic, it only took them ten minutes to get there. "Children's Hospital," Felty read. "Oh, those poor little kids who have to be in a hospital at Christmastime."

They drove through the Children's Hospital parking lots and then around all the medical center lots. Tyler pulled his undivided attention from Beth long enough to help look. They only needed two more, for goodness sake. They found another Hawaii and four Floridas, but no Rhode Island or Nevada.

After half an hour, they decided it would be best to look elsewhere.

"Let's try over there one more time," Felty said. He tapped his forehead. "I have a sense about these things."

Max maneuvered the car down another row and slowly drove between cars. Felty called out as if he'd been struck by lightning. "There they are!"

It was good the car was crawling, because Max slammed on his brakes. Beth would have gone right through the windshield otherwise.

Felty unbuckled his seat belt and leaped out of the car like a twenty-year-old. The others followed. He rested his hands on his hips and stared at two cars parked right next to each other.

Rhode Island and *Nevada*.

"If that's not a miracle, I don't know what is," Max said.

Tyler could think of a few, like the woman standing next to him, the miracle of love and laughter that had flowed into his life because of her.

But the license plates were good too.

Savoring the moment, Felty meticulously wrote them down in his notebook and then closed it with finality. "A Christmas to remember," he said, smiling as if he would erupt into laughter at any moment. He clapped his hands together. "Now, if you will help me, I need to get a box out of the trunk."

Raising his eyebrows, Max unlatched the trunk, and Tyler opened it and pulled out a cardboard box. "What's in here?"

"Annie-banannie insisted I bring these today, just in case. That woman is smarter than all the presidents of the world put together."

Felty opened the box. Inside, along with an impressive assortment of potholders, were four beautiful little baby blankets.

"Knitted by Anna?" Tyler asked.

Beth grinned. "With an extra dose of love."

Felty was already halfway across the parking lot. He turned back to look at them. "Well, don't just stand there. Let's go do some good." He sang as he marched away. "*Each day I'll do a golden deed, by helping those who are in need.*"

Please turn the page for an exciting sneak peek of
Jennifer Beckstrand's next
Matchmakers of Huckleberry Hill romance,
HUCKLEBERRY SPRING,
coming in February 2014!

Felty's eyes did not stray from his newspaper as Anna Helmuth laid a four-inch stack of brochures on the table next to his recliner.

"Take your pick, Felty," Anna said sweetly, plopping herself into her rocker and taking up her knitting. "What kind of surgery would you like to get?"

"Hmmm," Felty said, not paying attention as he perused the death notices.

"Sometimes you squint. Maybe you'd like to get Lasik."

Felty lowered *The Budget* so he could spy his wife over the top of it. "What are you saying, Anniebanannie? You think I squint?"

Rocking back and forth, Anna inclined her head towards the thick stack of papers without missing a beat in her knitting. "It's that purple brochure on the top. I don't know. You might be too old for Lasik."

"I'm only eighty-four——not too old for anything." The newspaper crunched as Felty set it in his lap.

He stared curiously at Anna's potpourri of brightly colored brochures. "What is Lasik, and why do you have a brochure about it?"

"I already told you, dear. You need to pick what kind of surgery you want. Lasik is just one of many choices."

"Do I need surgery?"

"Of course you do, dear. Spring is the busiest time of the year on a farm, and I need you laid up and unable to work for at least a month."

Felty took off his glasses and cleaned them with his handkerchief as if this would help him decipher what Anna was talking about. "You want me laid up for the spring work?"

"You're squinting, dear. You need Lasik."

"What will become of the chickens?"

Anna lifted her eyebrows, pursed her lips, and nodded as a gesture of reassurance. "I've got it all worked out. Our grandson Ben will take over the farm while you're indisposed. And look after the chickens."

Felty furrowed his brow as if someone had taken a plow to his forehead. "You're not still scheming to get Ben and Emma Nelson back together, are you? It's a lost cause, Banannie. A lost cause."

"Lost causes are my specialty," Anna insisted, as her fingers and knitting needles seemed to meld together in a blur of fuzzy pink yarn. "Ben and Emma belong together, and if anybody can make it happen, we can. We've never missed yet."

"It would take a miracle to get Emma to set foot on Huckleberry Hill ever again."

"Leave that to me. I have a few tricks up my sleeve."

Felty frowned as if he'd already lost this debate. "But Ben lives in Florida. What young man in his right mind would trade Florida for Wisconsin?"

"Ben would, if he knew his *dawdi* needed him. If he knew the farm would fall to pieces without his help."

"Ben's got twenty cousins living in Bonduel who could help with the garden and the animals. He'd wonder why we couldn't use one of the other grandchildren."

Anna's ball of yarn tumbled off her lap. "Don't you worry. I'll see to it that all of the other grandchildren are excessively busy on their own farms."

"And how will you see to that?"

"Now Felty. They all want Ben to come home. If I tell them my plan, the cousins will be perfectly happy to neglect their grandparents. Ben has such a tender heart. He'll come back when he knows we need him desperately, especially when you're going to be feeling so poorly."

Felty leaned back in his recliner and raised his arms in surrender. "I'm feeling worse already."

"That's the spirit!"